Meant to Be

SWEETBRIAR COVE
BOOK 1

MELODY GRACE

ONE.

$\mathcal{P}$OPPY SOMERVILLE BELIEVED in soulmates.

Call her crazy, or naïve, or hopelessly romantic if you want—she'd heard it all. But ever since she sneaked her first drugstore romance novel to read under the covers at night, she'd believed. That there was someone for everyone; a pot for every lid. A place her heart could find a home.

It's what made her race through the works of Jane Austen by the time she was fifteen, and sing along with every love song on the radio, and sit up nights watching classic old windswept movies while her college friends were out drinking in the rowdy bars on State Street on a Friday night. It's why, when she finally sat down to write her very own book, a love story was the only thing on her mind. Now, a few years and half a dozen novels later, she had millions of readers all over the world—because they wanted to believe, too.

Some people rolled their eyes, but Poppy didn't care. She figured there was something brave about that kind of hope, especially with so much darkness in the world. Love was worth taking a risk on, no matter how easy it seemed just to play it safe and settle for something less than The

One.

So why did she have a tight knot in the pit of her stomach just thinking about the wedding that should have been happening twenty thousand feet below her right now?

She could picture it perfectly—she'd selected every detail. She knew the music that would have been playing, the white roses decorating the chapel pews. It was her dream wedding from start to finish—and it was all still just a dream. Because she'd broken things off just two weeks before the ceremony. Now, instead of saying her vows and entering into holy wedded matrimony, she was squished into the coach section of a last-minute puddle-jumper flight, trying to put as many miles as possible between her and the wedding-that-wasn't.

"Don't worry, it's nearly over."

Poppy snapped her head around.

The lady in the next seat paused her knitting and offered a sympathetic smile. "We'll be landing soon. This is always a bumpy ride, those Atlantic winds."

"Uh huh." Poppy managed a faint reply. She was gripping the armrest so hard, her knuckles were turning white. Her stomach had been churning for an hour now, but she didn't know if it was the choppy flight making her feel so uneasy—or regret that she'd thrown away what could have been her one chance at happiness, someone to share her life with forever.

The plane lurched, and Poppy bit back a whimper.

It was the turbulence, she told herself. Definitely the flight.

"Do you want to try and take your mind off it?" the woman asked, friendly. "I have a book you can read, if you'd like."

She rummaged in her purse, then pulled out a paperback. Poppy recognized the cover in an instant. It was her first book—the one that had propelled her from beavering away at a tiny cubicle at a temp job in the city, to ... beavering away in a tiny office in her apartment, instead. Contrary to popular opinion, bestselling authors weren't all jet-setting around the world to exotic locations. The advance on that book had barely paid off the last of her student loans and bought a good bottle of wine to celebrate. But still, toasting the deal that night, she'd never been prouder. And even though her deals had grown along with her readership, Poppy knew that doing what she loved every day was the real prize.

And sharing her stories with readers around the world.

"Thanks." She took the book and pretended to look over the jacket, even though she knew every word by heart. She'd bounced for joy when those first advance copies had arrived, holding it in her hand for the very first time. "Are you enjoying it?" she couldn't help asking. She always loved to get reviews, no matter how hard she tried to stay away.

"Ooh yes," the woman said promptly, and Poppy glowed with pride. "I love all her books," she continued. "She has a way of writing, you really feel the passion of the relationship. I bet her husband's one in a million, to make her write like this."

Poppy came back down to earth with a bump that jolted more than the plane. She knew all her fans thought she was having breathless affairs, or settled with the man of her dreams, but the woman in Seat 12B couldn't have been further from the truth—especially now.

Luckily, before she could reply, the overhead announcement switched on. *"Ladies and gentlemen, we're ready to make our descent into Boston International. Thank you for joining us on this red-eye flight, if you could stow all baggage . . ."*

Poppy let out a sigh of relief. She could see the city lights spread out below them now, still dark before sunrise. She'd only been able to get a red-eye flight from New York at the last minute, she'd been in such a hurry to get out of town.

"There you go." Her companion smiled. "You've almost made it! Just a few bumps and we'll be back on solid ground."

Poppy wished it could be so simple. When they disembarked at the gate and she switched her phone back on, she found a dozen text messages waiting for her—all of them marked with the capital letters of increasing urgency.

Don't look at your messages.

Seriously – DON'T LOOK

I'M BANNING YOU FROM FACEBOOK.

(call me, I love you)

Her best friend, Summer. Poppy knew she meant well, but now there was no way she wasn't going to look. She stepped back from the scrum at the baggage carousel and took a deep breath, bracing herself before she clicked through to Facebook and saw the notifications waiting for her.

Congratulations, Owen and Poppy!

Poppy felt a weird out-of-body sensation, like she was looking at herself in another life. Her inbox was full: best wishes from distant relatives and old co-workers and old grade-school classmates she hadn't seen in twenty years. *Best of luck for your life together. Here's to a beautiful bride!* In all the rush to cancel everything and make sure all their guests were notified, Poppy hadn't thought to update her social media profile. It was just the same as it had been two weeks ago, with her engagement photo beaming out from the front page and a wall full of excited wedding countdowns from her family.

But the photo didn't show the doubts whirling in her mind, even then. Or the sinking feeling in the pit of her stomach every time she looked at her engagement ring, and picked out a wedding dress, and tasted cake samples with their moms cooing over every slice. It felt like the walls were closing in on her, crushing her with icy panic, until she'd woken up in a cold sweat and known without a doubt she couldn't go through with it. She didn't love Owen, not the way she needed to if she was going to say those vows. And as much as she longed for a life with someone, building the kind of forever she wrote about every day, every instinct in her body was screaming at her, Not this time.

Not this man.

She guessed her instincts were right, because now the sinking feeling was gone—replaced by an epic black hole of guilt. It still made her sick with shame, remembering the look on Owen's face when she'd told him it was the end. Maybe he should have seen it coming—things had been distant and tense between them for months—but still, it didn't make it any easier saying the words "it's over" and ruining his life the way she did.

Aunt June would say she was being dramatic. She did, in fact, when she reached out and offered Poppy a lifeline: her beach cottage on Cape Cod.

"Trust me," June had said down the phone line, in her usual no-nonsense tone. "If you stick around, you'll let them talk you back into it. You need a nice change of scenery. And don't you have that book that needs finishing?"

Poppy didn't need reminding. Even now, hauling her bags off the conveyer, her deadline loomed large. Her already pushed three times, editor leaving panicked voicemails, black cloud of a deadline. The final book in her series, the installment all her readers had been waiting for. She'd been avoiding that blank page for weeks now, so Aunt June's offer couldn't have come at a better time. She could shut herself away miles from all the drama, and focus on giving her readers the happily-ever-after they deserved.

Even if her own happily-ever-after seemed further away than ever before.

IT WAS STILL dark by the time Poppy claimed her rental car (and an extra-large coffee) and hit the road. She was worn out from travel, and counting the minutes until she could collapse into Aunt June's guest-room bed, but as the reassuring voice of GPS guided her down the wide freeway, she couldn't help but feel her tension ease. The miles disappeared in no time and the sky was turning pink as she crossed the Sagamore Bridge. It was the unofficial gateway to the Cape, where the bicep of shoreline arced in a lazy curl against the mainland, and Poppy could almost feel the change in the air. Six lanes narrowed to just a sandy two-way road, and then suddenly, the sun lifted over the horizon, glinting through the lush green woods and glittering on the dark ocean. Even though she had the car heater blowing on full against the early-morning chill, Poppy wound down the windows to inhale a lungful of crisp, tangy sea air.

It tasted like summertime.

Melting ice-cream cones and sticky sunscreen, the shriek of cold water, plunging into the pond—the memories hit her in a rush, and just like that, she was ten years old again.

The last time she made this drive, she was curled in the backseat, her head in a book while her parents bickered up front. They told her it would be an adventure, a whole summer at Aunt June's, but she knew well enough they just wanted her out of the way so they could fight at full volume back home. As she stood on the porch and watched their car disappear back up the bumpy lane, she was surprised to hear June say, "Ten bucks says they'll be divorced by the time they come pick you up again."

Poppy had stared at her in shock. Of all the things they didn't talk about those days, the D-word was the biggie, something they tiptoed around like an elephant slap-bang in the middle of the house.

June gave her a knowing look. "C'mon kid, you're smarter than anyone, all those books you've been reading. It'll be alright," she added, patting Poppy on the shoulder. "Some things just aren't meant to be."

Poppy learned a lot of things that summer, like how to swing out over Blackbottom Pond to hit the water just right with the biggest splash, and the secret ingredient that made Aunt June's sweet iced tea so sweet (a splash of maple syrup), but that one stuck with her the longest. Because if some things weren't meant to be, then that meant there was plenty that *was*. True love existed, and maybe her parents hadn't found it with each other the first time around, but she had to believe it was still out there, for everyone.

Except you.

She pushed away the whisper of doubt in the back of her head, and focused on finding the blink-and-you'll-miss-it turn off the highway. She'd been up all night, and exhaustion was hitting hard. She had to force herself to keep her eyes open as she wound her way down past clapboard houses and white picket fences, bright with hydrangeas in the early morning sun. When she finally found the blue-shingled beach cottage sitting squarely at the end of the lane, she could have cheered out loud.

Poppy parked out front and grabbed her purse from the front seat. She had a suitcase in the trunk, but the only thing she needed right now was a soft mattress and sleep, so she fished the spare key from under the ceramic whale on the porch, let herself in, and crawled straight upstairs to collapse face-down on the nearest bed.

She kicked off her shoes, buried her face in the nearest cool pillow, and let out a sigh of satisfaction.

Then the hammering began.

TWO.

*W*HAT FRESH HELL was this?

Poppy dragged herself over to the window and squinted at the morning sun. From there, she could see out into the side yard, to Aunt June's vegetable patch, and the riot of wildflowers trailing down to the shore—and the house next door.

Although, to be honest, calling it a house felt like an insult to other homes, ones with four solid walls and a roof. This was barely standing, stripped back to the frame and wide open to the elements. She could see into the back room, from the cords of raw wood stacked on the foundation, to a tangle of power cords and equipment. And she could definitely *hear* everything inside, too.

The banging got louder.

Please, she sent up a silent prayer. *Just let me have an hour or two of sleep.* And then, like the Gods of Slumber were smiling down on her, the banging stopped. Yes!

Poppy collapsed back into bed and closed her eyes to—

RRRREEEEOOOORRRR

The high-pitched whine of a saw echoed through the window, followed by the screech of metal against metal.

Every one of the hairs on Poppy's skin stood on end.

She leapt out of bed. Enough! She stormed downstairs and out through the yard. "Excuse me!" she called, approaching the house next door. "Hey?"

The sawing cut out, and a moment later, a man strolled out onto the deck. "What's all the racket?" he demanded, safety goggles pushed up over his head and a power drill in his hands.

Hello.

Poppy stopped. Even through her sleep-deprived anger, she could still register cornflower-blue eyes, and a strong jaw, and chiseled arms straining under that plain white T-shirt . . .

"Well?" he asked again, scowling impatiently. "I'm kind of busy here."

"I know, I heard," Poppy recovered. "Every last hammer, in excruciating detail. Do you know what time it is?" she added, plaintive.

The man glanced at his watch. "Seven-oh-three," he drawled.

"On a Sunday morning!" Poppy exclaimed. "Aren't there rules or regulations about this kind of thing? Some of us are trying to sleep."

"Oh yeah, late night was it?" The man arched an eyebrow and gave her a head-to-toe smirk that made Poppy flush. She knew she must look a mess, in sweatpants and an old ball shirt with a stain from where the flight attendant had spilled cheap red wine during a bumpy patch.

She smoothed down her tangled hair and straightened

up. "I just got in on a red-eye. I'm staying at my aunt's, right next door."

"June said something about that." He hoisted some wood over to the workbench. "But then, you always did like to boss everyone around, right pipsqueak?"

Hearing her old nickname triggered a sense of déjà vu. There was only one person who'd ever called her that, even when it drove her crazy. *Especially* when it drove her crazy.

"Wait, Cooper?" she asked, blinking in disbelief.

"The one and only." He gave her a lazy grin, and even with stubble on his jaw and a smudge of sawdust on his cheek, that smile still wiped all her anger from her mind.

"The last time I saw you, you were . . . shorter." She managed to recover in time. That was saying something. She remembered a gangly kid, constantly tormenting her with bugs and boogers and lord knows what else.

Now, Cooper Nicholson was all man.

"How have you been?" she asked, still stunned. "What are you doing these days?"

"I'm good. I stayed around town, started a business fixing up old houses," he replied, then gave her a look. "At least, when I don't have nosy neighbors interrupting me."

"I'm sorry," Poppy exhaled. "I've just been travelling all night, and I'm so tired I could cry. Is there any chance you could keep it down, just for a couple of hours?"

"OK, OK." Cooper seemed to soften. "Wait here."

He disappeared back into the house, and Poppy tried to catch her breath. Who knew Cooper, Spitball King of

Sweetbriar Cove, would grow up to be so . . . so . . .
Delicious.

After a moment, Cooper emerged with something in his hand. "Sorry about the noise." He flashed her a wide, easy smile. "This should take care of it."

Poppy looked down.

Earplugs.

The man had kept her up, taunted her, and now presented her with two tiny knobs of bright orange foam like that was any help at all.

"You're not going to keep the noise down?" she asked, exhausted.

"Sorry, pipsqueak," he said, sounding anything but apologetic. "Just count yourself lucky you got a lie-in today. Usually my crew starts at six!"

Before she could say anything, he turned back to his saw. The high-pitched whine started up, and Poppy turned on her heel and fled.

So much for small-town neighbor charm. It looked like she was on her own.

COOPER NICHOLSON WATCHED POPPY hightail it back across the yard. She was pissed, he could tell.

Pissed, and cute as hell.

He remembered her from the summer she'd spent at her aunt's. Back then, she'd been a tiny thing, with bright red glasses almost bigger than her face. Not that you ever saw it, she was too busy with her nose stuck in a book. She could be out on the beach, surrounded by ballgames and playful dogs, and a dozen splashing kids, and nothing would ever shake her fascination with whatever she was reading that day. And to a mischievous ten-year-old like Cooper, that was like waving a red rag in front of a bull.

He chuckled, remembering all the ways he tried to distract her. Most of them involving spider crabs, seaweed, and spitballs. No wonder she gave him such an icy glare when he called her by her old nickname, "pipsqueak." But what could he say? Something about Poppy Somerville made him want to get under her skin.

He turned back to the workbench and started sawing again, but this time, he felt a twinge of guilt. She looked like she hadn't slept in a week—but he was on a schedule here. She couldn't just come waltzing over and demand he put all his plans on hold for her to get some beauty sleep.

Not that she needed it. Even stressed, stained, and sleep-deprived, Poppy still looked effortlessly beautiful. She must have hit a growth spurt somewhere along the way, because she sure wasn't a scrawny little girl anymore.

The saw hit the bracket with a screech.

Focus.

He was barely a few weeks into this project, and had another month left, at least. More if the dry weather didn't hold and they got their usual spring rainstorms. He knew the house didn't look like much now, but under the sawdust and rotting shingles, there were great bones, and he was determined to restore it to its former glory.

Renovating the historic houses along the Cape had started out a hobby, but it had grown into a thriving business for him. Most developers wanted to tear the older homes down and use the prime ocean-front plots to built new, modern mansions, but Cooper had always loved the history in buildings like this. He studied old craftsman techniques and researched the original materials, and soon the word spread about his skill and classic architectural designs. When a reporter from *New England Quarterly* had featured him in an article about historic preservation, his phone had started ringing off the hook and hadn't stopped yet.

But this project was special. He'd had his eye on the house for years. When he was a kid, they'd always cut through the yard down to the beach, and as a teenager, he'd gotten up to all kinds of mischief in the woods backing onto the edge of the property, but it was the house itself that appealed to him now. A classic colonial saltbox, it was built in the 1800s and was one of a disappearing breed on the Cape. It had sat empty for years, falling into disrepair, until finally Cooper had finally been able to track down the owner's family after digging through old land records in the dusty archive at the town hall. He'd sunk his life savings into the crumbling foundations and acre-plot of beachfront land, but once it was finished and sold to some lucky buyer, the proceeds would set him up right for a long time. The view alone was worth a million dollars: nothing like the gentle curve of the bay and the sparkling blue ocean stretching out to the horizon.

Yeah, the house would be spectacular when he was finished, it was just going to take a heck of a lot of elbow

grease to get there. Which meant he was working weekends, up at dawn, and keeping on right through to
sundown, no matter who was trying to get some sleep
next door.

Still . . .

Cooper reluctantly shut off the saw. Poppy had looked
exhausted, and besides, he'd been meaning to head into
town to pick up supplies before the stores closed early.
The noisy work could wait, for a couple of hours, at least.

Never say he wasn't a generous guy.

He grabbed the keys to his truck and drove the winding lane back towards town. He was practically a resident
at the hardware store these days, and Hank had everything he needed for once.

"They say there'll be rain by next week," the old owner warned him, as he totaled up Cooper's supplies. "I'd
get that roofing done sooner rather than later."

"That's the plan," Cooper agreed.

"How are you finding the siding?" he asked. "Still
think you should be using the original shingles?"

"Remember termites," another regular, Larry, pitched
in. He paused by the register. "Those little bastards are
lurking everywhere, especially older wood like that."

It was always like this. You couldn't stop by Hank's
without a debate about everything from wood to the
weather.

"Your pop knew all about termites," Larry added.
"Didn't he use to make up a special paint?"

Cooper nodded. "My dad knew all about a lot of
things." It's how he learned most of the tricks of his

trade—those summers in high school working right alongside his pops on contracting jobs. At the time, he'd wanted to be anyplace else, but looking back now, he wished he'd appreciated that time together when they still had it.

"Before I forget," Hank added, "keep an eye out for June's niece, won't you? She said she's arriving today."

"Already here," Cooper replied. "Came in off a red-eye and stormed straight over to ask me to keep it down."

The men chuckled. "Sounds like she takes after her aunt," Hank said, and Cooper would have sworn he saw a twinkle in his eye. "We're under strict instructions to make the girl feel welcome."

"Well, she's more than welcome to come pitch in with construction," Cooper joked. "Like you said, there's rain coming."

He headed back outside and loaded up the truck. There was a bigger chain hardware store just an hour away that stocked everything cheaper, but he always stayed loyal to Hank. He liked dropping by to hear the gossip from the regulars, and it made him feel closer to his father, in a way, spending time with all his old friends like this.

He'd never planned on sticking around in Sweetbriar Cove. He went to college over in Boston, studying engineering, and made plans after graduation to move out farther west. Chicago, maybe, or Dallas, some big city where your neighbor didn't know everything about your business, and even the clerk at the grocery store hadn't heard all about your date with that girl from Truro last

Friday night. But he was finishing up his final semester when his dad had got sick. Stomach cancer. There had never been any question in Cooper's mind about what to do. He'd finished up his classes and moved straight home, driving Bill to his appointments, making sure he took his meds on time. He even took over Bill's contracting jobs to keep the money coming in, watching as his dad's good days got further and fewer in between, until finally his legendary stubbornness was no match for the cancer in his gut.

After that, Cooper had thought about leaving again for a big city, but it never had the same appeal. The town had pulled together for them, looked out for them, sent casseroles and prayers, and sat with him through the worst of it. He would never admit it to anyone, but they were the only family he had left. So, he'd stuck around, and worked hard on the business, and built a reputation as the guy you could count on to come in on time and under budget, and soon enough he'd even started thinking about settling down and starting a family of his own.

And that's when it had all gone to hell.

Cooper paused at the red light. He was so deep in memories that when he saw a flash of blonde hair up ahead, it felt like he was back there again.

He caught his breath. There was a familiar woman climbing out of her car, her face bent away from him.

A tide of regret slammed through Cooper, the same guilt and shame that hit whenever he was reminded about the biggest failure of his life. Then she lifted her head, and he realized it was a stranger he'd never seen before.

He exhaled. He was gripping the steering wheel so tightly, his knuckles were white. Cooper yanked the wheel around and pulled over to park.

It looked like his new neighbor was getting her beauty sleep after all.

He needed a drink.

THREE.

To HER SURPRISE—AND RELIEF—the earplugs actually worked. Or maybe she was just too tired to let a little light chainsaw action ruin her slumber, but Poppy barely heard a noise from next door. She slept all day, and by the time she'd enjoyed an epic hot shower and unpacked her things in the pretty guest bedroom, she felt just about human again.

And hungry. She couldn't even remember the last time she'd eaten, her stomach had been tied up in knots during the flight, and before that . . . some chips from a vending machine, maybe?

Either way, she needed sustenance, and fast. She pulled on her jeans and a sweater, then headed off into town on foot. It was a bright, blue-skied afternoon, and even though it wasn't quite summer yet, the sun was faint and warming and the breeze danced with a salty ocean tang.

Poppy finally felt herself start to relax. She'd been tense for months, it felt like—with the wedding plans hurtling towards the finish line, and her deadline too— but as she strolled the winding country lane with the ocean glinting on her right, and the leafy woods rising up the hill to Main Street square, for a moment all that stress felt a thousand miles away.

Sweetbriar Cove always had a way of making you feel right at home.

Set in a hollow, mid-way up the Cape, Sweetbriar had been settled by early English colonists—at least according to the town historical society. She hadn't been back in twenty years, but Poppy was pleased to find everything exactly as she remembered. The winding country lanes lined with old Colonial buildings, the green of the town square, and the church spire rising from the top of the hill. She could even swear it was the same flyers advertising the Spring Fling Literary Festival peeling in the grocery store window, and the same calico cat perched on a fencepost outside the hardware store. On closer inspection, there were some new improvements—a chic art gallery tucked next to Franny's Gift Shoppe, a new coffee shop she mentally bookmarked for her morning cup of joe—but the true spirit of Sweetbriar was still alive and well.

Poppy was tempted to stop and browse for a while, but the rumble in her stomach drove her on, until she found the tavern on the corner with a chalkboard outside promising the best fish and chips on the Cape.

Sold.

She ducked inside. It was a homey pub, with traditional wooden beams, old black-and-white nautical photographs on the walls, and a big fireplace across the room. She made a beeline for the bar, which was being tended by a scruffy, surfer-looking man with tousled blond hair. "Is it really the best on the cape?" she asked, nodding to the menu. He grinned.

"According to Big Pete," he said. "And he's the only authority we need."

"He's still around?" Poppy exclaimed. Even she remembered the town mayor, presiding over the Fourth of July fireworks with a flourish, decked out in a top and tails printed with the American flag.

"Still alive and kicking, although slower these days," the man grinned. "They'll have to bury him right here in the square. Really, I think the town hall voted on it last year."

Poppy laughed, just as a familiar voice came from behind her.

"Flirting again, Riley? You should know, pipsqueak here doesn't like boys. We've all got cooties."

Poppy turned, and found herself staring into Cooper's teasing blue eyes again. She felt a flush—then immediately scolded herself. "Only some of them," she said with a glare. "And can you please stop calling me that?"

"Sleep well?" he asked, undaunted.

"No thanks to you." She heard a chuckle, and when Poppy turned back, she found the bartender looking amused.

"Friend of yours?" he asked Cooper.

"She wouldn't put it like that," he said. "Poppy, this is Riley," he introduced them. Riley gave her a wink, and Cooper let out a snort. "Don't mind the smooth talk," he told Poppy. "He flirts with everything that moves."

"Excellent." Poppy smiled, just to get a rise out of

him. "I haven't flirted with anyone in forever."

Riley smirked. "I like this one. Food? Beer?" he asked her, and won her undying affection. At least someone had priorities.

"All of the above," Poppy answered, and he gave a salute.

"Coming right up."

Riley disappeared in to the back, and Cooper slid easily onto the stool beside Poppy. "So how's life as a big-shot romance author?" he asked.

"How do you—? Oh, June," Poppy realized. "I should have guessed." She remembered the time her aunt came to visit—and then proceeded to move all her books to the front section of the store, proudly telling everyone within earshot that her niece was the bestseller. Poppy loved her enthusiasm, just wished it wasn't quite so . . . public. "Tell me she doesn't brag too much," she said, just imagining what the town must think of her.

Cooper gave her a sideways look. "It depends if you classify sending out a town newsletter about your new book 'too much.' She told everyone to keep an eye out for you this week. I'm surprised she didn't make us roll out the ticker-tape and put on a parade." He tossed another peanut up in a lazy arc and caught it in his mouth.

Poppy gulped. "So much for keeping a low profile."

"In hiding, are you?"

"Something like that." She changed the subject fast. "What about you? I can't believe it's been so long. The last time I saw you, you were running around dropping seaweed down everyone's shirts."

"Not everyone," Cooper corrected her. "Just yours."

"Gee, thanks." Poppy gave him a sideways look. It was still a shock to see him all grown up, the teasing memory in her head replaced with someone so broad-shouldered and solid, with stubble on his jaw and worn cotton stretching over the muscles in his back—

Poppy dragged her gaze away. She shouldn't be looking at anyone's muscles, let alone the guy who'd made an art of tormenting her. "So, what's new with you?" she asked instead. "Wife, kids, white picket fence?"

The smile slipped from Cooper's face, and Poppy had a feeling she'd just said the wrong thing, but before he replied, Riley returned with her beer, and another for Cooper.

"Thanks." She gave him a smile. "Although I probably shouldn't drink this on an empty stomach."

"Lightweight?" Riley asked.

"The worst," Poppy admitted.

"Well, just so you know, my place is right upstairs. If you ever can't make it home." Riley gave her another wink.

Cooper grumbled beside her. "C'mon. Now you're just being desperate."

"I like to think of it more as 'charming' and 'irresistible,' " Riley corrected him, and Poppy couldn't help but laugh.

"Thanks for the offer, but I'll be sleeping in my own bed," she said firmly. "For the foreseeable future."

"Our loss," Riley said, unruffled, and headed back towards the kitchen and—Poppy hoped—her food.

"Interesting," Cooper drawled. "The Queen of Hearts hasn't found her perfect soulmate yet." His words were light enough, but there was a sarcastic note in his voice that made Poppy feel like he was mocking her.

"Not yet, no," she replied, cooler this time.

"Yet you figure it's your job to lecture everyone else on true love," he said, and took a swig of his beer. "Huh. Don't you think that's kind of hypocritical?"

"I'm not lecturing anyone." Poppy frowned, wondering how the conversation had suddenly taken a turn. "People are free to read whatever they want. I just write my stories."

"Full of happy endings and lightning strikes," Cooper challenged. "You ever think you're setting them all up to fail? Chasing after some big happy ending that's never going to come their way?"

Poppy paused. His words hit a nerve deep inside her, the same whispered doubts that kept her up at night, taunting her with the questions she wished she had an answer for.

He was wrong. He had to be. Otherwise everything she'd spent her life believing was a lie.

"What's it to you?" she challenged him, trying to keep her cool. She felt weirdly vulnerable, her raw wounds open for everyone to see. "Have you even read one of my books?"

"I don't need to," Cooper shrugged. "It's all the same. Building up some fantasyland of love and forever so people can't help but be let down with the real world. You know, I feel sorry for the suckers who believe it, they don't even realize what a scam they're buying into. No offense," he added, like an afterthought.

He had to be kidding. Poppy clenched her fists and got down from the stool.

"Where are you going?" Cooper asked, sounding confused.

"Well, you've just insulted me, my life's work, and every woman who's ever bought one of my books, so I figure I better get out of your hair. Unless you want to start in on my mom?" Poppy demanded. "My pastor? No? Good."

She turned on her heel and stalked across the bar. She would have walked out altogether if she hadn't been so hungry, but as she sat down at a corner table, she was fuming. What the hell was his problem? She didn't even know the guy, and he thought he could just dismiss her career as some kind of elaborate con on the readers of America. Poppy was used to dealing with snobbery—you didn't get to write romance without people looking down their noses at you—but usually that was easy to brush off. Literary elites scoffing at happy endings, like a book had to be five hundred pages of misery to be worth a read (but funnily enough, didn't have a bad word to say about all those trashy crime books for men). She'd stopped paying attention to those kinds of comments years ago, since she figured nothing would convince them that they were the ones missing out. Sure, she wasn't going to win any literary prizes, but that wasn't the point. Her readers didn't come to her looking for the real world, they wanted an escape from it. A place to disappear in between school pick-up runs and double shifts at the hospital; a place where fate wasn't cruel, hope won out, and love was never in vain.

A place to believe.

So Poppy built that world for them—and for herself, too. No matter what else was happening in her life, she could guarantee that everything would work out in the end. At least, it did between the pages of her books. And this year in particular, her writing had been her main escape, as the juggernaut of her wedding barreled on towards "I do."

Until the day she looked at her own words and realized if she married Owen—if she settled for their life together—she would be giving up on everything she'd told her readers to fight for all these years.

"What did he do this time?"

Riley's voice cut through her thoughts, and Poppy looked up to find him setting a plate of delicious-looking food in front of her. "Sorry, what?" she asked, her mouth already watering.

"Cooper," he explained. "I just saw him go storming out with a face like thunder, although, that's just a normal Sunday for him."

Poppy pressed her lips together. "Just a small disagreement," she said lightly, and Riley snorted.

"Why am I not surprised? Don't take it personally," he added with a sympathetic smile. "I love the guy like a brother, but he can be a grumpy asshole when he sets his mind to it."

"I'll remember that. Thanks, and for the food," she

said.

"My pleasure." Riley turned to go, but then Poppy remembered something.

"Wait. Did I put my foot in it earlier? We were catching up earlier, and I asked Cooper if he was married."

Riley looked uneasy. "You'll have to talk to him about that," he said, as some new customers came in. "I better go. Let me know if you need anything."

Poppy watched him walk away. It sounded like she had touched a nerve with Cooper without even meaning to, but even so, it didn't give him the right to tear her down like that. Maybe it wasn't personal for him, but it sure felt that way.

Enough letting Cooper Nicholson get under her skin, she decided, and reached for a crisp, thick-cut fry. For some reason, he'd been in her face since the moment she'd arrived, but that didn't mean she had to let him ruin her day. She was here for a reason, after all.

No drama. No conflict. Just the happily-ever-after her readers were waiting for.

Simple.

Right?

FOUR.

*A*NY HOPE THAT COOPER had been joking, saying his crew usually started at six a.m., was shattered the next morning when Poppy woke to what sounded like a pneumatic drill boring straight through her skull. A peek out the window confirmed it: the construction site was a hive of activity. Even those earplugs weren't going to help her now.

Time for Plan B.

She took a shower, dressed in jeans and a pretty peasant blouse, and turned on the radio loud to try and drown out the racket next door. "*One way, or another . . .*" she sang along, as she unpacked the rest of her things in the antique bureau. Aunt June always had eclectic taste, and the old house was filled with trinkets and souvenirs from her travels—from the tribal masks in the staircase to the Australian didgeridoo leaning up against the hall. Downstairs, the beachy living room opened up to a big butter-yellow kitchen with windows out to the back porch. Poppy scavenged in the cupboards and found some instant coffee, which she poured into a polka-dot mug and took outside to sit on the back steps in the morning sun.

She breathed deeply, the sea air whipping her wet hair around her face. It really was beautiful out here: the ocean was glinting, blue and wide across the horizon, and the early-morning fog was already clearing to bright skies. Aunt June's garden was full of climbing roses, lavender, and grass, with a winding path all the way to the sand. If it weren't for the yells and banging breaking the calm, it would be a picture-perfect scene.

Almost pretty enough to make her forget everything she'd left behind in New York.

Poppy's heart sank. The guilt was still digging away, hard behind her ribcage. She could only imagine what Owen and his family were saying about her now, and she didn't blame them. Walking out on a wedding with only a few weeks to spare was unforgiveable, but what was she supposed to do?

It wasn't supposed to be like this.

They'd met online two years ago, after such a long, lonely spell of bad first dates and lackluster fix-ups that Poppy had almost given up hope she would find someone. She was twenty-seven, spending every day writing great love affairs for her characters, and her weekends at new baby showers or engagement parties, watching those love stories come to life right in front of her. But at the end of the night, she always went home alone.

To the apartment she loved, in the life that she was proud of, sure—but it still filled her with that lonely ache when she looked around and wished she had someone there to share it with her. To snuggle up in bed with on a Saturday morning, and bicker with over the TV remote at night. She wanted holiday traditions, and pet names, and, one day, a family of her own. So when Owen sent a message through the latest online dating site—with actual punctuation, and no lewd photos attached—she was ready. True love might take a little effort, but she was willing to try.

And it worked. He was sweet and steady, and sure, he preferred to read thick military histories, and his eyes glazed over a little when she tried to talk to him about the chapters she'd written that day, but it wasn't the end of the world. She didn't really understand his work, either (something to do with cyber-security and systems administration, she thought), but not every couple had to share each other's passions. They had fun together, the relaxed, easy kind of conversation that made it feel like she'd known him for years, and slowly, Poppy wondered if maybe this could be the forever she'd been looking for.

Still, it took her by surprise when he proposed— getting down on one knee during his parents' anniversary picnic. It seemed to come out of nowhere, and for a split second, she'd almost turned him down, but looking at his excited expression, and hearing the gasps and whispers all around them, she couldn't help but tell him yes. After all, it made sense: they'd been together a year already, and it was all going fine. Great, even. This is what you did next—got married, moved in, built a life together—and it would have been foolish to throw it all away just because her stomach didn't flip when Owen walked into the room or slid into bed with her at night.

But as the months passed and the wedding plans

reached fever pitch, her doubts became impossible to
ignore. The whispers in the back of her mind became
shouts, and she found herself sitting in front of the TV at
night beside him, trying to imagine if this was her forever.
If this was it, the rest of their lives just like this, would it
be enough for her?

Or would her heart still ache, imagining a great love
that was out there for her, somewhere?

Owen deserved more than that. They both did. And as
much as she felt guilty now, practically stranding him at
the altar, Poppy knew that it would have been even worse
if she'd said "I do" when her heart wasn't in it. She'd
saved them both from heartache. She just had to hope
that one day, Owen believed it too.

Her phone buzzed in her pocket, and Poppy pulled it
out, glad of the distraction.

Or not.

"Quinn," she greeted her literary agent. "How's it
going?"

"What do you mean, 'how's it going'?" Quinn's voice
demanded. "I log on to look at photos of the happy
couple, and find a bunch of people bitching about how
you walked out on him. How do I not know this?!"

"You were at that conference in Germany," Poppy
protested weakly. "I was going to tell you when you got
back."

"They have wifi in Germany!" Quinn exclaimed, then
calmed herself. "What happened? Are you OK? Did you
walk in and find him in bed with that bridesmaid—you
know, the step-cousin who was giving you attitude about

the shoes? Bastard!"

"Whoa, it's not his fault," Poppy interrupted quickly. "I promise. I just realized he wasn't the one for me."

"Oh." Quinn paused, then changed tacks. "Then you did the right thing. You're so much better off without him. Plenty more fish in the sea!"

"Oh, yes?" Poppy couldn't help replying. "How's that working out for you?"

Quinn groaned. "Don't ask. What's Owen's number? Maybe I'll give him a call. Kidding," she added, but Poppy wouldn't put it past her. Quinn was a force of nature who let nothing stand in her way. It made her a great agent, but her love life was more like a crime scene: full of bad accidents and tape reading "do not pass."

"Anyway," Quinn moved on quickly, like she had another ten calls to make that morning. "Does this mean I can tell your publisher they'll be getting a manuscript soon? Since you'll be writing now, instead of feeding him chocolate-covered strawberries on honeymoon in Bora-Bora?"

"I hope so," Poppy said. "I'm at my aunt's place for a few weeks, trying to get it finished."

"Hallelujah," Quinn cheered. "I didn't want to say anything, but I've been fielding angry calls all month. I've held them off as best I can, but even I can't work miracles. Are you sure I can't send them any pages?" she added, her voice taking on a pleading note. "I know you hate showing your manuscripts until they're finished, but even just a few chapters would go a long way to buying us some time."

Poppy gulped. "Sorry," she said, trying to keep her voice even. "The first chapters need some major rewrites. It took me a while to settle into the voice, I don't want anyone seeing it like that."

Quinn sighed. "OK, whatever you need. Just remember, they've pushed your deadline twice already. Any longer, and they'll have to move your release date back next year."

"I promise, I'll have something for you in a few weeks," Poppy vowed. "I'm actually in the middle of a scene right now, so I should get back to it."

"Don't let me keep you. Laters, babe!"

Quinn rang off, and Poppy lowered her phone. Lying to her agent? Just add it to her growing list of crimes. Everyone at her publisher thought she was already halfway through the book, but the truth was, she hadn't written a single word.

Poppy had writer's block, and she had it *bad*.

But all that was going to change, starting today. She jumped up and headed back inside, retrieving her laptop then heading to the old study. It was a shady room lined with old bookcases, and it also happened to be the farthest room away from Cooper's construction site. Still, the shouts and banging echoed through the windows as Poppy sat down at the desk, opened her screen, and started a new document.

Chapter one.

The cursor blinked at her, taunting. This part should be easy. It was the final book in her series, the conclusion to a love story that had spanned a century and three continents. She knew these characters inside out—and knew exactly what her readers were expecting from her. Still, as Poppy stared at her notes, all the careful plot ideas and outlines, she still couldn't find those first words.

What did she know about true love?

A whole lot of nothing.

The banging came again, louder. She slammed her screen shut. She was going about this the wrong way. Back home, she'd treated writing like a real job: getting up every morning, getting dressed, and going out to write at the library or coffee shops around the city. No wonder she couldn't start writing—she was sitting there in her pajamas, messing up her usual routine!

Poppy headed back upstairs. She grabbed some towels from the linen closet, and stepped into the bathroom. June must have had it updated since she was there last, because the chipped sink had been replaced with a gorgeous expanse of blue tile, with a deep tub and a walk-in shower. Poppy turned on the water, feeling determined. A shower, some fresh clothes, and then she'd find somewhere to hunker down and write. The words would pour out of her, then.

They had to.

She stripped her clothes off, tied up her hair, and stepped under the hot water. Ahh, that was better. She would get back on track in no time, she just had to—

"AHHHHHHHHHHHHHHHH!"

COOPER HEARD THE SCREAMS clear from next door, even

over the sound of construction. For a long, panicked moment, he thought something terrible had happened. Poppy had fallen down the stairs, or been attacked by a drifter, or cut off some vital limb . . .

He dropped his tools and raced across the yard. "Poppy?" he yelled. The back door was open, so he charged inside and up the stairs. "Poppy? Are you OK?"

"I'm going to kill you, Cooper Nicholson!"

Maybe not.

He was at the top of the stairs when a door opened and Poppy came barreling out, straight into him. "Whoa," he said, automatically putting his arms out to steady her. His hands closed around silky, wet skin, and he realized she was wearing nothing but a towel.

A very small towel.

Cooper stepped back. "Christ, woman, I thought you were getting murdered up here." He cleared his throat. He didn't know where to look. Her hair was pinned up, revealing the slim arch of her neck, glistening with water. The postage stamp of a towel was barely covering her long legs and the swell of her—

He dragged his eyes back up to her face. Her furious, shooting-daggers face.

"You wish," Poppy looked as if she wanted to be inflicting bodily harm on him. "But I've half a mind to throw you down the stairs myself."

"What did I do this time?" Cooper frowned. "I told you, my guys need to work. I'm sorry about the noise, but—"

"It's not the noise!" Poppy exclaimed. "Here." She

grabbed his hand and yanked him into the bathroom before he could object. Poppy turned on the shower, and for a moment, a parade of X-rated images flashed in Cooper's mind. Like what it would be like under the spray with her.

Without that towel.

"Well?" Poppy demanded. He tried to push those thoughts away. She was staring at him expectantly, like he was supposed to know what the hell she was going on about.

"You're going to have to spell it out," Cooper said, annoyed now.

"There's no hot water!" Poppy cried. "You know anything about that?"

Cooper blinked, and then it all came rushing back. "Oh yeah. We had to shut off the gas this morning, we're rerouting the main pipe."

Poppy scowled. "And you didn't think to warn me about it, or—I don't know—ask if that was OK?"

Cooper knew he should apologize, but man, she was cute when she was spitting mad. Her brown eyes were flashing, and she'd completely forgotten about that towel, which was slipping lower with every angry gesture, revealing inches more of that pale, wet skin.

"Sorry," he shrugged, trying not to smile. "Don't worry, it's only going to be another couple of days."

"Couple of days?" Poppy's voice went up an octave.

"Tomorrow," he corrected, taking pity on her. He was used to roughing it—pitching a tent to sleep in the yard on some of his projects and living off the grid on

vacation—but clearly, Poppy needed her creature com-
forts. "I promise, hot water will be back tomorrow. Hey,
it's not so bad," he added. "Cold showers are good for
the circulation. And it looks like you could use a little
cooling off."

Poppy grabbed her towel tighter. Her cheeks were
flushed, and she was sexy as hell, her hair falling down
around her bare shoulders. "What I could use is some
peace and quiet to get my work done."

"And I could use two weeks on a boat in the Caribbe-
an," Cooper drawled, knowing it would turn her pink
cheeks even redder with rage. "But as the Stones said, we
can't always get what we want."

He turned and left her in the bathroom before he was
tempted to do something he'd regret. Like kiss the mouth
that was spluttering insults behind him.

Now that would really heat things up around here.

FIVE.

$\mathcal{P}$OPPY DECIDED IT was better to take herself far away from Cooper and the construction site, before she picked up one of those hammers and did some damage to more than just the walls. She knew the hot water issue wasn't a big deal—she wasn't some kind of diva who couldn't make it through the day without luxuriating in a bubble bath. No, it was the look on Cooper's handsome face that made her blood boil: that infuriating smirk that got her riled up, until she was just about ready to explode.

Note to self: Cooper Nicholson was a hazard to her blood pressure. And her creativity. Because even once she'd braved the ice-cold shower, dressed, and thrown her laptop in her bag to head into town, Poppy still couldn't get focused to write.

She took a sip of tea and let out a sigh. The coffee shop she'd seen yesterday was the perfect writing spot: a bright, modern café just off the town square, equipped with comfortable couches, cozy nooks, and plenty of outlets for her power cord. She'd been camped out there for most of the day, but how many words had she produced?

Exactly zero.

Well, two, if you counted "chapter one," but Poppy knew that wasn't going to cut it with her editor back home.

She looked around the room in search of inspiration. She'd already updated her author blog, checked twitter, and set up boards on Pinterest for all of her characters, so she was all out of time-wasting tactics. Unless she checked Facebook again—

No. Focus. She had everything riding on this book. She couldn't let her readers down.

Which was the problem. Poppy had never suffered writer's block before. She loved to write, and even on her worst days, she'd always managed to get words on the page. After all, it was only a first draft, and everyone knew first drafts were made for fixing. But somehow it felt different this time. This was the final book in the series, the ultimate happily-ever-after. She and her readers had spent years with these characters, watching them laugh, and cry, and fall in love, and she couldn't bear the thought that anyone would close the book disappointed and wishing for more.

Not that there would be a book if she didn't find a way to break this block and get writing. But every time she forced her hands to the keyboard and started typing, the same fears bubbled up in her chest.

What did she know about love?

It had never held her back before. Somehow, her own inexperienced heart never seemed to matter for the other books. She was writing something to believe in, a vision of the love she wanted for herself, as if by writing it down, making that dream real, she could somehow conjure it out of thin air. Even when she was dating Owen, that future vision of love remained, promising in the distance, helping fuel the last book she'd turned in, just the week before he'd proposed.

And she hadn't written another word since.

It didn't take a genius to realize the two were connected. The wrecked wedding plans, her break-up, and Poppy's current writer's block. But it didn't make sense: she'd turned her life upside down because she believed in a true love like the ones she'd written, but now that she had distance, her fears were back in force.

What if the love in her books were just fiction?

What if she'd thrown her shot at happiness away on a fantasy?

What if, after everything, Poppy would always be alone?

She gulped. That was the worst fear of all, the one that kept her up late into the night. The lonely vast horizon, years passing one after the other, just as empty as the one before—

"Refill?"

She looked up. The server was clearing a table nearby and nodded to her empty mug. Poppy snapped back to reality. "Thanks, but I shouldn't," she said reluctantly. "Any more caffeine and I'll never sleep tonight."

The server moved off, but the woman at the next table caught Poppy's eye with a smile. "Lucky you. I'm immune now, it takes me at least four espressos to get a decent hit."

Poppy smiled. The woman was about her age, with curly blonde hair, wearing a funky print skirt and boots that laced up to her knees. "Not so lucky," Poppy said. "All it takes is a slip-up from the barista, and I'm cleaning the kitchen at three a.m."

"I'm Mackenzie," the woman said, friendly. "You're June's niece, right?"

"How did you—?" Poppy stopped herself again. Of course, small-town news travelled fast. "Did she put out a news bulletin before she left?"

"Not quite," Mackenzie smiled. "But actually, I heard about it from Riley at the pub. He said you and Cooper went a couple of rounds last night."

"And this morning." Poppy sighed, then caught Mackenzie's eyebrows shooting up. "Not like that!" she yelped, blushing. "He's working on the house next door, and it's like he's trying to get in my way."

"Cooper can be . . . stubborn," Mackenzie said. "But he's a good guy, really."

Poppy's doubts must have shown, because the other woman laughed. "Really!" Mackenzie insisted. "When my roof was leaking last year, he came out and fixed it for me, in the middle of a snowstorm. He likes to act tough, but really, he's a sweetheart."

"We'll see about that," Poppy said, but she wasn't convinced.

"So how long are you in town?" Mackenzie asked.

"I'm not sure yet. A few weeks, maybe?"

Or longer, if she didn't get her book written and needed someplace to hide from her editor's wrath.

"Great," Mackenzie beamed. "This place is always so quiet before tourist season starts up. We could use the fresh blood."

"You make it sound like you're secretly vampires," Poppy joked.

"Who needs blood when you've got caffeine?" Mackenzie cracked back. She nodded to Poppy's laptop. "Are you working on the final book? Sorry," she said, looking embarrassed. "I didn't want to be a total fangirl, but I love your series. I started reading them when I got food poisoning last year, and they made it almost bearable to be vomiting on the bathroom floor."

"That's high praise," Poppy laughed. "Thank you."

"So, can you tell me what happens?" Mackenzie asked, her eyes wide. "No, wait, don't. I want the surprise. Or maybe just a hint?"

"I'm afraid not," Poppy lied. "My editor would kill me if I let anything slip."

Not that she had anything yet to reveal.

Mackenzie sighed. "I totally understand. I'm just impatient. I'm always reading spoilers online about my favorite shows, and then I get disappointed that it's not a surprise."

"I promise, this book will stay a surprise," Poppy swore. To the both of them, at this rate.

"You know, if you have the time, you should come by our book club," Mackenzie suggested, brightening. "We get together every month at the bookstore. It's basically just an excuse to sit around, drink wine, and gossip, but I know the others would be thrilled to have an actual author come chat. Marcie Bringham self-published a children's picture book about her cat," she added. "But it's not exactly the same thing."

"Maybe . . ." Poppy hesitated. She loved meeting book groups and readers, but wasn't sure what she'd have to say right now, when she was deep in a creative crisis.

"No pressure," Mackenzie reassured her. "Think about it. If anything, you should come for the food. We put on a mean dessert potluck."

"Well in that case . . . let me know when the next one is, I'll see if I'm still in town."

"Perfect." Mackenzie beamed. "Well, it was nice meeting you. I won't interrupt your work anymore." She got to her feet and wrapped a long patterned scarf around her neck.

"You too, see you around." Poppy watched her leave, glad to have made a new friend. Aunt June was always saying how friendly everyone was in Sweetbriar, and she was right. All the people Poppy had met so far had welcomed her with open arms.

Except Cooper, of course.

She flushed, remembering their run-in that morning. All the cold water in the world wasn't enough to cool her down after how infuriating Cooper had been.

And how hot he was, too.

Poppy tried not to recall the feel of his body against hers, when he'd reached to steady her. Those strong hands on her bare arms, just inches away. The towel she'd grabbed still left her feeling completely exposed, and she'd been painfully aware of his eyes slipping over her body, his gaze like a caress on her cool, wet skin.

Why did someone so annoying have to be so handsome? As much as she hated the sight of that teasing smirk on his lips, she had to admit, it looked pretty good there.

It was just as well, because she had a feeling she'd be seeing a lot more of it.

AFTER ANOTHER HOUR staring at her empty screen, Poppy admitted defeat. Clearly, a coffee shop wasn't where she needed to be to get her creative juices flowing, so she packed up and began to head for home. The sun was just starting to go down, casting the streets in a rosy dusk light, and even though it was still spring, and tourist season had yet to begin, the main street was still busy with locals, picking up groceries on their way home from work and pausing to chat on the corner.

Poppy looked around, still half-hoping inspiration would strike. Her eye caught a handwritten sign, almost buried under the foliage surrounding a squat old cottage, half-hidden down a side street.

Books, rare & usual.

This must be the store Mackenzie had mentioned. In her life, Poppy had never been able to resist a bookstore, and today was no exception. She veered across the road and ducked under the low arbor, following a paved pathway through an overgrown garden. It looked more like somebody's house from the outside, but there was an *open* sign propped in the window, and when she pushed open the door, it opened with a musical *ding* from the bell.

She stepped inside and was immediately hit with that same sense of belonging she'd felt the first time she'd stepped into her local library as a child and found—oh, the magic!—an entire temple devoted to books. Here, the tiny rooms seemed to spill into each other in a dense warren of low doorways and hidden nooks. Creaky bookcases packed with books lined every wall, and the last of the day's sunlight filtered through the windows and pooled on the polished wooden floors.

Poppy breathed in the scent of old books, and, just like that, her stress and deadline panic melted clean away. Now, this was heaven. She must have spent half her life browsing in bookstores just like this, but she never got tired of it. She never knew what treasures she would find—an old paperback by her favorite author, or a new title that for some reason caught her eye. She lost track of time, browsing among the stacks, until her arms were full of titles, and a voice pulled her from her reverie.

"We're closing now."

She looked up. There was a guy loitering in the door-way, jingling keys impatiently in his hand.

"This is your store?"

"For my troubles," he replied. He had a gruff English accent, with messy brown hair and a thick winter beard.

"It's amazing," Poppy gushed, following him out to the front. "I could spend all day here."

"As long as you buy something," he said abruptly, ringing up her purchases. "Some people browse for hours and never spend a penny. I've half a mind to start charging rent."

Okay. Poppy made a note not to get on this guy's bad side.

Just as she was paying for her stack, the doorbell dinged, and she was surprised to see Cooper walk in, with Riley and a couple of other guys behind him. Cooper stopped when he saw her, and resignation was clear on his face.

"Should have known I'd find you here," Cooper drawled. Poppy tried to ignore the flush that prickled across her skin from seeing him again. He still hadn't shaved, so his strong jaw was stubbled, glinting bronze, and he was wearing a faded plaid shirt, and jeans that fit him just right . . .

Not that she should be noticing how his jeans fit. Poppy dragged her eyes back up. "Don't tell me you've got a book club," she asked. "What is it this week: *How to Make Friends and Influence People?*"

Riley laughed out loud as Cooper narrowed his eyes. "Poker night," he said. "Don't let us keep you."

"You should stay," Riley interrupted. "Do you play?"

"A little," Poppy said, tempted. It looked like a fun group, and the owner was already setting up a table with snacks and beer. "But I don't want to intrude . . ."

"Good," Cooper said, at the same time as Riley insisted,

"No way, the more the merrier."

Poppy knew it was a guys' night, and any other time, she would have left them to their manly bonding, but

Cooper's smirk was still bugging her. "Sure, why not?" she said brightly. She put her books down, and headed over to the table—ignoring Cooper's groan.

"Deal me in."

SIX.

*A*N HOUR LATER, Cooper's smirk was wider than ever. He lounged back in his seat like he owned the poker table—which he did, if the stack of M&Ms in front of him was anything to go by. Poppy should be infuriated, but this time, she didn't mind his cocky smile.

Her plan was working.

"I'll see your five, and raise you . . . ten." Cooper carefully counted out from his hoard and pushed them to the center of the table.

Riley recklessly tossed in a handful of candy. "What the hell, I'll see that bet. Grayson?"

The bookstore owner shook his head. "This is getting too rich for me." He folded, tossing his cards down. Cooper turned to Poppy.

"Remember, face cards beat numbers," he said, patronizing.

"Thanks." She smiled sweetly, even though she was boiling at his tone. "I can't believe I forgot that last time!"

"Hey, we all make mistakes starting out," Riley said, encouraging. Poppy flashed him a quick smile, then checked her cards again. She was finally sitting on an unbeatable hand, which meant the past hour of acting totally clueless was about to pay off.

Big-time.

Maybe it wasn't fair, acting like she'd never played before, but it was their fault for assuming she didn't know a royal flush from a pair. Aunt June had taught her everything she knew at family holidays—and June was a card shark in goldfish's clothing.

Poppy hid a smile, and eyed the massive stack of candy in the middle of the table. Her aunt had always told her to pick the right moment to play to win, and it looked like that moment was now.

"Any time soon would be great," Cooper reminded her, impatience flashing in his blue eyes.

"Hmmm." She pretended to think about it. "I guess . . . I'll see your bet." She pushed some M&Ms over. "And raise you . . . twenty." Poppy counted her candy and added it to the pile.

"Are you sure you want to do that?" Riley frowned, leaning in. "If you bust now, you're out of the game."

"Go big or go home," Poppy said brightly. "What do you think, Cooper—want to fold?"

He gave her an arrogant smile. "Nope, I'm good. I'll see you on that. And raise it, too."

The pile of candy grew. Riley let out a whistle, and threw down his cards. "I'm out."

"Guess it's just me and you, pipsqueak." Cooper grinned across the table.

"I guess so." Poppy made sure to bite her lip and give an anxious look at her cards.

Cooper's smile couldn't get any wider. He must think he had this game locked down, and Poppy couldn't blame him. She'd spent all night betting carefully—and losing every hand. But she hadn't been paying attention to her cards, she'd been watching the other players instead, learning all their secret tells. And they had plenty. Riley scratched his beard on a bad hand, Grayson gulped his beer to hide a smile when he was on a winning streak, and Cooper?

Cooper got impatient when he was bluffing. His knee bounced, just beneath the table, and he always pushed the other players to make their move before they had a chance to figure it out.

Like now.

He made a show of sighing. "You can still fold," he offered, like he was doing her a favor. "Keep those last chips for one more game."

"Thanks for the advice." She smiled again. "But I'm all in." She pushed the last of her candy forward. "I call."

Cooper raised an eyebrow. "If you say so." He lay down his cards. "Four of a kind."

"Decent." Poppy celebrated inside. She'd been right about his tell. He'd been bluffing all along. "That would be a winning hand . . . if I didn't have a royal flush. King, Queen, Jack, Ace. Boom!"

She laid her cards out. Jackpot.

Riley let out a whoop, and even Grayson chuckled. "You dark horse, you," he said approvingly.

"Face cards beat numbers, right?" she echoed Cooper's helpful advice.

"How did you . . . ?" he spluttered, looking totally shocked.

"Must be beginner's luck," she said, putting her arms out to sweep the massive stash of candy closer. "Or maybe it's the fact you're a terrible bluffer. Just some advice," she added, "but try not to tap your cards like that. It's a sure sign you've got nothing over sixes."

Riley hooted with laughter. Cooper scowled. "So you've been playing us all this time?" he demanded.

"You say 'playing,' I say 'letting you underestimate me.' " Poppy beamed. She tossed an M&M in her mouth and crunched. Delicious.

"This is your fault," Cooper grumbled to Riley. "You invited her."

"Yeah, well, I didn't know she had a secret life as a Vegas hustler." Riley looked impressed. He put his hand up to Poppy, and she high-fived him. "What are you doing next week?" he asked. "There are some guys out in Provincetown we could take to the bank."

Poppy laughed. "Sorry, I only play for chocolate."

"Too bad," Riley grinned. "We would make a mean double act."

Cooper cleared his throat. "Are we going to get on with the game?" he said, frowning.

Grayson laughed. "Game's over, man. And you lost." He got up, and went to the tiny kitchen in back for another beer. He brought one for Poppy, too. "To the victor," he said, toasting her.

She smiled. Aside from Cooper acting like a sore loser, she was having fun. She ate a couple more pieces of candy, and smiled at Cooper across the table. "What's the matter?" she teased. "Can't handle being beat by a girl?"

———————

"SURE I CAN." Cooper stared back across the table at Poppy, trying not to notice how damn cute she looked. Her cheeks were flushed and her eyes sparkled; she was clearly happy from her win.

He couldn't help but be impressed, even if his ego had taken a hit from that performance. He didn't think she'd had it in her to bluff and play him like she had, but he'd always been a bad judge of women.

His track record spoke to that, alright.

"I guess I shouldn't be surprised," he said ruefully. "You're a storyteller, right? And telling stories is just another way of hiding the truth."

Poppy looked thrown. "You lied, too," she pointed out, "Bluffing a bad hand."

Cooper shook his head. "That's not the same."

"Isn't it?" Poppy glared at him. "So I'm the liar and you're, what, just playing a game?"

"Hey," Riley interrupted. "Who wants to deal another hand?"

Cooper shook his head, still focused on Poppy. "I'm just saying, telling stories is all fine and good, until people wake up and realize they're in the real world."

They weren't talking about poker anymore, but it was needling him how she didn't seem to care what happened to her words once they were out in the world—those books she thought were so innocent giving people false hope and expectations. He could still remember the way he'd felt seeing that woman on the street yesterday, the sinking sense of dread when he'd thought she was Laura.

He'd believed in happily-ever-after once, and look where that had gotten him.

But Poppy clearly disagreed. She looked as if she was about to go to war to defend her right to sell an impossible fantasy. "For someone who hasn't read my books, you sure have a lot of opinions about them." Her voice was tense, and Cooper shrugged.

"I know what it's like to be fed a fairy tale, some happily-ever-after image of what life is going to be like. And all of that, it's just a lie. Maybe if you told the truth about love, people wouldn't be so disappointed in the end."

"Someone was disappointed with you?" Poppy snapped back. "Gee, what a surprise."

Her words were a kick in his gut. "Says the Queen of Hearts," Cooper replied, before he could stop himself. "Didn't I hear you were supposed to be getting married?" he asked. "I guess happily-ever-after isn't working out so great for you, after all."

Right away, he knew he'd crossed the line. Hurt flashed across Poppy's face, and she got to her feet.

"C'mon, take it easy." Riley tried to diffuse the situation. "How about we settle this on the table? Dealer's choice."

Poppy shook her head. "Thanks for the game," she said shortly. "I'll see myself out."

She walked quickly to the door, and let it slam shut behind her. The sound made him flinch. He'd really blown it now.

"You're an ass."

Cooper turned to find Riley scowling at him. Even Grayson, who usually steered clear of any drama, gave him a look. "Seriously," Riley continued. "What the hell was that? We were having a fun game, and then suddenly it's like World War 3 up in here."

Cooper sighed. "Sorry, man."

"I'm not the one you need to apologize to."

Cooper's conscience pricked uncomfortably. "I was just teasing," he lied. "It's not my problem if the girl can't handle a joke."

"Whatever you say." Riley shook his head, "Anyway, I guess that's game-over."

"I should be getting home anyway," Cooper said, finishing his beer. "I've got another early start tomorrow."

He said his goodbyes and headed out, but his guilt only grew. There was no good excuse for the things he'd said. He could see Poppy's face now—the way she'd pressed her lips together in that thin line, emotion flashing in her eyes. He may have meant every word he said to her, but it wasn't her fault. It wasn't anything to do with her.

Yup, he'd screwed up again.

With a sigh, he yanked the wheel around. His place was on the outskirts of Sweetbriar, deep in the woods, but he found himself driving back along the main road in the other direction, towards the shore. He could let Poppy cool down and sleep it off, but his father had taught him never to go to bed on an argument, and he'd learned the hard way how right the old man was about that. The least he could do was apologize and offer her a ride home.

Sure enough, as he followed the winding lane out of town, he saw a lone woman walking along the edge of the road in the dark. His headlights caught a slim figure with her arms wrapped around her. Poppy.

He slowed to a crawl alongside and rolled his window down. "Want a ride?"

Poppy barely glanced at him. "No thanks."

"Come on, it's cold out. You'll catch a chill."

"I'm fine." She paced on, stubborn.

"Consider it an apology," Cooper tried again. "I'm sorry I went off on you back there. It wasn't your fault."

"I know," Poppy snapped back, and despite his guilt, he had to stop himself from smiling. She hadn't changed at all. Still as stubborn as she was at ten years old.

"I'm trying to extend an olive branch here," he said. "Or are you going to make me beg?"

"Would you even know how?" Poppy's voice was still clipped, but he could see the edges of a smile on her lips.

"I'm a little out of practice, I'll admit." Cooper smiled. "Come on. I'd never hear the end of it from June if you went down with pneumonia your first week here."

Poppy paused, like she was assessing the road—and the chilled wind that was picking up off the ocean—then sighed. "OK. Thanks," she added reluctantly, as Cooper stopped the truck and she scrambled up into the passenger seat.

"There, look at us, building bridges," he said, trying

again to make her smile. He still felt bad for being such an ass earlier, but he couldn't bring himself to explain why. Why her simple belief in happy endings and true love brought out the devil in him. He'd wanted to lash out, and she'd been an easy target.

Poppy sat silently as he drove back towards the coast. The mile passed quickly, and the beach house appeared in front of them, the porch lights casting the house in a warm glow. Cooper pulled up outside the front door. "Here you go."

Poppy reached for the door handle.

"Wait, I've got that." Cooper found himself getting out and circling round to get her door. Poppy blinked, clearly surprised he was being so chivalrous, but she let him help her down from the truck cab.

"Thank you."

He walked with her up the front path. "You didn't say how long you were staying in town," he said, trying to make polite conversation.

"A few weeks, maybe. I'm trying to finish one of those bullshit romance novels." Her voice was still icy.

He winced. "I didn't mean it like that. I'm sure yours are great."

"Great for a lie, you mean."

Cooper clenched his jaw. "Maybe I shouldn't have said anything, but you have to admit, it's not exactly real life you're writing about."

"So what if it isn't?" Poppy protested, turning. "Maybe people deserve an escape."

"But what happens when they buy into that?" Cooper

asked. "And wind up believing that's what their lives should look like? Soulmates. True love."

"You don't believe in love?"

Cooper flinched. "Yeah, but not like it is in the books. Real love is messy, and broken, and hard. Not all fairy tales and Prince Charming."

"Says you." Poppy's gaze was determined. "If you want your life to be messy, and broken, and hard, then go right ahead. But don't judge the people who want something different."

Cooper exhaled. He didn't have an answer for that. Sure, he'd love to believe in a world like the ones in her books, but his life had shown him that was just a fantasy. In her books, your mom didn't walk out when you were just a kid, and you didn't have to watch your father die of cancer, and the one woman you tried to build a future with . . .

Well, let's just say they didn't write a happy ending together. No, she saved that for some other lucky guy.

"I guess we'll agree to disagree," he said, not wanting to fight anymore. "But I am sorry, for giving you a hard time. I'll try not to be a total ass like that again."

"I won't hold my breath," she replied, but still, her expression softened. Cooper guessed that was about as much as he could hope for, considering.

He'd take it.

She climbed the front steps, then turned back, her face level with his. "What was her name?" she asked. Her eyes were illuminated in the porch light, compassionate and steady. "The woman who hurt you like this?"

"What makes you think someone hurt me?" Cooper shot back, even as a knot twisted in his gut.

Poppy smiled ruefully. "I like to think you weren't always such an ass," she said. "Although, now that I think about it . . ."

Cooper laughed, hollow. He shouldn't have said anything, but there was something about the way she was looking at him, like somehow she understood the disillusionment that had carved its way deep into his chest.

"Laura." Her name stuck in his throat. "We were . . . going to get married. Start a family. Then she made other plans."

"I'm sorry." Poppy reached out and rested her hand on his arm for a moment. "Some things aren't meant to be."

Her touch was light, gentle on his, and despite everything, her words slipped past his defenses. For a moment, Cooper could almost believe her. That it wasn't his fault. That he hadn't destroyed his own chances of happiness.

That somehow, this was all part of a bigger story, instead of the same ending he was doomed to repeat.

Cooper reached for her. He didn't understand it, the instinct that suddenly surged through him. His body moved on its own, bypassing every rational thought as he stepped closer and reached to take her face between his hands.

Poppy's mouth fell open in surprise, but she didn't make a sound.

He kissed her.

Her lips were soft, already parted, and damn, so sweet

it was like a rush of pure sugar flooding his system, drowning out the darkness for one glorious moment as he reveled in the taste of her mouth, the soft touch against his hands, and the way her body swayed against him, closer, all heat and warm curves.

It felt right. Even as his brain caught up with him, it felt too good to be holding her in his arms. She let out a breathy sound against his mouth, and then she was kissing him back—as lost to the moment as he was, as their tongues intertwined in a sensual dance and he felt every last synapse in his body come screaming to life.

Wanting her. Wanting *more*.

What the hell was he doing?

He stepped back. Poppy looked dazed, her skin flushed and her eyes still half-closed. It was the sexiest thing he'd ever seen.

"I, uh," Cooper coughed. Poppy Somerville wasn't for kissing—or anything else. She'd already made it clear what she thought of him, and "incompatible" didn't even begin to cover it. "I'm sorry," he said gruffly. "That was . . . I don't even know. Sorry. Forget it even happened."

He turned on his heel and left, before he took leave of his senses and did anything stupid.

Like taking her to bed.

SEVEN.

FIVE DAYS LATER, Poppy could swear she still felt his lips on hers. It was like a dream. A weird, confusing "fallen asleep in front of the TV after eating too much Thai food" dream: one minute, she'd been arguing with him like usual, and the next?

She'd been deep in the most sensual, bone-melting kiss of her life.

With Cooper Nicholson.

Poppy shook her head, trying to shift those hot, toe-curling memories. It didn't make sense. Was it a joke? A game? Or maybe she should just chalk it up to temporary insanity—for the both of them. Cooper had made it clear he was as baffled as she was over what had just happened, and since he'd left her on the doorstep that night, he'd gone out of his way to steer clear. All week, she'd only seen him from a distance—hurrying straight to the construction site next door in the morning, or speeding past her in his truck as she browsed in town.

She should be relieved. The more space between them, the better. No chance of any more arguments—or heart-stopping kisses, either. But every time her mind wandered, it took her right back to that kiss, and how good it felt to be wrapped in his strong arms, giving in to the burning heat—

Nope. Poppy dragged her attention back to her laptop screen. She didn't have time to obsess over those delicious ten seconds, not when she had thirty chapters waiting to be conjured out of thin air.

Any time now.

Poppy sighed. She'd done everything she could to shift this writer's block—from brainstorms and writing exercises to rereading her older books in the series, hoping the familiar characters would take voice in her mind like they always had before. But the days were passing fast, and she was no closer to having even a hint of a book to send her editor. She was going stir-crazy from staring at her computer screen, but every time she got even a few pages of writing done, she knew in her bones it was all wrong. She hadn't found *it* yet—the heart of the story, the thing she wanted to say—and until she figured that part out, it was all just empty words.

She got up from her comfy seat in the den and went to go make dinner. It was a cloudy Sunday, overcast and spitting rain, but somehow she wasn't surprised to see Cooper's truck parked next door as usual, and the sound of occasional hammering coming from the bare-bones house. He definitely worked hard, even without the rest of his crew on site to lend a hand.

She paused at the kitchen window. The ocean was stormy, the foam-tipped waves surging up against the shore. Cooper emerged from the main structure to haul some wood in from the truck, bending his head against the wind. He was bundled up in a jacket and scarf, and for a moment, she thought about inviting him in for a hot drink or some dinner. Then she remembered how his mouth had felt against hers, sure and certain, and she prickled with embarrassment all over again.

Soup. She'd make soup. That would kill some time. Poppy set about pulling ingredients from the fridge: last night's chicken, celery, carrots—Aunt June's chicken soup could solve any problem, and she didn't even need a scribbled recipe as a guide. This one she knew by heart. Poppy had just diced the vegetables and added them to the pot when her cellphone rang. "Summer," she smiled, lodging the phone against her shoulder so she could keep stirring. "Hey."

"How's beach life?" Summer asked, her voice bright. "I'm so jealous, I've been working around the clock at the restaurant. Tell me how sunshine feels, all I have is those fluorescent strip lights burning down on me."

She smiled. Summer was a chef at a high-end restaurant back home, and for all her complaining, she loved her work. "No sun today, but you should take a break, come visit. Cash in all that vacation time you never use."

Summer sighed. "I wish. I booked time off for your wedding, but now . . ." She trailed off. "Whoops, sorry."

"It's OK," Poppy reassured her. "I'm not going to break down every time someone mentions marriage or weddings."

"I know, it's just . . . have you been on Facebook?"

"No, why?"

"Nothing!" Summer said brightly.

"Summer," Poppy prompted her.

"OK, don't flip, but Owen posted a bunch of photos. From Fiji."

Poppy paused stirring. "He went on our honeymoon without me?"

"Well, you weren't exactly going to go with him," Summer pointed out.

"I know, I just . . . didn't expect it. But I suppose it makes sense," Poppy said slowly, still trying to process the news. "We managed to get our money back for the venue and catering, but those flights were non-refundable. At least the trip didn't go to waste."

"Listen to you, so practical." Summer laughed. "Ever thought about writing non-fiction? You could do a how-to guide on cancelling your wedding."

Poppy didn't reply. She should be relieved that Owen had taken the honeymoon tickets; if anyone deserved a week on the beach in Fiji, it was him, after everything she'd put him through. She'd insisted on being the one to call around cancelling their wedding plans, but still, there were things they both had to take care of, like returning all the early wedding gifts to everyone, along with a polite note explaining that Owen Hendricks and Poppy Somerville were no longer due to be married.

"Poppy?" Summer asked, and she realized she'd been silent a while. "I'm sorry, it's too soon to be joking about this stuff. I know it hasn't been easy on you."

"It's OK," Poppy said. "I'm doing fine. And I mean it," she insisted. "I probably should be more devastated. I mean, we were together nearly two years. But mostly, I just feel . . . relieved."

Relieved she wasn't on her honeymoon as planned, with a ring on her finger and that sick feeling still heavy like a stone in her stomach. The fact that she hadn't even missed Owen once since getting on her flight said it all. She'd been so caught up in her deadline panic, she'd barely thought of him at all, not even when Cooper kissed her.

Cooper had kissed her.

Poppy remembered it all over again—in glorious Technicolor. She'd already been making out with another man, not three weeks after breaking her fiancé's heart.

Poppy groaned. "I'm a terrible person!"

"You're not!" Summer protested. "You did the right thing. And Owen will see that too, one day."

"I hope so." Poppy felt a pang. "I never meant to hurt him."

"Well, a week in a luxury resort getting waited on hand and foot probably helped soothe the blow," Summer said. "Hell, I'd call off a wedding if it got me out of the kitchen before seven. On a weekend."

"You love it," Poppy teased. "You'll be the youngest executive chef in town if you keep this up."

"I don't know." Summer sounded tired. "These hours, all the petty kitchen in-fighting . . . Anyway, listen to me, this is supposed to be *your* pep talk!"

Poppy laughed. "I told you, I'm fine."

"You're better than fine," Summer insisted. "You're amazing, and you've done the right thing. Now both you *and* Owen get to find the person you're supposed to be with, instead of spending years trapped in an empty marriage resenting every time he chews too loudly."

"Well, when you put it like that . . ."

"Anyway, I better get back to work," Summer said. "I'm trying to plan the menus for next week, and I'm running short on inspiration."

"How about chicken soup?" Poppy suggested. Her pot was simmering nicely now, filling the kitchen with the delicious smell of herbs and broth. "Didn't I read somewhere that comfort food is the new big trend?"

Summer laughed. "I wish. If I dared serve that at Chez Andre, they'd probably throw down their silver spoons and storm out. But maybe a deconstructed coq au vin . . ." she mused. "With rosemary and gorgonzola soufflés . . ."

"There you go." Poppy smiled. "Good luck!"

"You too, babe."

She hung up and moved the pot off the flame. Outside, the spatter of rain had turned to a steady drizzle, and the clouds were darkening fast. Poppy paused at the window. Cooper's truck was still parked there, but with all the tarps flapping about where his roof was supposed to be, he couldn't be getting much shelter from the rain. It would be the neighborly thing to invite him in. After all, she had plenty of soup.

But he'd kissed her.

And insisted it was a mistake that meant nothing, she reminded herself. If he could pretend like it never happened, then she could, too.

As she deliberated, there was a rumble of thunder in

the distance. The skies opened, and the drizzle became a deluge, pouring down and battering the bare construction frame next door. She saw a flash of movement, and then Cooper came hurrying through the storm towards his truck.

Poppy opened the back door. "Cooper!" she yelled, waving across the yard. "Come inside."

She beckoned, and he paused for a moment. Then the thunder rumbled again, and he changed direction, and veered across the yard towards her. He sprinted up the back steps and inside just as the sky flared with lightning.

She closed the door fast. Cooper was dripping wet, his hair plastered to his head and water running in rivulets over his cheeks. "You're soaked!" Poppy exclaimed, trying to ignore the fact he looked like some kind of Gothic romance hero, striding in out of the rain. "Here, let me get you a towel." She found one in the clean laundry pile and handed it to him, taking his wet jacket in return. She hung it by the door, and then moved some newspaper underneath to catch the drips of water. "Boots?" she demanded, and Cooper pulled them off. A smile played on the edge of his lips.

"Yes, ma'am," he said.

She groaned. "God, don't ma'am me. I've got another ten years of 'miss,' I swear."

Cooper toweled off his wet hair and face. Even under his jacket, his clothes looked soaked. Poppy beckoned for them. "Let me put those in the dryer, before you catch a cold."

Cooper raised an eyebrow in amusement. "Trying to

get me naked? At least buy me dinner first."

Poppy flushed. "I'll find you a bathrobe, or something to wear." She scurried out before he could see her cheeks burning red. She suddenly realized that for all her neighborly good intentions, she'd just invited the wolf through her door. The handsome, sexy wolf.

And told him to take all his clothes off, too.

Poppy ignored the slow flip in her stomach, and busied herself tracking down dry clothes for him to wear. Even her slouchiest clothes would be way too small for him, but buried in the closet in one of the guest rooms, she hit the jackpot: an old Indiana State T-shirt and some men's sweatpants, sized large.

"Success," she said, entering the kitchen with her bounty. She was braced for some kind of tension or awkwardness, but instead, Cooper was by the stove, with a spoon already dipping into the pan of soup. He paused, looking so much like a guilty schoolboy, she couldn't help but laugh. "Go change," she said, "I'll fix us a couple of bowls."

"Angel." Cooper flashed her a smile on his way out, so bright Poppy was thrown off balance.

Wow.

It was a good thing he was so grumpy, she thought. Otherwise that smile could do some serious damage. As it was, she had time to pull herself together—setting out two bowls, and a board with some hard cheese and the crusty loaf she'd bought in town the day before. When Cooper rejoined her, dressed in the sports gear, she didn't even notice the way the T-shirt pulled over his muscular torso, or how the loose sweatpants inexplicably hugged his ass.

Didn't notice for long, at least.

"That smells amazing," Cooper said, eyeing the soup hungrily. His hair was damp and rumpled, dark strands in his eyes, and Poppy felt an inexplicable urge to push it back.

Down, girl.

"You have good timing, it's just ready." She ladled it between their bowls, then took a seat at the old kitchen table. He cleared a stack of magazines off the other chair and joined her.

"Thanks. For the shelter, and the soup." Cooper said. He shot Poppy a rueful smile. "I don't know what I was thinking, trying to work through this. Everyone said the rain was coming."

"But you thought you knew better?" she said, half-teasing.

"Something like that."

They started to eat. Cooper devoured his first bowl, barely coming up for air, then went to fix another. This one, he ate slower, sopping up the juices with bread. "Damn, nothing beats Aunt June's soup," he said, sounding satisfied. "I talked her into bringing it to a town potluck last year, I swear I stood guard by the table all night, making sure everyone only took one helping."

Poppy smiled. "Once, my college boyfriend dumped me in the middle of finals, and she shipped me a jar of it, wrapped up in tissue paper so the glass wouldn't break."

He laughed. "I keep asking for the recipe, but she says

it's family only."

"Really?" Poppy arched an eyebrow. "Then you better be extra-nice to me."

"I can do that."

Cooper caught her eye with a roguish smile, and just like that, Poppy forgot what they were even talking about. Her stomach turned a slow flip, and she felt her cheeks flush.

She knew how those lips felt, soft against hers.

She looked away. "Are you done?" she said, her voice coming out high-pitched. She got up and reached for his empty bowl, but Cooper waved her hands away.

"I've got this." He cleared their things, and ran hot water to do the dishes. "Coffee?" he offered.

"Thanks. The pot is—"

"Right here. You go put your feet up," he ordered her lightly. "Consider it my thanks for dinner."

"OK." Poppy didn't know quite what to do with herself, so she went to the living room and curled up on the couch. The worst of the storm had passed, but rain was still drumming lightly on the porch roof, and it felt warm and cozy inside. She pulled a blanket down and tried to relax, but it was impossible with the awareness humming through her body. She could hear Cooper moving about in the kitchen, and wondered if he felt it too. Or maybe he'd meant what he'd said the other night, and the kiss really didn't mean a thing to him. So why had he leaned in and claimed her lips like that?

And why had it felt so good?

Poppy was still puzzling when he emerged a few

minutes later with two steaming mugs. "Milk and sugar OK?" he asked, handing her one.

"Great. Thank you." Poppy wrapped her hands around the mug, as Cooper casually sat down on the other side of the couch. He stretched his legs out in front of him and yawned.

"I hope this doesn't last all week," he said, looking out the window. "We need to get the roof on, or we'll be way behind schedule."

"Your client cracking the whip?" she asked.

"Something like that." Cooper looked over. "It's my place," he told her. "For now, anyway. I figure I'll fix it up, then find some rich summer people to take it off my hands."

Cooper seemed to be working too hard for it to just be a flip project, but Poppy didn't push. "Sounds like a plan," she said instead. "You shouldn't have any problem finding a buyer. I've been here a week, and already I never want to leave."

Cooper grinned. "Even with all the noise?"

She tossed a cushion at him. "Don't. The next time my agent calls demanding pages, I'll sic her on you."

"How's the writing going, anyway?" he asked, taking a sip of his coffee.

She let out a pitiful groan. "It's not."

"What do you mean?

"I'm blocked," she admitted sadly. "Completely and utterly blocked."

Cooper seemed amused. "Hazard of the trade, right?"

She shook her head. "Not to me. Not like this. It's the

most important book of my career, the one everyone's waiting for, but all I can do is sit at my computer screen and panic." Poppy could feel it all over again, the crushing weight of expectations pressing down on her chest. "And then I beat myself up for panicking, and feel guilty for letting everyone down, and then the whole feedback loop starts again."

"Whoa there." Cooper looked surprised. "Is this what you've been doing all week, just sitting here in your loop?"

She nodded. "Sometimes I go to the café in town and sit and panic there, too. I'm a failure," she said. "And an imposter, too. Maybe you were right before," she added, looking over at him in defeat. She'd been fighting her doubts and insecurities all along, but maybe it was time to admit the truth. "What do I know about happily-ever-after?" she said. "I mean, just look at me. I've written a dozen romance novels, but I don't have any clue what I'm doing when it comes to my own love life."

Poppy cringed to hear the words out loud. "God, I'm such a cliché—the romance author who's never been in love."

Cooper quirked an eyebrow, and Poppy braced herself for the questions about what happened with Owen, but instead, he suddenly got to his feet. "You've been sitting in this house way too long," he announced. "We need to break this cycle. Come on."

"What? Where?" Poppy blinked. "It's storming out there."

"Not anymore." Cooper paused, listening, and Poppy

realized he was right. The steady drum had stopped, but it was still dark out, and late now, too.

"I don't know . . ." she said reluctantly. "I figured I would just curl up with a book. Is anything even open on a Sunday night?"

Cooper grinned. "Ye of little faith. Come on, grab your coat and let's get out of here. It'll be fun, I promise."

Poppy hesitated. It wasn't the cold and dark she was worried about, it was the man standing in front of her: tall and broad-shouldered, and looking way too tempting. But Cooper flashed her that irresistible smile, and she knew, she didn't stand a chance. Between Cooper and another night in staring at a blank screen, there was no contest.

"Fine," she agreed, and got to her feet. "But don't think this will win you Aunt June's secret recipe."

Cooper laughed. "You'll change your tune by the time I'm through with you." He winked, and Poppy felt her stomach turn that slow, delicious arabesque.

The problem was, she would.

EIGHT.

COOPER STARTED THE ENGINE, waiting for Poppy to get herself together. His clothes were dry, his belly was full, and he was feeling something he never expected to for his infuriating new neighbor.

Sympathy.

He'd thought her tantrums over the construction noise were just some kind of prima donna routine, but watching the sadness and fear in Poppy's eyes as she described her writer's block, he realized it went much deeper than that. She was cracking under a ton of pressure—and he'd been making it worse. One more thing to add to the list of things he needed to make amends for, right below picking fights at poker games, and kissing her on the front porch.

That kiss . . .

Cooper paused. He'd been trying to banish it from his mind all week, but somehow, it always came back to him. The feel of her lips, soft and yielding. The look in her eyes, dazed with desire . . . He'd lost his mind even reaching for her in the first place, but damn if it hadn't been the best ten seconds of temporary insanity he could remember.

"OK, I'm all set." Poppy climbed up beside him into

the truck. She was bundled up in a red winter coat now, her hair peeking out from under a knit cap; cheeks flushed from the cold. She looked over expectantly. "What's this big outing you've got planned?"

"Wait and see." Cooper put the truck in drive. The truth was, he didn't have a plan yet, he just knew he needed to get Poppy out of that house. It looked like she'd been holed up there all week, going stir-crazy as she battled that blank page. She needed something to snap her out of it and make her loosen up a little. The question was what.

Sweetbriar on a Sunday night didn't exactly have many options. Most stores had shut hours ago, and even Riley didn't keep the pub open past nine. Besides, he and Poppy didn't have the best track record when it came to pleasant conversation, so they needed something distracting . . . noisy . . . preferably in a public place where he wouldn't be tempted to go kissing her again . . .

He had it.

Cooper drove up through town then turned onto the highway, heading towards Wellfleet, just a few miles away. Poppy turned the stereo on beside him, and his CD of old classics started to play.

"I love Elvis." She sounded surprised.

"My dad used to play these CDs in the car all the time," he explained. She turned the volume up a little and sang along. He tried to hide a smile, but she caught it.

"I'm terrible, I know," Poppy said cheerfully. "I swear I'm tone deaf."

"You'll fit right in at karaoke," Cooper grinned.

"There's a karaoke place in Sweetbriar?" Poppy asked. "Why am I not surprised?"

"Riley got a system, a couple of years back. If it were up to me, I'd smash the thing, but he says it's good for profits. People need a couple of extra beers before they get up the courage to sing," he explains.

Poppy laughed. "Smart guy."

"He can be." Cooper nodded. Riley was a good friend, but sometimes Cooper wondered what the guy was doing sticking around someplace as small as Sweetbriar. He'd made his fortune in tech and social media, and now he was killing time pouring beers, but Cooper would never ask. Just like Riley didn't ask about his past, there were some things guys just kept to themselves.

Cooper saw the turn up ahead, and pulled off the main highway. The neon sign loomed up above them, bright against the dark sky: *Wellfleet Drive-In.*

"Oh my god!" Poppy exclaimed, seeing the lettering. "I didn't think this place would still be running!"

"It's a Cape institution," Cooper said. He'd remembered seeing her there as a kid, when a parent would pile them all in the back of a car, and they'd run riot, fueled by popcorn and candy. He'd figured she might enjoy it again, and seeing the grin on her face, he'd chosen right. "I'm not sure what's playing tonight, so don't hold it against me if it's nothing but Disney cartoons."

"Let's see . . ." Poppy peered out of the window at the display board. "It's an oldie night. *Vertigo.*"

"Works for me." Cooper paid the five bucks entrance fee to the kid at the front gate, and then slowly drove into the field that doubled as the drive-in lot. There was a screen set up at the far end, and a few rows of cars already parked in place. He picked a spot in the middle of a row and pulled in. "You want popcorn?" he asked, turning off the engine.

"We just ate!" Poppy laughed.

"And?" Cooper reached to open his door, but Poppy acted first.

"I'll go," she said, hopping down. "Sweet or salted?"

"Surprise me." He could have sworn she blushed, but maybe that was just the headlights.

"I'll be right back."

He watched Poppy head across to the concession stand, her red coat bright in the dark. He hadn't planned on spending his evening like this, but he had to admit, he was having fun. An old movie, some conversation—there were worse ways to pass the time. As long as he kept his head and stayed in control this time, there wouldn't be any repeat of the madness of last week.

Poppy was just a friend. A neighbor. His platonic acquaintance.

At least, that was the plan.

Another car pulled into the spot next to him, and he turned to find a couple of teenagers in the front seats. The boy shut of his engine, then promptly reached over to start making out with his date.

Cooper averted his eyes. OK, so maybe he could have picked a more platonic spot than a dark drive-in movie theater, but he was a grown man, not some hormone-addled teen. Just because Poppy's lips were undeniably kissable didn't mean he was a slave to attraction. She hadn't even mentioned what happened between them, and for all he knew, it hadn't crossed her mind. He should be relieved she was being so relaxed about everything, instead of making a scene. He'd said to forget about it, that it meant nothing at all.

So why did it burn that she'd been able to do just that and move on?

POPPY STOOD IN LINE at the concession stand and tried to ignore the butterflies spinning in her stomach. Movie tickets, popcorn . . . Had she and Cooper accidentally wound up on some kind of date?

No. She quickly shook off that thought. He was just being friendly, that's all. Surprisingly friendly, given their history, but she wasn't complaining. He was right, she'd been going crazy in that house, and she was feeling better already just getting out into the crisp night air for a few hours of welcome distraction.

"Popcorn, please," she asked the boy manning the stand. "Sweet and salty, just mix it all together. And a couple of sodas . . . and red vines . . ." Poppy hadn't been to the movies in months, and she got carried away; by the time she returned to Cooper's truck, her arms were laden with snacks. "Maybe I went a little wild," she said, passing the bounty before she climbed back up.

"A little?" he echoed, looking at the spread. He reached for the box of candy. "I guess I better step up to the plate."

"Aim high. I believe in you." Poppy laughed. She looked past him, and saw the windows of the next car steaming up. Inside, she could just about make out a couple of teenagers necking—hard.

"Ah, romance," she quipped, and Cooper shot her a grin.

"You think they'll catch a single frame of the movie?"

"No way." Poppy munched on a handful of popcorn. "God, when I was a teenager, we used to drive out to this abandoned farm in the middle of the country to park. You couldn't move for beat-up old Hondas."

"We would all go to the woods," Cooper said. "The property I'm working on now, actually. There's a whole acre back there, and if those trees could talk . . ."

Poppy grinned. "Is that why you bought it? All those fond memories."

"Something like that." Cooper grinned. "Actually, it's the rest of its history. Old saltbox houses like that are disappearing these days. Most people don't want the hassle of restoring when it's easier to just knock them down and build from scratch. But you lose all the historical details, the craftsmanship . . ." He was talking animatedly, and Poppy could see the passion on his face. He'd played it off before like just another money-making flip, but it was clear he cared about the house far more than that.

"Seems like a lot of work for something that's just a paycheck," she said carefully.

Cooper shrugged. "Call it a work ethic," he said. "I can't help but get the job done."

She snorted. "Ha!"

"Excuse me?" he looked over.

"The Cooper I remember would find any excuse to get out of chores," Poppy said, shooting him a mischievous grin. "Your dad had to come drag you off the beach to go do laundry."

Cooper grinned. "He wasn't exactly paying me sweat equity back then."

Poppy took another handful of popcorn. The trailers were playing on screen, local ads for lobster shacks and pottery classes. "How is he these days?" she asked.

Cooper paused, and a shadow slipped over his face. "He passed a few years back. Stomach cancer."

She gasped. "Oh God, I'm so sorry. I didn't know." She looked at him anxiously, hoping she hadn't just put her foot in her mouth and dragged up painful history, but Cooper just gave her a quiet smile.

"It's OK. I mean, I still miss him, but . . ." He paused. "Life goes on."

It did. The summer they'd all run wild as kids seemed a lifetime ago. Twenty years, gone in the blink of an eye. Poppy sighed. "We were babies back then."

Cooper chuckled. "We're not over the hill just yet." He nudged her elbow. "You've got a few good years in you yet."

"Gee, thanks." She laughed. "I'll need them. My mom is already sending me links about the likelihood of finding a husband after thirty."

"Ouch." Cooper looked over at her. "So what happened, with your wedding? You don't have to talk about it if you don't want," he added. "I just heard it all got called off."

Poppy let out a breath. She didn't want to drag it all up now, not when she was finally getting some distance. "Let's just say it wasn't meant to be."

"Fair enough."

To her relief, Cooper didn't push. He reached for the radio instead, and tuned it to the movie soundtrack. The cab filled with the opening music as the movie started on screen. But Poppy couldn't focus. She still felt jittery, like she'd been drinking too much coffee. Maybe that cup she'd had an hour ago was wreaking havoc on her system. Or maybe it was being alone in the dark, just an arm's length away from the man who'd kissed her senseless.

She snuck a look at him beside her, his features illuminated in the light from the movie screen. Why did he have to be so handsome?

"Everything OK?" Cooper turned and caught her looking.

"Yes. Great!" Poppy snapped her gaze back to the screen. "I haven't seen this movie in forever."

"It's a classic," Cooper agreed. "Are you comfortable? I can put the seat back if you want."

"I've got it." Poppy grappled around for the lever, until Cooper chucked.

"Here." He reached across her, sliding his hand down the side of her seat. "It's temperamental," he said apologetically. "You have to yank it just so . . ."

"Uh huh." Poppy's reply was faint. He was leaning in, so close she could smell the rain still on his hair.

"There!"

Suddenly, her seat tilted back so fast Poppy let out a yelp and grabbed hold of him for balance.

"Whoa." Cooper braced against the seat. For a moment, they were almost horizontal. His blue eyes were dark in the shadows, and she was so close, she could feel his breath on her cheek, hot. *If she just slid her arms around his neck* . . . The thought slipped recklessly into Poppy's mind, and her gaze dropped, drawn to his mouth. His lips were just inches away—

"Sorry." Cooper pulled himself up and shifted back to the driver's seat. "I told you it was temperamental."

"Right." Poppy gulped. "Thanks."

"No problem." Cooper grabbed another handful of popcorn. He was staring straight at the screen, like nothing had even happened. "Let's enjoy the show."

POPPY HAD ALWAYS loved Hitchcock, but by the time the credits rolled, she couldn't have told you anything that happened on screen. She'd spent the movie sneaking furtive glances at Cooper, wondering if he felt the electric tension between them, or if it was all in her mind.

None of this would have happened if he hadn't kissed her. It was like how they said a bell could never be unrung; he'd kissed her, and now she couldn't be un-kissed. In an instant, he'd gone from being Cooper, the gruff neighbor keeping her up when she needed to sleep, to *Cooper*. The man who had pulled her into his arms and made her feel something she hadn't in a long, long time. And for all their casual conversation that night, Poppy still knew something between them had shifted, and it wasn't ever shifting back.

"What did you think?"

Cooper's voice pulled her back, and she realized the movie was over. The other cars were rolling out, and the concession boy was pulling up the screen.

"Oh. Great. It was good," Poppy blurted. "Thanks for bringing me."

"Any time." Cooper turned on the engine and joined the snaking line heading back across the field to the highway. They drove back towards Sweetbriar in companionable silence, but Poppy couldn't help but feel the tension still crackling between them. Unless she was delusional and conjuring something out of thin air. She glanced over again. Cooper looked perfectly at ease, like he was probably thinking about rivets and hammers, or whatever sports game was on tomorrow night.

"Feel any better about that book?" he asked.

She sighed, and he shot her a sympathetic look. "I guess not."

"I'll figure it out. I *have* to," she vowed. "I just need to decide what it's about. Not the plot," she explained, "but the theme."

"What do you mean?" Cooper asked as he pulled up back outside the cottage.

"It's hard to explain, but there's always a question I wind up asking in my writing, or some argument I want to explore," Poppy said. The truck stopped, but she didn't move. "My last book was about forgiveness—how you can heal and move on with someone you love. But when I try to think about what matters to me right now, the message I want to send my readers, I just come up a blank. It's like everything that's happened with Owen and the wedding just drained away my inspiration. I don't know how to get that back," she said sadly. "Not when I wonder sometimes if chasing my soulmate is just a childish dream."

Poppy stopped herself, too late. Listen to her, blabbering her deepest insecurities—to someone who had already made it perfectly clear he thought she was a naïve con-artist peddling lies. "Anyway, thanks for this. I needed to get my mind off everything." She opened the door and got down, wanting to put as much distance as possible between herself and that confession, but Cooper followed, shutting off the engine to walk her to the door.

"Maybe that's your question," he said finally. Poppy turned. "How you can keep believing in something, even when you don't have any proof it's going to work out," he explained. "And what about if you believe it?" he added. "If you think you have everything, and it doesn't work out. Are you supposed to just do it all over again, like nothing ever happened? Offer up your heart for someone to stomp all over because, what, they might be the real one this time?"

Poppy saw the emotion flashing across his features, then he shrugged, looking self-conscious. "Or, something like that. What do I know?"

"No . . . you're right," she said slowly. She was wondering if her faith in happily-ever-after would ever be rewarded—or if she was just a foolish romantic for hanging onto that dream. Well, plenty of her readers could relate to that dilemma. And what Cooper said about starting over . . . that was the real risk. The highest stakes of all. To love, even when you'd been hurt before. Even when you knew the price of watching it all fall apart around you.

For the first time in months, Poppy felt a shiver of inspiration. Cooper was right. The story had been inside her all along. She'd been holding back, not wanting to throw all her personal issues onto the page, but maybe that was the only choice. Write through her fears and insecurities, and see if she could find the answers that way.

Relief crashed over her. She wasn't doomed, after all.

"Thank you!" Poppy threw her arms around Cooper, smothering him in a hug. "Seriously, thank you!"

Cooper froze, clearly surprised. For a moment, his body was solid against hers, and even separated by their layers of bulky winter wear, Poppy could swear she felt the heat from his body, all the way to her bones.

Her breath caught. They were back on her porch, the place it had happened. Only this time, she knew what was coming.

She knew how good it would be to taste his lips again.

Releasing him, Poppy slowly stepped back to solid ground. She caught his eyes, and she could see it there: the same desire that was singing in her veins. A low heat burning, ready to flare brighter in the dark.

Oh God. This was it. Time seemed to slow as she parted her lips and took a breath, and leaned in to—

"I'll see you then."

She felt the gust of cold air replacing his nearness as Cooper stepped back. He jammed his hands in his coat pockets, looking at the ground. "Good luck with the writing," he said gruffly, then turned and hurried back to his truck before she could get a word out.

Poppy quickly turned and let herself in, slamming the door shut behind her. She sank back against the solid wood and took a trembling breath.

What just happened there?

Nothing. A whole lot of nothing—exactly the way it should be, she reminded herself. She hadn't come here to get entangled in romantic drama with Cooper, she was here to leave all of that behind her and work. And for the first time in too long, Poppy finally had words dancing in her brain, sentences waiting on the tips of her fingers.

No more distractions, however tempting.

She grabbed her computer, turned on the study light, and got to work.

NINE.

*I*T RAINED ALL WEEK, and Poppy loved every minute of it. With the outside world damp and grey, she had the perfect excuse to hide herself away at the cottage again—except this time, instead of staring at her blank screen with a sense of looming dread, she was writing.

All day long.

This was when she loved her work: when a story finally took flight, and she was so caught up in spilling the words onto the page that she didn't even notice the time passing. She surfaced briefly for food, and to shower, but aside from the essentials, Poppy blocked everything out and just wrote. No distractions, no calls; she ignored her emails, let her phone go to voicemail, and just threw herself into the book.

It felt good to be back on her game again. Sure, the chapters were messy, and she was sprinting to make up for lost time, but that crushing panic was finally gone, and it felt like a weight had been lifted from her shoulders.

Speaking of . . . Poppy paused to massage her aching neck. She'd been hunched over her laptop for days, and even though she tried to take breaks to stretch and walk around, she felt the tension running tightly across her shoulders and back. She glanced outside. The rain had finally passed, and she'd woken that morning to find clear skies and a bright horizon. Maybe she should take a real rest, and walk into town. She'd pretty much lived off store cupboard pasta and soup all week, and she needed fresh groceries and supplies if she was going to keep up this pace.

The phone rang, and Poppy reached for her cellphone before she realized it wasn't hers, but the landline. She picked up the retro red handset Aunt June had in the corner. "Hello?"

"Hi, Poppy," a friendly voice said. "It's Mackenzie, we met the other day? Caffeine addict, fan-girl . . ."

"Hey." Poppy smiled. "I remember, how's it going?"

"I'm great. I didn't have your cell number, but I figured I'd give you a call," Mackenzie said. "My book club is meeting tomorrow, and I know you're probably busy, but Franny's made her plum cobbler, and it would be a crime for you to miss out."

Poppy hesitated. She didn't want to interrupt her progress on the book, but she knew a break would be good for her. She'd been holed up for so long, she hadn't had a chance to meet any more Sweetbriar citizens, and Mackenzie seemed like fun.

Besides, home-baked plum cobbler was too good to resist.

"I'd love to," she said.

"Yay!" Mackenzie exclaimed. "It'll be fun, I promise. It's my turn to host, so just come by Fired Earth around four. It's the pottery studio on Main Street."

"I know it." Poppy smiled. "Can I bring anything?"

"No, you're good," Mackenzie said. "Unless you have a bottle of wine or two knocking around."

"Wine?" Poppy was surprised—especially because they were meeting in the afternoon.

"Like I said, we're not your usual book club."

Poppy laughed. "Wine it is then. See you later."

She hung up, smiling. With all the work she'd done, she'd earned some drinks and cobbler tomorrow—and maybe the chance to make a few friends, too. Aunt June would be back from her cruise in a week, but Poppy was already thinking about staying longer, and taking her time to enjoy the local area and all its attractions.

Like the attraction next door.

Poppy listened to the sound of hammering and tried not to imagine Cooper at work. They'd been on a rain break all week, but he'd arrived with his crew first thing in the morning, and Poppy had taken all her self-control not to find a reason to cross that property divide and say hello.

She couldn't stop thinking about him.

Ever since that night at the drive-in, feeling that strange electric tension shimmering in the air, Poppy hadn't been able to get him off her mind. Her days were filled with writing, but when she closed her laptop at the end of the night and climbed into bed, somehow, thoughts of him were always waiting. The solid, confident movement of his body. The way his eyes crinkled at the corners when he smiled.

His kiss.

She shivered at the memory. He was probably work-ing there now, wearing that pale blue T-shirt that brought out the blue in his eyes . . . and those jeans that hugged his ass just right . . . his muscles rippling under the fabric of—

Nope. Poppy dragged her mind out of the gutter and back to her screen. She was clearly rebounding from her failed engagement—looking for love in all the wrong places. And Cooper Nicholson couldn't be more wrong.

There was a knock at the door, and Poppy leapt up, glad for another distraction. "Coming!" she called. She went to go open the door, and stopped dead when she saw who was waiting on the other side. "Cooper." She flushed, wondering for a second if she'd conjured him up with all her lustful thoughts. "Hi."

"Hey." Cooper looked concerned. "Sorry, I didn't mean to interrupt. Are you sick?"

Poppy glanced down. She was still in her pajamas, at two in the afternoon. "No, writing," she said, embar-rassed. "I guess I lost track of time."

"You broke through your block? That's great," Cooper congratulated her.

"So far, we'll see. I don't want to jinx it," Poppy add-ed, but she couldn't keep from beaming. After so much stress and insecurity, it was a relief just to wake up in the morning with an idea for the chapter ahead. "What can I do for you?"

"Well, it's actually the other way around." Cooper shifted on the doorstep. There was a boyish smile playing on his lips, like he was excited about something. "I have something to show you. But, you'll need to get dressed first."

"OK." Poppy was puzzled. "Give me five minutes."

"Take your time."

She went back inside and upstairs, but as she headed for her bedroom, she caught sight of her reflection in the mirror. *No!* She groaned. It was no wonder he thought she was sick: she looked a mess. Her hair was tangled, her skin had that pale zombie look about it, and was that . . . ? Yup, strawberry jam smeared across her jaw.

Poppy jumped in the shower and rinsed off in record time, then she pulled her hair up into a ponytail, dressed in jeans and a red knit sweater, and bounced back downstairs. Cooper was waiting there, out on the porch. "You must be relieved the weather changed." Poppy said, as she sat on the bottom stair and pulled on her boots.

"It put a dent in my schedule, that's for sure." Cooper pushed his hair back from his blue eyes, sounding rueful. "I worked on some plans and internal sketches, but yeah, there's only so much you can do."

"It's gorgeous out today." Poppy felt the warm temperature and left her jacket on the rack. "I always love it after the rain clears, everything seems to fresh and new."

She was babbling, she knew. And about the weather, too. How much more awkward could you get? But Cooper didn't seem to notice, and she followed him outside and into the yard.

He led her past the construction site, to where a sandy path led away from the house, meandering along the shoreline.

"Are you sure you aren't just leading me astray?" she joked, and then cringed again. Cooper seemed perfectly relaxed, so why couldn't she do the same? It wasn't like they'd had a torrid affair; it had been one kiss, weeks ago now. She should have done study abroad in France, Poppy thought. They knew how to deal with casual *liaisons*. That, and all the delicious cheese.

She was so busy scolding herself for her lack of chill, Poppy barely registered their surroundings, until she realized they were passing through a wooded area, with pine needles carpeting the sand underfoot. The air smelled fresher here, a mix of the tree scent and salty air, and they were far enough from the house that she couldn't hear the construction noise over the steady swish of the waves against the shore.

"It's beautiful out here," she said, looking around. "I've been cooped up inside for so long, I haven't even had a chance to explore the beach."

"I figured." Cooper still looked strangely excited—like a kid who had a secret he was just dying to tell. "I also figured you might need some peace and quiet for your writing. And since I can't exactly give you that back at the house . . ."

He came to a stop beside what looked like an old cabin: the wooden frame nestled on the edge of the trees, overlooking the dunes and ocean. The wood was bleached and weathered, and bluebells were growing wild, half-covering the old frame with creeping vines and sprigs of blue flowers. "Surprise."

Poppy was confused, but Cooper just chuckled. "Look inside."

Poppy moved closer and cautiously swung the doors open. She was expecting rust and dirt, but they swung open smoothly to reveal a tiny cabin, barely thirty square feet.

"I forgot this was even standing," Cooper explained behind her. "But I was out checking the property line the other day, and found it. I thought it could be your writing cabin."

Wait, what?

She turned and looked at him in surprise. "This is for me?"

"If you want." Cooper looked bashful. "I know it's not much, but I swept it out and brought down some furniture, too. I figured, it's away from everything, so even if we have to drill the foundations, you won't hear the noise."

Poppy stepped inside. It was tiny, but surprisingly homey. The walls were wooden boards, with a single window, and there was barely enough room for an armchair and an old bistro table, but Cooper had put a knitted throw over the chair, and fit a rickety bookcase in the back.

"This is amazing," Poppy breathed, looking around. With the doors open, it was like she was right there on the beach, nothing between her and that incredible view, blue water and clear skies as far as she could see. She could drag the chair out and have her toes in the sand all day long while she wrote.

"You like it?" he asked, looking hopeful.

"I love it!" Poppy exclaimed. Cooper looked pleased. "Thank you so much," she told him, beaming. "Seriously. I can't believe you did this for me."

Cooper cleared his throat. "It's not a big deal, it was just sitting here, getting dusty. And this way, you won't be complaining about noise all day."

He was trying to play it off as an afterthought, but Poppy was still touched by the gesture. He'd put thought into this, and care, too, and knowing he'd done it all in secret to surprise her gave Poppy a sudden burst of confidence.

"Have dinner with me," she asked suddenly, before she could take it back. "As a thank you, for this. To-night?"

Cooper looked thrown, and for a moment, she won-dered if she'd made a massive mistake. Her heart beat faster. Then he gave her a thoughtful smile. "OK."

"OK," Poppy echoed, full of relief. "Great. Pick me up at seven?"

"It's a date."

He said the words casually, but as they sunk in, Poppy realized for the first time what she'd just done.

She was going on a date. With Cooper.

Gorgeous, infuriating, argumentative Cooper.

And lord knows what was going to happen next.

TEN.

*W*HAT HAD HE gotten himself into now? Cooper spent the rest of the afternoon a daze, wondering how he'd managed to go from "keeping his distance" to "pick you up at seven" in barely ten minutes flat. So much for staying platonic. He'd managed to resist temptation last time around, only to throw that self-control out the window the minute she smiled up at him with those hopeful brown eyes and asked the same question he'd been biting back all week.

Dinner. A date. Damn, what was he thinking?

What was he thinking *with*, more like? He should never have fixed up that cabin for her. It wasn't even supposed to be a big deal; he'd stumbled over it, just like he said, and for some reason, an image of Poppy had dropped into his mind: sitting out there with her laptop, curled up while the ocean breeze lifted her hair around her face. He told himself he needed to clean the place out sometime, and if he did it now, it would save him having to deal with her marching over to complain every time he needed to drill a support beam or hammer the joists in place. But sweeping out the sand had turned to polishing the window, and nailing that old shelving unit to the wall, because he was guessing she liked to have books with her wherever she went. Before he knew it, the place was all spruced up.

And the smile on Poppy's face when she saw it had just about made his week.

Cooper knew he was playing with fire. If she was anyone else, none of this would be a problem. He wasn't a monk—he'd had his share of flings these past years, with women who were in town for the summer, or just passing through. Casual, fun arrangements where they both knew exactly what the rules were, and nobody got hurt.

But Poppy was different. For all the red-hot chemistry between them, she was searching for the real thing. Cooper may not know much about women, but he knew he wasn't it. After Laura, he'd steered clear of relationships, and for good reason. He'd screwed up the one thing that had mattered more than anything to him, and he knew that given half a chance, he'd do the same to the next woman who came along. Some people were made for togetherness, and some people were just an emotional ticking time bomb—set to detonate and destroy everything in their path. Cooper knew which he was now, and he wasn't about to throw that grenade into anyone's life.

No, he was the last thing Poppy needed right now. If he was a gentleman, he would just call her up right now and take it back—feign some last-minute emergency, or say he'd forgotten he already had plans. Rain-check, another time, no harm done.

"OK if we clock off now, boss?" one of his crew interrupted his thoughts. Cooper was up on the roof, hammering the last of the shingles in place. "We finished spreading the concrete if you want to check."

"Sure, go ahead," Cooper called down to him. With the rain gone, they were finally making some progress on construction, and had spent the day getting the exterior sealed up tight in case of another storm. "We'll pick it up tomorrow."

The site cleared out. Cooper always stayed later than his crew: getting some takeout and then working late into the night with nothing but the radio for company, but tonight, he clocked off with the others and headed for home. But as he passed the pub in town, he had a second thought. It was early, and still quiet, and he found Riley polishing glasses at the bar, one eye on the TV screen in the corner.

"Playing hooky?" Riley sounded surprised to see him.

Cooper snorted. "Some of us have been working since dawn."

"Yeah, yeah." Riley smirked. "And some of us had the sense to go into a trade that doesn't open until noon."

He took a glass and pulled at the tap of Cooper's favorite ale, pouring a pint so smooth, Cooper couldn't find it in him to offer any smart retort. He took a drink instead, and raised his glass in thanks. "You're a mouthy bastard, but you can pour a pint."

"My mom would be so proud," Riley quipped. He leaned back against the counter. "So what's this I hear about you and Poppy?"

"What?" Cooper's head snapped up. Surely word about their date couldn't have spread already. Sweetbriar's gossip tree was good, but not that good.

"You were at the drive-in the other week," Riley replied. "So says Franny, anyway."

"Oh, that." Cooper took another gulp. "Yeah, she was going stir-crazy at the cottage, so we went to a movie."

"Really?"

He could hear the suggestion in Riley's voice, but he ignored it. "Yup."

"Huh."

Cooper managed to last another minute of silence before sighing. "What?"

Riley smirked. "Nothing."

He rolled his eyes. "Aren't we kind of old for this?"

"Speak for yourself, grandpa." Riley grinned. "I'm just hitting my prime. Like a fine wine, I get better with age."

Cooper shook his head. "One of these days, you're going to meet a girl who doesn't buy your bullshit lines, and then I'll be there to watch you fall."

Riley laughed. "Never going to happen. But this isn't about me. This is about you and our new resident romance writer. I didn't think happy endings were your style."

"They're not. It's not like that," Cooper replied, even as he remembered Poppy's brilliant smile. "We're friends."

Friends who kissed. Friends who were going out to dinner in an hour.

Friends who had red-hot dreams about peeling off the

other friend's clothes and doing wicked things with them all night long.

"Good," Riley said, casually turning to clear some glasses. "So you won't mind if I ask her out?"

Cooper tensed. "I thought she already shot you down."

"I'm nothing if not persistent," Riley said cheerfully. "Anyway, she hasn't seen me go all out yet. Turn the charm on full. Show her all my assets, if you know what I mean."

Cooper glared at him. The thought of Poppy out with Riley—laughing with him, flirting, *kissing* him . . . It made him want to wipe that smirk off Riley's face and set him right, for good.

"Unless you have a problem with that," Riley added, his smile turning sly. "Do you?"

Cooper gritted his teeth. He knew exactly what Riley was doing, pushing him to admit there was something between him and Poppy. "You do whatever you want," he growled out in response. "It's a free country."

"You're right, it is." Riley grinned, like he could see exactly how worked up Cooper was under the surface. "And a beautiful woman like that isn't going to stay single for long."

Cooper downed the rest of his drink in one. "I need to get going."

"Big plans?"

"Something like that."

Cooper slammed down the empty glass and left, before he said or did something he regretted. Riley was trying to get under his skin—and it was working. He knew he wasn't the man for Poppy, but it still burned to think of her with anyone else.

But why?

Outside, he turned his cellphone over in his hand, torn. He still had a chance to call it all off, but for some reason he couldn't bring himself to cancel their plans. She'd looked so happy, discovering the cabin, and even opening the door in her ratty sweatpants and tangled hair, she was beautiful enough to take his breath away. Call it selfish, but he wanted another evening with her, enjoying her feisty sense of humor, and figuring out what made her tick.

All he had to do was find a way *not* to kiss her senseless the minute he had a chance.

How hard could that be?

ELEVEN.

*P*OPPY STARED AT her meager wardrobe that evening and despaired. What was she supposed to wear?

She hadn't packed for dating; she'd barely remembered to throw clean underwear in her suitcase along with five books, her laptop, and an extra power charger. Back home, her closet was stuffed full of cute dinner outfits: little black dresses, or va-va-voom pencil skirts, her lucky lace bras, and those heeled pumps that made her butt look amazing. But here? She'd packed for the cold weather and seclusion, and her array of chunky knit sweaters and comfy sports bras didn't exactly scream, "Kiss me now, lover!"

She was doomed.

She wrapped herself in a bathrobe and started towel-drying her hair. Maybe by the time she was done, one of her slouchy gym sweatshirts would have magically transformed into a sexy fitted tank top. Her phone rang. Quinn again. This time, Poppy answered.

"You're alive, then." Quinn didn't bother with a friendly greeting—she sounded stressed. "Tell me you've been blowing off my calls because you're too busy writing the next international bestseller."

"I have," Poppy answered, and for once, she wasn't bending the truth. "I'll have you pages by the end of tomorrow."

"I've heard that before."

"But I mean it this time," Poppy promised her. "Five chapters. They need fixing, but you can send them to my editor, that should keep them happy for a while."

"Thank God!" Quinn cheered. "You had me scared for a while. I thought you'd had some kind of breakdown, and we'd be scraping your career off the bargain book section floor."

"You and me both." Poppy felt the relief wash over her again. It had been close, but she was out of her downward spiral and back on solid ground. "Tell them I'm sorry, and I'll deliver on schedule, I swear. It doesn't matter if I have to write around the clock, I don't want to let them down."

Quinn laughed. "They'll live. To be honest, this might be a good thing. They've been getting scared you might cancel the book and leave altogether for another publisher. I've had three calls this week from different editors, asking if you're back on the market."

"Quinn, no." Poppy knew that tone, and quickly shut her down. "I'm happy where I am. They just pushed my deadline three times because I needed it, that's the kind of loyalty I want."

"OK, OK," Quinn sighed. "I'll let them know. Oh, before I forget, I got something inviting you to speak at this literary festival, it's local I think . . . hang on . . ." Poppy heard her clicking at her mouse. "Here it is, the

Cape Cod Spring Fling Festival. It's usually more literary, you know, Franzen, Atwood, Zadie Smith, but I guess someone cancelled at the last minute, because they want you to come."

"I'd love to!" Poppy exclaimed, pleased. "I've seen the flyers here in town."

"I'll tell them you're in," Quinn said. "And then maybe we can start talking about your next deal . . ."

"Bye, Quinn." Poppy cut her off before she could laugh—or cry. Next deal? She wasn't even going to think about that. Not while she still had this book to deliver—and an outfit to assemble before Cooper arrived.

She checked the time. Six forty-five. Crap. She tore through her suitcase again, and—*hallelujah*—found a plain black tank buried in the bottom. It wasn't much, but with her fitted pair of jeans, a pair of ankle boots, and a cute necklace, it would work. She wouldn't cut it at a hot restaurant in the city, but this was Sweetbriar Cove: a sheer layer of red lipstick was about as dressy as she needed. Poppy gave her hair a final rumple, brushed a quick dusting of blush on her cheeks, and was throwing her keys in her bag the doorbell sounded.

"Coming!"

She forced herself to pause. *Breathe.* It was just dinner, she told herself, going to open the door. Just dinner, with Cooper. A friendly dinner with no expectations and—

"Hey."

Poppy's jaw dropped. Cooper was standing on the porch, but not the scruffy, work-boots-and-plaid Cooper she'd seen for the past couple of weeks. No, this man was smart and clean-shaven, with his hair brushed back out of his blue eyes, which somehow looked even brighter against the cornflower cotton of his crisp button-down shirt.

He leaned in to kiss her cheek, and Poppy could have sworn her stomach turned a slow pirouette.

"Um, hi," she stammered, and then immediately scolded herself for acting like such an idiot. "You look . . . smart."

"And there you were, thinking I didn't own a razor." Cooper flashed her a devastating smile. "Ready to go?"

"Yes!" Poppy blurted. "Except, I don't know where. I meant to look up some restaurants around here, but then I was writing, and—"

"You lost track of time," Cooper finished for her. "That's OK, I figured you might not know the area. I have a place in mind, it's pretty casual, but they do the best seafood around."

"Casual's good," Poppy said, relieved. "I'm not exactly dressed for anywhere fancy."

"I don't know." Cooper gave her a quiet smile that made her blood run hot. "You look beautiful to me."

Oh god. Poppy turned away to hide her blush, and busied herself pulling on her coat and scarf. But she couldn't avoid his gaze for long, and soon they were in his truck, heading out along the coastal road, as Poppy tried to take deep breaths and keep her cool.

Why was she so flustered?

It was the rebound thing, she decided. This was the

first guy she'd been out with since Owen, so of course she was nervous about doing it wrong. But even as she tried to convince herself it was totally normal to be melting down over a man's smile, she knew this wasn't about Owen. It was all Cooper.

"Did you get much writing done today?" he asked, glancing over.

"Yes, lots," Poppy replied, ignoring the afternoon she'd spent frantically obsessing over their date. "I think I'm going to be OK—thanks to you."

"What do you mean?" Cooper looked surprised.

"What you said to me the other night, about making my own fears the theme, it really helped. Unlocked something, I guess," Poppy explained. "I'm always nervous about putting too much of myself in my books, but you made me see I have to try this time around. I need to be honest about what I'm feeling, otherwise, how can I expect my readers to really connect?"

"That's . . . brave." Cooper chuckled. "I can't imagine pouring my heart out to millions of people."

"The strong, silent type, huh?" Poppy asked, a teasing note in her voice.

"I'll take that over 'emotionally blocked and distant,' " Cooper replied. He smiled, but Poppy could tell there was something behind his words.

She didn't push. They'd barely gotten the evening started, and her stomach was still spinning in an excited dance. Real talk could wait—until after the appetizers, at least.

"I felt that way too, to begin with," she answered

instead. "It seemed like everyone reading my books would be judging me, thinking everything I wrote about my characters was really just about me. But it turned out to be the opposite. I guess if you call it fiction, you can get away with anything," she added, smiling.

"I took a look at one of them, you know." Cooper gave her a sideways glance. "This afternoon, I figured I should know what I was getting myself into."

Oh god! Poppy felt her face burning up. "Which one?" she asked, wracking her brain to figure out how bad it was. Some of her romances were sweet and innocent, but some of them . . . weren't.

Cooper chuckled. "Let's just say it was *revealing.*"

Definitely one of the steamy ones.

Poppy thought about throwing herself out of the moving truck to escape the humiliation. She'd never had to deal with this before. Owen was the only guy she'd really dated since her career took off, and he'd never looked twice at her books. Now memories of all the sexy scenes she'd written flashed in her mind, those sensual descriptions and heated moments. They'd seemed so safe on the page, but now she had to look him in the eye and pretend like he hadn't just read some of her most private fantasies.

What did Cooper think of her now?

"So, we're going to forget you ever said that," Poppy announced brightly. "And just move right along. How's the house coming along? What are the plans like? Do you have a buyer lined up?"

Cooper grinned. "Relax. I stopped reading when I got to the good stuff. Figured you'd prefer it that way."

"Oh, thank god," Poppy exhaled in a rush. "It's bad enough knowing my mom reads it, I never really had to think about being around guys who'd read . . . you know, *that stuff*."

"No?" Cooper looked amused. "It would probably be a draw for some guys. Especially since you just said a lot of it is based on your life . . ."

Poppy covered her face with her hands. "Let's just forget I ever said anything!"

She heard Cooper laugh, and then a moment later, felt the truck turn off the main highway. She lifted her head as they pulled into a brightly-lit parking lot, beside a barn-style restaurant with a sign reading *Fresh Catch Daily!* They parked out front, and Cooper went around to get her door. "Like I said, it's nothing fancy," Cooper said as he led her to the main doors. "But they do the best lobster around—and that's saying something on the Cape."

Poppy stepped inside after him and looked around. It was a big, homey space set with communal-style benches, already half-full with families and other couples. There were photos of sailboats, and old anchors hung up on the walls, and the windows on the far wall looked out over the twinkling lights of the bay. Poppy's mouth watered as she watched a waitress pass by with a massive platter of fresh-baked rolls and butter. "To tell the truth, I prefer this kind of place over fancy restaurants," she confided, as they waited for the hostess. "My friend Summer works at a really high-end place in the city, but every time I go there, I start worrying about using the wrong fork, or annoying the snooty maître d'."

Cooper chuckled. "Let me guess, they serve everything with weird foam and freeze-dried shavings."

"Yes!" Poppy exclaimed. "Half the time, I don't even know what I'm eating. Summer isn't like that," she added quickly. "She's the most amazing chef, and her pastries . . ." She trailed off with a lustful sigh. "One day, she wants to open a bakery, but I guess she's still paying her dues."

"I get that." Cooper nodded. "I didn't go out on my own until just a few years ago. They don't tell you how running your own business isn't just about the fun stuff, it's all the extra work as well—keeping the books, and dealing with suppliers, and marketing."

"And you can't play hooky, either, when you're boss," Poppy agreed, laughing.

"See, I told you." Cooper grinned. "Work ethic."

The hostess showed them to a table by the windows, and they got settled, the salty sea air mingling with all the delicious food smells wafting from the kitchen.

"Can I bring you some menus?" the girl asked, and Cooper looked to Poppy.

"Usually, I just get the platter, but if you want . . . ?"

"No, it sounds good to me," she agreed quickly. "And can you please bring some of those rolls? Lots of those rolls. And butter," she added, before the waitress departed. She caught his smile from across the table. "It's hungry work!" she protested. "All that sitting around, typing."

"Working up a sweat." Cooper gave her a wink, and

Poppy cringed again.

"I said we were forgetting about that."

"We were," he replied, looking amused. "But now you're blushing so hard, it makes me wonder what I missed."

"That's for me to know, and you to find out," Poppy said, realizing too late how flirtatious the challenge sounded. But thankfully, the waitress returned with their beers, so Cooper just quirked a knowing eyebrow and let that one slide.

Poppy sat back, trying to relax. "I still can't believe you're here in town. You were always so . . . restless," she smiled, remembering him when he was younger. "I figured you'd be on the other side of the country by now."

Cooper gave a knowing smile. "Is that a polite way of saying I was a loud-ass brat?"

"Hey, take the pass," she said, and he laughed.

"You're right, I couldn't wait to get the hell out. I left for college, but then my dad got sick, and, well . . ." He shrugged. "It turned out Sweetbriar had something going for it, after all." He toyed with his beer bottle. "They really pulled together for us, and after a while, I guess it just feels like home."

Poppy felt a pang. She couldn't imagine losing a parent, especially like that. "I bet he'd be proud of you," she said softly, thinking of everything he'd achieved.

Cooper looked bashful. "I don't know about that. What about you?" he changed the subject. "Where's home to you these days?"

Poppy hesitated. "New York, I guess. Brooklyn. At least, that was the plan. I was going to move into Owen's apartment," she admitted. "And then we'd start looking for a place outside the city, maybe upstate."

"Ah yes, the famous fiancé." Cooper tilted his head, fixing her with an unreadable look. "So what happened there?"

Poppy let out a sigh.

He chuckled. "That bad?"

"No," Poppy quickly defended him. "He wasn't bad at all. He was great. I just... didn't love him," she said sadly. "Not the way I should."

She couldn't even explain why. Owen was a good guy: thoughtful and serious, kind of obsessive when it came to *Star Wars* movies and all the comic books he had stacked neatly in their basement, but Poppy figured she was the same with her romance book collection. Sure, he could get stressed and distant when he had a big project at work, and forget to call her when he travelled every other month, so sometimes they would spend a week barely exchanging a text, but not every couple had to coo sweet nothings over the phone every night. They were independent adults, with their own lives to lead. At least, that's what Poppy told herself.

"The truth is, I wanted it to be right," she admitted, meeting Cooper's steady gaze. "I wanted it to be him, so badly. I'd been on my own for so long before I met him, I thought, finally, this is it. Someone to be with, to share my life with. We would get married and start a family, and everything would work out. I could see it all, you know? The life I wanted more than anything. I knew deep down, he wasn't the one for me, but I ignored it for too long." She looked away, feeling foolish. "You probably don't understand."

"I do." Cooper's reply was quiet. "You thought that if you just pushed through, ignored all the warning signs, you could make him the one."

Poppy nodded. "Until the wedding was right around the corner, and those little whispers in my head started screaming at me, and I couldn't ignore it any more. So, I called it all off."

She sighed. She wasn't proud of what she'd done, but there hadn't been any other way. "Now I just have to hope I was right, and I didn't throw away something good and solid, for . . . what was it you said?" she asked, remembering his scornful words when they first met. "A fairy-tale fantasy that's only going to leave me disappointed in the end."

Cooper grimaced. "I'm sorry, I should never have said that."

"But it's what you believe, isn't it?" Poppy found herself hanging on his answer, hoping he wasn't as downbeat on love as he seemed. It shouldn't matter to her, but somehow, it did.

Cooper paused and looked down. "I don't know. Not like that. But either way, I had no right to be such an ass to you." He glanced back up and met her eyes with a rueful, sincere smile. "I'm sorry."

"Apology accepted," Poppy said slowly. She wanted to ask him more, about his past, too, and those glimpses of bitterness she saw still lingering at the edges, but the waitress suddenly returned, depositing two massive platters on the table.

"Alright you guys, I have two mixed, extra rolls, extra

butter."

Poppy took in the spread, and laughed. "Wow."

"Need anything else?" the girl asked.

"A bib?" she joked, but the waitress just nodded.

"On the table. Enjoy."

She dashed away, leaving Poppy to survey the feast in front of them. "There's no elegant way to do this, is there?" she said, her mouth already watering. There were whole crabs, clams, and even lobster tail, so fresh she could smell the ocean.

"Go crazy, I won't judge." Cooper grinned, handing her a plastic bib. Poppy laughed and fastened it around her neck, and he did the same.

Cooper held up his beer in a toast. "Here's to starting over."

She smiled and clinked the glass to his. "To starting over."

Their eyes caught, and Poppy felt a slow shiver of anticipation bubbling through her veins, the champagne promise of something sweet, just on the horizon. She'd spent all year questioning her choices, wondering if she could trust her instincts—or if they were sending her spinning off track, away from the truth. But as Poppy took a sip, she felt perfectly content. She was starting a new chapter in her life, and it was scary, but exhilarating, too, to leave her past behind and strike out in search of something more.

Maybe there was hope for her, after all.

TWELVE.

*D*INNER FLEW BY as they caught up on the past twenty years, until the platters between them were almost empty, and Poppy didn't think she could ever move again.

"Save me," she groaned, pushing her plate away. "You'll need to roll me out of this place like a wheel."

Cooper laughed and took the last of the fries from her abandoned tray. "Does this mean you won't stretch to dessert?"

Poppy wavered.

"They do a mean apple pie," Cooper said temptingly. "Or chocolate, if that's your poison . . ."

"You're a bad man," she scolded him, and he laughed.

"How about we get a portion to go? You'll rally for round two by the time you're home."

"And if I don't, pie works great for breakfast," Poppy agreed, as he beckoned the waitress over and gave her their order. Soon, they were packed up and back in his truck with a crisp delivery box of pie, headlights cutting through the dark night. Poppy relaxed and let the motion of the drive wash over her, soothing as the engine hummed. She'd enjoyed herself, and despite all her nerves, she and Cooper had fallen into an easy rhythm.

If only she could forget how handsome he was.

She breathed in the buttery scent of pastry from the box and tried to distract herself. "You were right," she said. "I'm rallying fast."

He laughed. "Told you so."

"Why don't you join me for a slice at the cottage?" she asked, without thinking. "I could put on some coffee, or even make some hot chocolate."

There was a pause. "Sure," Cooper said eventually. "I could go for that."

There was silence, and Poppy realized why: she'd just invited him in. After their date. For coffee. She may have been rusty when it came to dating, but she was pretty sure that meant she'd just offered him an open invitation to come back to her place and take her to bed for a night of limitless passion.

Or something like that.

Poppy's heart stopped. Oh God. She hadn't meant it like that—had she?

Memories of their kiss flooded her brain all over again: the sure, confident heat of his mouth and the feel of his body pressed against hers. All night, her stomach had been tied up in knots. It was undeniable; there was something between them, and even if Poppy couldn't make logical sense of it, she couldn't hide from the truth.

She wanted him.

Her heart beat faster. She snuck a look at him, illuminated in the headlights in the driver's seat. The strong line of his jaw, the curve of his bicep under his shirt, the way his hands rested on the steering wheel . . .

Poppy took a breath. His presence beside her was suddenly charged, the distance between them shrinking with every passing minute.

God help her, she was getting turned on by the way the man shifted gears.

The miles passed, and Poppy's anticipation grew, until by the time they turned off the highway and began to follow the winding lane down to the shore, she was certain her cheeks were flushing red from all her illicit thoughts. "Are you working early tomorrow?" she blurted, searching for something to say.

"The regular time," Cooper replied. "But if you need to call an early night, we can take a rain-check on that dessert."

Poppy gulped. Did he want to cancel? Did he want her to want to cancel?

"No, I'm good," she replied, fighting to keep her voice casual. "But only if you want to."

"I want to."

The quiet certainty in Cooper's voice shot a bolt of pure electricity through Poppy's veins. She couldn't stop a smile curling on her lips as she glanced over again. This time, Cooper was staring straight back at her.

Oh.

There it was again. The heat of connection sparking between them, inexplicable. Undeniable.

She quickly looked away. This time, her heart was racing. The shadows blurred outside the window as Poppy's body prickled with new awareness. She was really doing this. Going home.

With Cooper.

The truck slowed as they reached the cottage, and Cooper pulled in to park—beside a gleaming BMW she'd never seen before. "Is June back?" she asked.

"It doesn't look like her style."

She got out, and walked up the front path, confused. The porch light was on, and as she approached the house, she could see a duffel bag on the ground by the door.

"Hello?" Poppy called, looking around. "Is anyone here?"

"Easy," she heard Cooper behind her, and then he drew level, putting a protective arm in front of her. "You don't know who it is."

"In Sweetbriar?" Poppy wasn't worried. She headed up the steps and peered around the side of the porch, expecting a friend of June's, or a local townsperson come to deliver fruit cobbler or fix the gutters. The last person in the world she expected to come strolling around the side of the house was the man she'd left a thousand miles away with a stack of wedding gift boxes and an apology.

Her ex-fiancé.

COOPER WAS STILL on guard for intruders when the newcomer stepped into the light. He was tall, dressed in a preppy overcoat, with dark hair cut neat and thin gold wire-rimmed glasses. He looked like he'd just stepped out of the office—and definitely like he wasn't lurking to case the joint and make off with June's collection of antique thimbles.

"Owen?" Poppy gasped beside him. "What . . . what are you doing here?"

Owen.

Cooper tensed. This was the guy Poppy had left back home, the one she'd broken up with. What the hell was he doing all the way out here? Poppy had said it herself: it was over. She was moving on.

Cooper drew himself up to his full height and casually stepped in front of Poppy. "Cooper Nicholson," he said, sticking out his hand. He held Owen's gaze, steady. "It's kind of late to be showing up unannounced. Maybe you should give Poppy a call in the morning and see if she'd like to talk then."

"Who's this guy?" Owen looked past him. "Poppy?"

"He's . . . just a friend," Poppy answered, sounding stressed. She rested a hand on Cooper's arm. "It's OK, I've got this."

Friend.

It shouldn't have hurt, but it did. One dinner didn't change a thing. He'd thought there'd been something building between them, and when she'd invited him back for dessert, it seemed like she felt it too. But clearly, one look at her old love and she wanted Cooper long gone and out of the way.

He tried to ignore the rejection that slammed over him like a shock of cold water. It was nothing, he told himself. She was free to pick whatever guy she wanted.

Still, he wasn't about to leave her there alone with some psycho ex. "Are you sure?" Cooper searched her face carefully. "Because I can stay."

"I'm sure. I'll talk to you tomorrow. And thanks for dinner," she added with a small smile. "I had fun."

Fun. The kind you had with a guy who was just friends.

Cooper resisted the urge to slam the door in this guy's face and show Poppy what "fun" could really mean. That kiss was just a preview. Now that he knew how sweet she tasted, he could spend days getting lost in her touch, making her gasp and moan for more.

But that was just a fantasy. The real world was staring him right back in the face, waiting politely for him to go.

He nodded brusquely. "I'll leave you guys to it. Owen, it was good to meet you." Cooper shot him a warning look that made it clear he was on thin ice. If Poppy said the word, he'd happily send Owen packing out of Sweetbriar Cove for good.

Owen cleared his throat and looked away. "You too."

Cooper checked with Poppy again, but it was like she didn't even see him. She was staring at Owen with a flood of emotion in her eyes.

He should have guessed it wasn't over.

"Goodnight," he said quietly. It felt wrong somehow, to be turning his back on Poppy, and even worse to leave her alone with another man, but Cooper wasn't about to cause a scene. Like she said, they were just friends. He didn't have any right to the disappointment burning in his chest, so he clenched his jaw and climbed back in the truck, driving away fast enough to make the tires spin on the gravel road.

He was a damn fool.

Of course Poppy thought of him as just a friend, he'd been combative and grumpy since the day they met. And sure, he thought they'd connected—that time at the drive-in, and dinner tonight—but he guessed that didn't do anything to overcome his bad first impression.

Or second. Or third.

Cooper slammed his hand against the steering wheel. He couldn't even be mad at Owen for showing up like that. Poppy was a woman worth chasing. No, he'd screwed this one up all on his own, the same way he always did.

He drove for home, but it was like his hands had a mind of their own: they steered him miles past his own turn, to where a lane curved into the woods and the bumpy track dipped and wove through the trees. He'd cursed this dirt road a hundred times over, getting stuck in potholes and rained out by the storm. It was near impossible to get the building supplies in, but he'd made it happen eventually.

Cooper bounced over the last fallen branch and turned the corner. There it was: a small, rustic house sitting squarely by the pond. The lights were all off, and he figured the tourists he'd sold to were still out of town until summer, but still, he turned off the engine and sat there in the dark for a moment, just remembering.

This used to be his house. His, and Laura's. He'd fixed it up for them, that first year, imagining the life they'd spend there together and the family they'd raise, right here.

"What about if you believe it? If you think you have everything, and it doesn't work out."

He remembered what he'd said to Poppy, the questions he'd asked the other night. She may have been talking about her book, but those were the questions he'd been grappling with ever since the night he'd come home to find Laura's engagement ring on the table, and her sitting right there beside it with nothing but defeat left in her eyes.

And just like that, his happily-ever-after crumbled into pieces, and Cooper realized it had always been a lie.

It wasn't perfect. Hell, even he knew that. The bickering that turned to fights—lasting too long, cutting too deep. The slamming doors and empty silences, the hours he'd work just to avoid coming home, and the late nights she'd disappear to do much the same thing. But nothing was perfect, right? You just made it work. You fought for each other, for the life you were building, and got through the tough times, somehow.

But Laura didn't see it that way. "It shouldn't be this hard," she'd told him, and just like that, she'd taken herself out of the fight. Cooper was left alone on the battlefield with the sad, painful truth: she hadn't loved him enough to keep fighting for them.

He wasn't enough for her in the end.

Cooper sat there in the dark, lost in old memories. Laura was still on the Cape; she'd met a guy up in Truro the year after she left him. He was decent, from what Cooper could tell: an accountant, running a small shop for the local businesses. Now, they were married, with a baby, too. He saw them all together sometimes, glimpses passing on the street. She looked happy, and Cooper was glad about that. She deserved happiness, even if it wasn't with him. Relationships failed, sometimes people couldn't make it work—he knew that. He'd heard it all before. But deep down, Cooper still blamed himself for letting it slip away.

He should have been able to give her the life she wanted. He could have fought more to make things right.

It shouldn't be this hard.

Cooper swallowed back the knot in his throat. Look at him, picking over ancient history. People moved on all the time, and brooding in the dark wouldn't bring back something already dead and buried, which is why he rarely let himself think of her at all. But tonight, with Poppy's rejection still a fresh wound, he hadn't been able to keep himself from the past.

But it wasn't Laura's face that lingered in his mind as he turned the engine on and finally head for home. It was Poppy's.

Her eyes bright, smiling up at him. Hiding her face in her hands with embarrassment when he teased her. Laughing over dinner, so hard she almost choked on her food.

She was beautiful. Honest, and sweet, and determined. Tonight, he couldn't help but get swept up in her hopeful enthusiasm, believing that better days lay ahead. Somehow none of the past mattered, and those old wounds seemed a lifetime ago. For the first time in a long while, Cooper had found himself wondering what it would be like to try again with someone, for real this time. Open up and take that chance, to hell with the consequences.

Until they'd arrived back at her place to find her past wasn't ancient history, after all.

It was for the best. Cooper hit the road again, trying not to think about what she was doing with Owen, right at that moment. He had no business wanting a future with anyone. If the definition of insanity was trying the same thing over but somehow expecting a different result, then Cooper could take a hint.

Poppy was better off without him. He was a man made to be alone.

THIRTEEN.

" *I* THOUGHT YOU were in Fiji."

Poppy headed for the kitchen, trying to collect herself. Seeing Owen standing there on the porch like a ghost from a previous life had scattered every thought from her mind. She busied herself putting the pie away and filling the tea kettle, nervously setting it on the stove as Owen leaned against the counter, watching her.

"I was," he replied. "You were right when you booked it. The honeymoon sunset cruise was magical. A little less magical being the only single man on a boat of happy couples whispering sweet nothings in each other's ears, but what can you do?" Owen shot her a rueful smile, and right away, Poppy was washed in a tidal wave of guilt.

She wasn't supposed to be out on dates, having fun, and walking on the beach at dawn breathing in the crisp salty breeze. She was supposed to be on that cruise with him. She was supposed to be his wife by now, setting out on their life together, instead of avoiding his gaze, her skin still flushed with desire for some other man.

Cooper.

Poppy felt a pang. She'd hated brushing him off like

that, but her worlds had been colliding in one unholy mess, and she couldn't focus on Owen with Cooper so close. When he was around, she couldn't see anything but him, and that wasn't fair to Owen, not after everything. She just hoped Cooper understood.

"So, that guy . . ." Owen continued, as if he'd seen it written all over her face. "He's just a friend?"

Poppy took a breath. "Yes. No. Nothing's happened," she said quickly, still feeling like she owed him an explanation. "We had dinner, and . . ." She gulped. "I mean, I just met him. Here. He wasn't . . ."

"The reason you left me," Owen finished.

Poppy cringed. It was bad enough when she'd sat him down that day to tell him it was over, but now, she had a different kind of guilt to reckon with. Standing here with Owen, he felt like a stranger. Part of a life she hadn't even thought about in weeks. They'd shared their hopes and dreams, spent years together, and picked out their future right down to the china pattern on the registry list, but all that had faded away, so far it felt like a dream. It was shameful just how fast she'd cast him aside, and even thought she knew it was a sign that their relationship had always been doomed to failure, Poppy still ached to see the sadness in his eyes.

"Owen . . ." She didn't know what to say. "What are you doing here?"

"I thought, maybe if we talked . . ." he began, his expression turning hopeful. "You got cold feet, and I get it. All the wedding plans, our families—it was crazy. You needed some time to yourself, to figure it out. But we can make this work."

"Owen, no." She shook her head. "I'm sorry. You know I never meant to hurt you, but I meant what I said. I can't marry you."

"So we don't get married." Owen closed the distance between them and took her hands, holding tight. "We stay engaged, or just together. Whatever you want. I don't need a piece of paper to know you're mine."

Poppy stepped back. "But I'm not. Yours." She looked up at him, searching for a way to make him understand. "You know I'm right. It's been wrong for a long time between us."

He shook his head stubbornly. "Things were fine."

"*Fine*," Poppy echoed sadly. "Is that what you really want? To build a life together on 'fine'? Don't you think you deserve more than that?"

Owen sagged. "We could try—"

"Please." Poppy stopped him. "Don't. I care about you, you know I do. But I need more than that, and you should, too. You deserve to be with someone who can't imagine a world without you, who wakes up every day filled with gladness that they get to share their life with you. Not just 'fine.' "

Owen dropped her hands. He slowly went and took a seat at the table, and Poppy could see the denial finally slip away. "You couldn't have figured all this out before we sent the invites?" he asked with a rueful look.

"I'm sorry. But imagine if we'd gone through with the wedding," she pointed out. "We'd be hiring divorce lawyers instead of just sending gifts back."

To anyone else, that wouldn't have been much consolation, but Owen was always the frugal one. He spent hours on the internet looking up bargain deals, and set up a whole system for her to track her budget. Now, he nodded, looking more cheerful. "You're right. New York is an equitable property state, too. That would have gotten messy."

Poppy let out a small breath of relief. She was the emotional one, but Owen had always weighed things with logic and fact. It was one of the reasons it would have never worked between them, but now she was relieved she had a way to make him feel better.

"And think about if we'd bought a house together," she continued. "Or combined our finances, too. I had to do this now," she said softly. "Before we went too far to take it back."

He nodded again slowly. "I figured it was worth one last try," he said, giving her a familiar smile. "In case I could talk you around. I had a whole list prepared of reasons why we should stay together."

"That's sweet." Poppy exhaled. "But this isn't like my retirement plan, or deciding whether or not to get a dog. A pro/con list doesn't really work for love."

Owen opened his mouth like he was going to argue, then stopped. "Not for you, no, it doesn't."

The tea kettle whistled, and Poppy poured them two cups. She joined him at the table. "Did you get the last of the gifts returned?" she asked, and he nodded. "I'll be sure to send thank-you notes, all the same."

"You might want to steer clear of my mom for a

while," he said, making a face. "You're not exactly her favorite person right now. Or my sister's."

"No, I'd imagine not." Poppy thought of Owen's over-protective family and breathed a sigh of relief. Maybe there was a silver lining to this break-up business, after all. "What about you?" she asked. "It's a long drive back to New York this late. You're welcome to stay here, there are plenty of rooms."

Owen shook his head. "I'd prefer to get on the road."

"OK." Poppy toyed with her mug. She felt like she should say something, but she wasn't sure what was left to say. Maybe Owen had imagined this last-ditch effort chasing after her would change her mind, but it had only made her resolve stronger. Looking at him now, she felt affection and regret, but the kind you feel for an old friend whose life has taken a different path. Not the excitement she dreamed about in a partner, the love she'd been writing for her characters all these years.

She'd felt more passion in one kiss with Cooper than she had in her whole relationship with Owen.

"We had it good though, didn't we?" Owen gave her a nostalgic smile. "For a while, at least."

"We did." Poppy reached out and squeezed his hand. "I'm sorry, for everything."

"I know." He squeezed back. "But you're right. I think a part of me has always known you're right." He looked rueful. "I guess just because something adds up on paper doesn't mean it's real."

"You'll find it," she reassured him. "You're a good man, and somewhere, there's a woman who can't wait to meet you. And hey, maybe she'll love *Doctor Who*, too."

He smiled. "It would be nice to share my hobbies with someone," he agreed. "I always felt like you didn't really understand."

"Oh, I didn't." Poppy grinned. "I tried, but I pretty much started zoning out every time you mentioned regeneration and the star wars."

"Time Wars," he corrected her.

"There you go."

Owen finished his tea and stood. "I better hit the road."

She showed him to the door again, and watched him pull his coat back on. "Thank you, for coming out here." Poppy felt a curious mix of sadness and resolve. "I think it was good, to see each other like this."

"Without passions running high." Owen nodded. "You take care," he said, giving her an abrupt hug.

"You too." Poppy hugged him back.

"And about that friend of yours . . ." Owen paused in the doorway. "It's none of my business, but the way he was glaring at me, I'm guessing there's more than friendship on his mind."

Poppy flushed. "Maybe," she admitted. "But I'm not sure we're compatible."

Owen raised an eyebrow. "Weren't you the one who said love can't be calculated by a pro/con list?"

There he was with the logic again.

"Take care," Poppy said, as he headed out into the dark night. "Travel safe."

She closed the door behind him, and it felt like she

was closing a chapter of her life. She looked around the cottage, warm and cozy, and felt a sense of peace sweep through her.

Whatever came next was up to her.

She saw her phone sitting on the entry table, and wondered what Cooper was doing. Was he home alone, kicked back watching TV? Or working on some project, late into the night?

Was he thinking about her, the way she was thinking about him—his smile, his body, his mouth . . . ?

Poppy shook away those tempting thoughts. She couldn't just call him up and invite him over now, to pick right up where they'd left off on their date. No, she sighed. It was late and the moment had definitely passed.

Then her gaze landed on the paper bag with the dessert box. She smiled, and went to cut herself a slice. She sat in the kitchen, and savored every bite. She may not have any idea what was going on with Cooper, but she had apple pie, and a whole new beginning.

The rest could wait until tomorrow.

FOURTEEN.

*P*OPPY SENT COOPER a text the next morning, thanking him for dinner—but there was no reply. She tried not to read into it. He was probably busy with work or some project, and besides, Cooper never struck her as the texting kind. She'd see him soon enough at the house, or around town.

At least, she hoped she would.

She got dressed and packed up her laptop, with a thermos of coffee and a couple of cozy knit blankets, then she set out along the beach path, eager to spend her first morning writing in her new beach hut-slash-office. The air was brisk, but the sun was out, and making her way through the fresh green of the woods, Poppy thought how lucky she was to be in Sweetbriar, instead of cooped up in her apartment back in the city, or camped out in the corner of some noisy coffee shop, wilting under the fluorescent lights. Here, it was so quiet, she could only hear the sound of the ocean, and a lazy gull circling overhead. The hut was waiting for her, sturdy on the edge of the sand, and soon she had the doors flung wide open and was snuggled up in the armchair, watching the slate blue waves break over the empty sands.

It was so inspiring, nothing but her, the ocean, and the bright horizon. How did Cooper know exactly what she needed?

Her mind drifted, and she felt that now-familiar skip in her stomach, remembering their date last night. How it had felt, sitting across the table, laughing for hours, sharing stories and old jokes, and gradually peeling back the layers of his gruff defenses until the real Cooper was revealed.

He wasn't the man she'd thought he was. Sure, he could be prickly, and seemed to enjoy getting under her skin, but there was so much more to him, too. He was kinder than he'd ever admit, and seemed proud to be a part of the community here in town. And as for generosity . . . Poppy looked around her snug little cabin. Not many guys would conjure up a perfect writing spot out of thin air like this.

She checked her phone again. No response to her earlier message. She was terrible at texting, and had never understood how her friends seemed to carry on whole relationships through their phones, but she tried her best to think up another casual message. In the end, she snapped a picture of the sand, with her boots sticking up at the bottom of the frame.

Writing hard, thanks for the view!

She hit send, then immediately wondered if she was being too pushy. Dating felt like a minefield, especially when she wasn't even sure if what they were doing was dating at all. Dinner, a movie, a kiss—with any other guy, she'd take them as signs he was interested. But Cooper? He played his cards too close to his chest to even tell.

Not that she had time to sit around obsessing. Poppy tucked her phone away and reached for her laptop again. She was meeting Mackenzie for her book club at four p.m., which meant she had another few hours to make some real progress on her book.

Men in real life might still be a mystery, but at least she knew exactly what would happen with the ones on her page.

COOPER WAS PICKING up groceries at the store in Provincetown when someone rammed into his cart from behind.

"Hey!" he turned, ready to give them a piece of his already-surly mind, but instead of a reckless frat bro, he found a familiar face.

"Hey, stranger." Mackenzie beamed. "How's it going?"

He relaxed. Mac was an old friend, but he'd been so busy lately with the construction job that he'd barely seen her around town. "Not bad," he said, "just stocking up."

"Me too. All the essentials."

He glanced over. Mackenzie's cart was filled with chips, salsa, and two cases of wine. "Things really that bad?" he asked, and she laughed.

"I'm buying up for book club," Mackenzie said cheerfully. "You know Franny likes her tipple. What about you, cooking for one?" She peered into his basket. Cooper saw a gleam in her eye, and knew it wasn't an innocent question.

"Last I checked," he replied casually, but she wasn't so easily dissuaded.

"You could invite Poppy over," she said with a smile. "Wow her with your grilling skills, or . . . other talents."

Cooper glared. "You mean sawing a two-by-four?"

"Is that what the kids are calling it these days?" Mackenzie grinned. She really was impossible. Cooper fixed her with a "subject closed" look and moved down the aisle, but Mackenzie dogged him all the way to the cereal shelves. "I mean it," she said, trailing him. "Poppy seems great, and she doesn't altogether hate you, which is an excellent start, don't you think?"

"Mac," he said, warning.

"What? She's pretty and smart, and if you got together, she might even give up June's soup recipe, and then you can stop coming to all the town events you hate."

"I don't hate them," he replied, irritated. "You, on the other hand . . ."

Mackenzie planted herself in front of him. "How long have I known you?"

Cooper sighed.

"Well?"

"Too long," he replied.

"Sixteen years, and counting," Mackenzie said, ignoring him. "And in that time, how many women have I tried to set you up with?"

"None." Cooper reached past her for some Wheaties. "I always thought it was because you knew better, but somehow here we are."

"It was because you were always too pig-headed to listen," Mackenzie said, grabbing the cereal box out of his hand. She fixed him with a look. "And I never met a girl I'd want to inflict you on."

"And that's changed?" Cooper growled.

"Yes." Mackenzie glared at him. "*You've* changed. You're turning into a grumpy old man, one of those guys we always laughed about. Ever since Laura, all you do is work, or drink, or bang tourists who won't be around come Labor Day. You're better than this, Cooper. You deserve good things, and Poppy could be it."

Cooper stared back, his bitter retorts dying on his tongue. She made him sound like a total bastard. He wasn't that bad, was he?

Mackenzie softened. "Look, it doesn't have to be much. Take her to dinner, see if there are sparks. Just be open to something, for once in your life."

"I did," Cooper found himself answering, before he could think better of it. "We went to dinner last night."

Mackenzie lit up. "And?"

"And, nothing." Cooper felt a twist of regret. "Everything was great, until her ex showed up. It turns out he's less an ex and more a current."

Mackenzie shook her head, frowning. "That's not what I heard. She called off the wedding, practically left him at the altar."

"Well, I left her getting cozy with him on June's front porch." Cooper took Mackenzie by the arms and gently moved her aside. "So thanks for the pep talk, but I gave it my shot."

"But you can't give up!" Mackenzie protested.

"Watch me. And it's not giving up if you were never in the game," Cooper corrected her. "This grumpy old man is leaving well alone."

Her face fell, and Cooper knew how she felt.

"Fine." Mackenzie pressed her lips together. "I have to get going, anyway. But I will say, it's not like you to quit so easy." She spun her cart and walked away before Cooper could have time to object.

He wasn't a quitter.

He scowled, and finished the rest of his shopping with a cloud hanging over him. He wasn't a quitter, and Mackenzie was wrong to imply that he was. But what was he supposed to do—make a fool of himself chasing after a woman who wasn't his to chase? He barely knew Poppy, and a couple of polite texts didn't make a difference. She probably felt bad for letting him down so abruptly. If she'd wanted to see him again, she'd have said so. For all he knew, she'd spent the day with Owen, making up for lost time.

Cooper felt the burn of jealousy just imagining it, but he pushed it aside. He knew all about wanting a woman who didn't want him back. And he wasn't about to make the same mistake twice.

POPPY WROTE UNTIL her battery went dead, then headed back to the house to change and dig a bottle of wine from Aunt June's cellar. She arrived at the pottery studio at the stroke of four, bearing a bottle of white, and some prosecco, too, for good measure.

"You made it!" Mackenzie greeted her happily, and whisked her inside. "Everyone, this is the famous Poppy Somerville! Poppy, this is Franny, and Debra, and Ellie, and Bert . . ."

"Hi!" Poppy tried to keep track of everyone's names as she went through the whistle-stop introductions, but half of them passed her by. It was an eclectic group gathered there, a few older women in their sixties and seventies, plus another girl about her age, and a lone man in a green knit sweater.

"Don't worry, we don't expect you to learn everyone's name," one of the other women—Debra, was it?—said with a wink. "Just call everyone 'honey' and you'll be set."

"Thanks for the tip." Poppy smiled.

"And you brought booze!" Mackenzie took the bottles. "See, you'll fit right in. Come on."

She led her through the front space, which was set up as a gallery, displaying beautiful ceramic bowls and sculptures. One of the sets caught Poppy's eye—the bright polka-dot design just like the ones she'd admired back at the cottage. "You made these?" Poppy asked, pausing to pick up one of the cute mugs. "June has a whole set at home. They're adorable."

"Thanks." Mackenzie smiled. "They're from my polka-dot phase, I went kind of dotty—pardon the pun. Polka-dot bowls, teacups, you name it. Now I've moved on to stripes, they're more nautical," she explained, pointing to a new set of blue-and-white bowls, painted with anchors and a ship design. "Plus, they sell like gangbusters to the tourists. I swear, I could put an anchor on a lump of unfinished clay and it would get snapped up."

"I love it. Remind me to come back another time and browse," Poppy said, looking around. "I know my friend back home would love this stuff. She's a chef, so she goes crazy when it comes to kitchenware. I swear, she has more mixing bowls than pairs of socks."

"My kind of customer." Mackenzie grinned. "Feel free to stop by anytime."

In the back, Mackenzie had pushed aside a workbench and potter's wheel and arranged a mismatched assortment of chairs in a circle. She dragged a bench closer, and began to unpack various Tupperware filled with dessert. "I told you," she said, catching Poppy's eye. "We don't mess around."

"I can see that." Poppy accepted a plate full of the famous plum cobbler and a glass of wine, and took a seat with the others.

"It's such a treat, having a real author join us," Franny beamed. She was one of the older women, wearing a voluminous knit caftan in bright pinks and blues. "You'll have to tell us all about your new book."

"Oh, I don't want to interrupt you," Poppy said quickly. "What book are you discussing this week?"

There was a pause, and then everyone laughed. Poppy looked around, confused. "We call it a book group, but most of the time, we just come here to natter," Franny explained.

"Because some people can't agree on what to read," Debra piped up.

"You're the one who didn't like our last pick," Bert complained.

"I just don't see why we have to read another thinly-veiled story about some literature professor having a midlife crisis and seducing his students!"

Poppy caught Mackenzie's eye. The other woman gave a rueful smile. "See what I mean?" she said. "Anyway, it's usually safer just to steer clear. They nearly came to blows over Karl Ove Knausgård last year."

"My money's on Franny. She looks like she fights dirty," Poppy said, and Mackenzie snorted with laughter.

"What about you, how is the writing going?"

"Good!" she said. "Finally. I was blocked for a while," she explained. "But I finally figured it out. With Cooper's help."

Mackenzie raised her eyebrow. "Grumpy dude, yay high, sworn against romance? Are we talking about the same guy?"

Poppy laughed. "I know, I was surprised too. But he's been really supportive. He even found me a spot to write, so all the construction noise doesn't interrupt me." She pulled out her phone, and showed Mackenzie photos of the cabin.

"Huh. He's just full of surprises," Mackenzie said, looking thoughtful. "I heard you guys had dinner," she added.

"Wow, news really does travel fast." Poppy paused. "Is there a flare that goes up, or a bell, like Paul Revere?"

"We move with the times." Mackenzie grinned. "Group texts, all the way."

She laughed. "Yes, we went out," Poppy admitted.

"And?"

"It went great . . . until my ex showed up." She made a face. "I had to straighten things out with him, but now I don't know if Cooper has the wrong idea about us. I haven't heard from him yet."

Mackenzie sighed. "Men can be dim sometimes."

Someone cleared their throat loudly, and Poppy turned to find Bert looking put out.

"Not you," Mackenzie said quickly.

"Have you tried texting?" Debra asked, and Poppy realized that they'd all been listening in to the conversation.

"No, don't text, it's so impersonal," Franny argued. "My grandkids are glued to their phone all day. There's no romance about it."

"Maybe you're doing it wrong," the other younger woman, Ellie, said cheekily. "Text can be plenty romantic if you know the right emojis."

"Shakespeare would be turning in his grave," Franny tutted. "Shall I compare thee to a summer's day? Heart emoji, sun, winky face."

They all laughed, but Poppy felt a little self-conscious, having everyone pitch in about her love life.

"Sorry." Mackenzie must have seen her discomfort, because she gave Poppy a sympathetic look. "Small town. We have problems with boundaries."

"Oh, hush you," Debra piped up. "We want to hear

more about this date with Cooper. Where did you go?"

"It can't have been around here, otherwise we'd have already heard about it," Bert remarked.

"He hasn't dated in a while, has he?" Franny mused. "Not since—"

"Why don't we talk about books!" Mackenzie interrupted. "If you can't share what you're working on now, how about telling us more about your career?" she prompted Poppy. "How did you get your first book published? Have you met Fabio?"

Poppy let out a sigh of relief. Normally, she didn't like talking about herself, but it was definitely better talking fiction than spilling all the details of her real-life love life.

"Well, it was years ago," she began, as they thankfully all turned their attention back to the wine and dessert. "I was working as a temp at an office, writing on my computer when I should have been working . . ."

THE AFTERNOON PASSED quickly in the warm glow of home-baked desserts, gossip, and a good few glasses of wine. By the time everyone said their goodbyes and headed off home, Poppy had promised to come back for the next meeting—and give them a mention in her acknowledgments page, too.

"Thanks for putting up with all our nosy questions," Mackenzie said when they were alone. "And I'm sorry if we got too personal, about Cooper."

"There's not much to get personal about." Poppy helped tidy away their glasses. "He still hasn't texted me back. I guess that means he's not interested."

"Or, he thinks you're holed up somewhere with your ex," Mackenzie corrected her. "Or his phone is dead, and he hasn't seen your messages. Or he took a boat out, and got lost in a freak storm—"

"OK!" Poppy stopped her, laughing. "I get it. But in fiction, and real life, the simplest explanation is usually the best. If Cooper doesn't suggest picking up where we left off, it probably means he doesn't want to."

Mackenzie shook her head. "No way. Remember, men don't take a hint. You need to make it clear you're interested. Make the first move."

She seemed strangely insistent, but maybe Poppy was just being too scared.

"You should just go over there."

"Tonight?" Poppy blinked. "Isn't that stalking?"

"Or a grand romantic gesture," Mackenzie pointed out.

"I don't know . . ." Poppy's stomach tied up in knots just thinking about making the first move.

"OK." Mackenzie shrugged. "Don't. Wait around for him to get his head out of his ass long enough to text you back. But I wouldn't hold my breath," she advised. "Cooper Nicholson is one stubborn man."

He was. Poppy's heart sank. If he had the wrong idea about Owen showing up, then Cooper could just act like their date had never happened. The chance could slip away if Poppy didn't take the risk and find out once and for all if their sparks added up to anything real.

Her pulse sped up. "I'm going to do it," she said, surprising herself. "I'm going to see him."

"Yes!" Mackenzie clapped her hands together in delight. "OK, I have his address right here. And you look great in what you're wearing. What about your underwear?"

"Mackenzie!" Poppy exclaimed.

"What? Come on." She grinned. "A girl has to be prepared."

Poppy thought back to getting dressed that morning. Pale-blue, lace boy-shorts and her favorite bra. "It's fine."

"Then you're good to go." Mackenzie presented her with a scrap of paper, scribbled with an address. She grabbed an unopened bottle of wine, and the leftover cobbler container, too, and thrust them into Poppy's arms. "For luck."

"Thanks." Poppy felt a nervous flutter. "I can't believe I'm doing this. Maybe I shouldn't. Or should I?"

Mackenzie pushed her gently towards the door. "You definitely should. One of us needs some romantic adventure, and it sure isn't going to be me. Not unless you count the hot night I have planned with ESPN."

"Thank you." Poppy paused at the door. "I had a great time this afternoon."

"Me too." Mackenzie beamed. "Be sure to come by tomorrow and tell me how it all went!"

FIFTEEN.

$\mathcal{P}$OPPY DROVE THE main highway out to Cooper's address, her heart racing and her head spinning with doubts. What if she showed up and he laughed right in her face? Or had another woman there? Or, worst of all, made awkward polite excuses until she turned and fled in humiliation?

Relax, she ordered herself. OK, so maybe she wasn't all that experienced when it came to seducing gorgeous men, but she was a grown, red-blooded woman. She wasn't going to get tarred and feathered and marched through town with a scarlet *A* affixed to her chest just for dropping by a friend's place unannounced with a bottle of wine.

And cute underwear.

Poppy took a deep breath, and then another. The turn took her off the highway, out through the woods, and she found herself looking curiously around in the dusk light. The sun was setting through the trees, and she didn't know what to expect from Cooper's residence, but when she pulled up outside an old red barn—weathered with age, with faded white shutters and ironwork curling at the windows—somehow, it made perfect sense.

His truck was out front, and the lights were on inside. No excuses now.

Was she really going to do this?

Poppy thought about heading back to the cottage and spending another evening alone. She'd curl up with a book, make some more soup, and spend the night warm and perfectly content—just the way she'd passed hundreds of nights before. Or she could knock on that door and take a risk, leap into the unknown.

She wanted more. She wanted *him*. And didn't her books always say you should fight for what you wanted?

Poppy climbed out of her car and marched up to the door. She knocked firmly, before she had a chance to take it back.

"Just a sec!" Cooper's yell came from inside, and Poppy was almost about to turn on her heel and race back to the safety of her car when the door opened, and there he was.

Her pulse skipped.

Cooper was barefoot, wearing jeans and a faded black T-shirt. He looked scruffy, and relaxed, and devastatingly handsome, and for a moment, Poppy's mind went blank and her blood ran hot.

She wanted him bad.

"Poppy?" Cooper looked at her with a cautious expression. "Everything OK?"

"Wine," she managed to blurt, holding out the bottle. *Think!* "I mean, there was leftover from the book group. I thought we could share a glass."

And a kiss.

And your bed.

Cooper paused. "Are you sure you don't have other plans?" he asked slowly. "Like with that ex of yours?"

His gaze searched hers, and Poppy silently groaned. She was right—he'd gotten the wrong idea about her and Owen, and thought something was still going on.

"No plans," Poppy said firmly. "Owen just needed . . . to talk it out. Tidy up loose ends. But he agrees it's for the best that it's over between us."

Cooper's lips curled in a smile. "So he didn't want to stick around?"

"Nope." Poppy shook her head quickly. "He left last night. He's probably back in the city by now."

"Probably for the best." Cooper grinned.

"For the best," Poppy echoed, smiling back.

She felt it again, that champagne anticipation that had shivered during their date last night. Her fears and insecurities melted away, and she sent up silent thanks that she hadn't let Cooper's misconceptions keep her away.

He wanted her, too.

"Well, come on in." Cooper stood aside and opened the door wider. "Sorry for the mess, I wasn't expecting company."

Poppy stepped inside, and looked around curiously. It was an old converted barn, with a wide open main living space with double-height ceilings, furnished in a rustic, comfortable style. There was a galley kitchen along one wall, a huge oak dining table, and a loft-style area up a flight of stairs. His bedroom, she guessed.

"Shall I open the bottle?" Cooper asked, strolling over to the kitchen. "Or did Mackenzie already get you drunk?"

Poppy dragged her attention back from his sleeping arrangements. "You've been to book club, then?"

"The first rule of book club . . ." he quipped, and she laughed.

"It was fun. Not that we did much reading." Poppy drifted after him, taking in the mess of papers covering the table. She paused, looking more closely. There were blueprints and sketches: construction designs, and artist renderings, too. They were beautiful and precise, and clearly showed hours of labor.

Cooper returned and handed her a glass of wine. He saw her looking and seemed embarrassed. "Sorry, I was just working on something. I'll get these out of your way."

"No, leave them. These sketches are amazing." Poppy studied them, impressed. The intricate designs, the attention to detail . . . "I didn't know you were an architect, too."

Cooper shrugged. "It's nothing. Just some plans, maybe. I love restoring the older houses, but it would be fun to build from scratch one day."

"Is this the house you're working on at the beach?" she asked, pulling out some sheets with the front elevation planned.

"Yup. I was thinking of adding dormer windows here, upstairs," he pointed out. "And then a balcony area with French doors off the master, so you wake up every morning to that ocean view."

"That sounds incredible," she said, envious that someone would get to enjoy all the product of his labors. "Your future buyers are one lucky family."

He chuckled. "Let's see if I can get the roof to hold before we talk about how lucky they are. These older houses are tricky, they just don't make them like this anymore. They can be amazing if they're restored right, but they come with a lot more baggage."

"Don't we all?" Poppy joked, and he laughed.

Poppy took a sip of wine to calm herself and looked around the room again. Now that she knew what to look for, Cooper's passion for classic old design came through clearly: the vintage photographs of old Cape Cod buildings, framed blueprints on the wall over the mantel, and the rustic-looking furniture she was sure were antiques. "This is a great place," she said admiringly. "It's hard to find, but I'm guessing you planned it that way."

Cooper gave a boyish grin. "There are advantages to being miles from town. Not so many calls to come fix someone's roof at the last minute."

"I don't know about that," Poppy said, remembering how Mackenzie had sung his praises. "Mackenzie says you can be counted on in a crisis."

"Mackenzie says a lot of things," he replied, with all the exasperation of an old friend. "We go way back," he explained. "She's like a kid sister to me, I guess. An annoying, pushy kid sister." He paused. "Although, she can be right about some things."

His eyes caught Poppy's, and she felt herself flush. She

had a feeling she knew exactly what he was talking about, but she couldn't find it in her to be annoyed at Mackenzie's blatant matchmaking.

She'd been right about them, after all.

Poppy took another sip of wine, her head already spinning in a way that had nothing to do with her drink. It was finally sinking in that she was alone with Cooper, with nothing to interrupt them this time. He went to put some music on, and she tried to calm the butterflies in her stomach, but when the slow, sultry strains of a classic Elvis Presley record began to play, and Cooper reappeared in the doorway—his smiling blue eyes fixed steadily on her—Poppy couldn't stop the heat that rolled through her body, jolting every nerve and synapse with pure desire.

Cooper crossed the room.

Poppy caught her breath. His gaze didn't waver, that playful smile on the edge of his lips as he came closer, closer, until he was standing right in front of her. Close enough to touch. He plucked her wineglass from her hand and set it on the table, then gently pressed his palm to her cheek.

"I'm glad you stopped by," he said softly.

His touch rippled through her, electric. Poppy felt like her body was humming, just to feel the warmth of his skin on hers. She wanted to reach for him, touch him, take everything she'd been fantasizing about ever since the night they kissed, but somehow she was suspended in the moment, feeling everything in slow-motion as he leaned in and grazed her lips with his.

Poppy shivered against him. Just the softest brush of his mouth was a revelation, and she swayed closer, eager to find his lips again. This time, the kiss deepened: slow and soft, his mouth exploring hers, tasting. She slid her hands up over his chest, savoring in the solid muscle as his tongue dipped between her lips, tantalizingly slow.

How could a kiss awaken every last sense like this? Poppy was overwhelmed by the feelings rushing over her: the heat from his body, the taste of wine on his tongue; the low, spicy scent of his aftershave, and her own heartbeat thundering over the music in the background. She was wrapped up in the moment, falling deeper into the kiss, and as his fingertips traced the slow outline of her jaw, something inside her let go. Free-fall.

She didn't care what came next between them. She just wanted more.

COOPER WAS DRUNK. He'd only had a sip of wine, but there was no other explanation. Not for the way his head spun to hold her, and his heart pounded in his chest with every touch.

One taste of her, and he was gone. She was the sweetest damn sin he'd ever known.

Poppy let out a breathy sigh against his lips, and Cooper felt a shock of lust barrel through his system. Her body was soft in his arms, pressing closer, and when he surfaced, he'd never seen her look so beautiful: her eyes had drifted shut, her lips parted as if begging for more.

Happy to oblige.

He kissed her again, fighting to take it slow, but damn, his control was fraying with every touch. He parted her lips and sank his tongue deeper into her mouth, stroking against hers in a sensual dance that set the world on fire. She felt too good in his arms, her curves molding against him eagerly as she pressed closer and moaned against his mouth.

That sound was his undoing.

With a groan, Cooper grabbed her by the waist and lifted her up on the table, setting her down with a jolt. Poppy gasped in surprise, then wrapped her legs around his waist, pulling him into the warmth of her body. Damn. Cooper dipped his head to kiss along the pale line of her collarbone, and Poppy shivered against his lips.

She was intoxicating. Everything was a blur besides her sweet mouth. To hell with the papers—he pushed them all aside as she looped her arms around his neck and pulled his mouth back up to hers. He wanted to lay her out on the table and take her right there. Lose himself in her sweetness and never come up for air. He wanted—

SMASH.

A crashing sound pierced the haze of lust. Cooper looked up, bleary, and found their wine glasses in pieces on the floor.

"Whoops." Poppy sat up. She was flushed and breathless, and so beautiful it hurt to look at her. So he kissed her again instead, teasing along her jawline and nibbling on her earlobe.

"But . . . the glass . . ." she murmured weakly. Your feet . . ."

"So I'll keep them off the floor." He scooted her further back on the table and tipped her horizontal, spread beneath him on the wood.

Poppy smiled up at him, hair spilled like a halo around her face. "So we're trapped up here?"

"Looks like it." He grinned back as she reached to hook her finger over the neck of his T-shirt. She slowly tugged him down to cover her.

This time, he didn't hold back. He kissed her deeply, probing her hot mouth as her body arched up against him, her tongue sliding to match his own wet strokes. It was incredible, the heat igniting, deep inside. He ran one hand down her curves and felt her tremble at his touch, and lord, he loved how responsive she was, how he could see the effect he had on her, just as wild as the fire burning in his own veins.

He dipped to kiss her neck, and she moaned again, sliding her hands over his back. She was his, totally wanton in his arms, and damn, he felt invincible, like a king; her touch and sweet whimpers urging him on. He nipped her shoulder lightly and slid one hand to cup her breast, teasing the tender swell through her sweater until he couldn't hold back any longer. He peeled her shirt up her body and slid his hands beneath the cotton to feel every inch of her smooth, hot skin.

Poppy wriggled beneath him, helping push her clothes over her head until she was bare beneath him in jeans and a lacy bra.

Goddamn she was gorgeous.

Cooper dipped to kiss her but Poppy pushed him

back. "Play fair," she said, breathlessly. Her eyes gleamed, and it took a moment for Cooper's brain to function, but when he realized what she wanted, he laughed.

"Yes ma'am," he said, and stripped his T-shirt off. "Better?"

"Much." Poppy bit her lip, her eyes roving over him with desire written all over her face.

What was that he said about feeling like a king? Make that a god.

Cooper leaned in and kissed her lips again, her neck. He trailed his tongue down to the hollow of her collarbone and swirled it over her silky skin. He was ravenous for her, he wanted to feast on every inch of her, but he forced himself to go slow and savor every taste. He kissed lower, over the swell of her chest, whispering at the lacy edge of her bra. Poppy trembled again, unconsciously pressing against his mouth, and he couldn't hold back another moment. He stroked her, teasing at the nub of her nipples as he closed his mouth over one stiff peak and sucked through the silk.

Poppy gasped, rising up against him. He toyed with her, nipping lightly through the fabric, and then turned his attention to her other perfect breast.

God, she was beautiful.

Poppy tangled her fingers in his hair, whimpering softly now. He skimmed lower, dusting her stomach with kisses, but couldn't stop himself returning to those gorgeous breasts. He needed to see her.

He wanted to see everything.

Cooper peeled off her bra, and then lavished her with kisses as he unbuttoned her jeans. Poppy helpfully pushed them off, and then she was spread on the table beneath him, naked save a tiny scrap of silk between her thighs.

Cooper stared down at her, dizzy with lust. He wanted to freeze this image so he'd always remember it.

But he wanted to taste her more.

He leaned in, gripping her hips and lifting her to meet his mouth. He nudged the silk of her underwear as Poppy's whole body went rigid with anticipation.

That's right, darling. You know what I want.

And how good it's going to feel.

Because Cooper wasn't a competitive man, but the memory of her ex was still too fresh for his liking. He wanted her screaming his name, and only his, and he wasn't going to stop until she was begging in his arms.

Starting now.

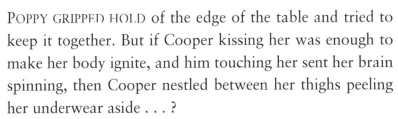

POPPY GRIPPED HOLD of the edge of the table and tried to keep it together. But if Cooper kissing her was enough to make her body ignite, and him touching her sent her brain spinning, then Cooper nestled between her thighs peeling her underwear aside . . . ?

She had no words.

And Poppy always had words. It was her job, for crying out loud—to put these feelings into sentences and chapters for her readers to enjoy, describe the way her characters felt even as their blood ran hot and pure desire sent their thoughts scattering to the far reaches of the universe.

She was a writer. She was supposed to use her words. She was—

"*Ooh.*"

Cooper licked up against her and Poppy moaned out loud. God. What was he doing to her? With his lips, and his hot mouth, and—

His fingers?

Poppy gasped, pressing against him for more. He lapped at her in a maddening rhythm, swirling and sucking at her sensitive nub as one hand pinned her down in place and the other stroked lazily over her stomach and bare breasts. He toyed with one nipple, lightly pinching as his tongue dipped inside her, and *god*. Poppy gave up trying to process the sensations crashing through her, she just lay back and reveled in the waves of incredible pleasure Cooper was giving, driving her higher with every stroke until she was teetering on the edge of something, holding on for dear life.

"That's right, darlin'," he murmured against her, the vibration of his words whispering against her most sensitive spot. "Come for me."

Poppy couldn't help it. He licked at her again, and sent her flying.

She let go.

Oh my god.

The pleasure slammed through her, waves of delicious heat that somehow didn't sate her, they just left her dizzy and gasping for more.

She wanted all of him. Now.

Before she could even try to pull herself together, Cooper was lifting her in his arms. He scooped her off the table like she weighed nothing and carried her up the stairs. "I always wanted to be swept off my feet," she joked, and Cooper chuckled.

"Baby, I haven't even started yet."

He gave her a look that was so smoldering, she practically melted right there in the hallway. *Oh boy.* Poppy held on tight as he took her into the bedroom and placed her carefully on the bed. It was a rustic, clean room just like the rest of the house, with soft bedding she would have happily snuggled into and slept—if it wasn't for the gorgeous man stripping off his clothing right in front of her, or the wild heat of desire still burning in her veins.

He glanced up and caught her watching him as he took off his pants. Poppy flushed, but she didn't look away. She held his gaze, her pulse racing.

Cooper leaned over her on the bed and captured her lips in a blazing kiss.

If she'd thought their chemistry could burn the house down before, now, she knew Cooper was right: it was only the beginning. Body to body, skin to skin, this kiss did things to her she didn't know were possible. Cooper slid his tongue deep into her mouth, and she moaned, reaching up to pull him closer. She ran her hands over his broad shoulders and taut muscles, greedy to touch as he returned the favor, stroking her body back to the brink with his roving fingers and strong, sure touch. Her hands moved lower, and Cooper groaned against her, making her bolder to tease and stroke at his hard length.

God, he felt so good.

Cooper pulled away, and Poppy let out a whimper of protest, but he was only reaching for the nightstand. He rolled on a condom, and then he was back, settling between her thighs—where he belonged.

He braced himself above her, teasing her mouth open as she felt him nudge at her entrance. Then slowly, he sank inside her.

Poppy gasped to feel him, filling her inch by glorious inch. She flexed around him, adjusting to the feel, and Cooper groaned against her.

Then he began to move.

God, she thought she'd felt pleasure before from his mouth and hands, but this was something else. He was surging inside her, stroking her so deep, she lost her mind. Poppy clung onto him, rising to meet every thrust, until they were moving as one, each new hot stroke driving her higher, setting her blood on fire. There were no words left, just the feel of him: hard, and deep, and so damn right she never wanted it to end. But her body couldn't hold back. Soon, she was cresting, right there on the edge again, his body bearing down on her and his mouth claiming hers.

"Cooper . . ." she moaned, lost to the sensation. "Oh god, I'm close."

He lifted his head, and the look in his eyes—that raw, animal need—stole what was left of her breath away. Over and over again, he surged into her, his gaze still fixed on hers so she was drowning in the sight of him, the overwhelming pleasure that rose, and crested, and—

god—shattered through her with a cry as he thrust deep one last time and sent them both over the edge, until she was spent and breathless in his arms.

And never wanted to let go.

SIXTEEN.

*P*OPPY TOOK A ragged breath, collapsed in a haze of pleasure. That was . . . He was . . .
Incredible.

Cooper rolled away and took care of the condom, but before she could even miss him, he was back beside her, holding her tightly, his chest rising and falling hard.

"Goddamn." His voice was thick with satisfaction. "You should come with a warning."

Poppy felt a glow of pride. "You weren't so bad yourself."

Cooper snorted. He suddenly rolled her beneath him again: pinning her to the mattress with his mouth just inches from hers. "You want to try that again?" he said, a teasing spark in his eyes.

"Give me five minutes," she grinned back. "And sure."

Cooper laughed, and collapsed beside her again. "Make it ten." He stroked her naked curves and yawned. "I'm not as young as I used to be."

"I don't know . . ." she mused, stroking circles on his chest. "You've still got moves . . . for an old man." She stroked lower, and Cooper caught her hand.

"Minx," he said, grinning. "Dangerous woman."

Poppy stretched. She rather liked the sound of that. She propped herself up on her elbows and looked around. "I like this place," she said. "It's very . . . you."

"Run-down and out the back of beyond?" Cooper arched an eyebrow.

She laughed. "Rustic and manly."

"You like that, huh?" Cooper's hands slipped under the sheets. Poppy wriggled, ticklish, and he leaned in, murmuring low and sexy. "You should drop by the construction site sometime. I can hammer a joist like nobody's business."

"I'll bet you can." She laughed and kissed him again, loving how easy it felt. How natural. His body was hot and deliciously naked against her, still sweaty from all their tanglings, and she was reminded of her thought that very first day she'd seen him, grown up from the boy she'd known.

He was all man.

Eventually, Cooper broke away. "What did you bring with the wine?"

Poppy took a moment for her brain to function again. "What?"

"The Tupperware. It looked like pie. Was it pie?" Cooper brightened, and she had to laugh.

"Cobbler. And I can't believe you're thinking about food when you have a naked woman in bed with you."

"You made me work up an appetite," he said, hopping out of bed. She was treated to the sight of his naked body in all its glory before he grabbed a robe. "Don't move an inch," he said, and headed down the stairs.

Poppy sank back into the pillows. She couldn't if she tried. Amazing sex and a man to bring her dessert in bed?

This must be what heaven was like.

And she would have missed out on all of it if she hadn't taken that leap and showed up at his door tonight. Poppy thought how close she'd come to just going home, and shivered. It just goes to show that working up the courage and taking that risk brought all kinds of unexpected delights. For once, she hadn't been content to disappear into the comforting fiction of her books—she'd gone after what she wanted in the real world, and it had worked out better than she could ever have dreamed.

Well, maybe she had dreamed this, late at night in those secret fantasies. But Cooper live and in the flesh was more glorious than even her most fevered daydreams. She'd found a man who could teach her romantic heroes a thing or two. Or three. Or more . . .

"You didn't say it was Fran's famous plum cobbler."

Cooper reappeared with the bottle of wine, the Tupperware container, and two forks. He dove onto the bed, bouncing beside her, and she laughed.

"Now, this is a feast," Poppy said. He offered the wine, and she took a gulp, sweet and straight from the bottle. "When I was a kid, I used to love all those books about British boarding schools. My parents even asked me if I wanted to go away to school, and I had to tell them no, I just loved all the midnight feasts they had, sneaking off in the middle of the night."

"I remember you always had your nose in a book."

Cooper fed her a fork of cobbler, and Poppy sighed with satisfaction. "You always seemed so . . . self-contained. Like it didn't matter what else was going on in the world, you had your books, so you didn't need anyone. I envied you for that."

"Really?" Poppy looked at him in surprise. "I read so much because I felt lonely all the time. Even that summer here, I was such an outsider. I felt like everyone thought I was such a nerd."

"We did." Cooper grinned, and reached to push back her hair from her eyes. "But a cute nerd."

She smiled. "You drove me crazy. If I'd had a dime for every time you dropped something slimy down my shirt . . ."

"Sorry. I couldn't help it," he said. "You got so flustered and angry when I called you—"

"Don't!" Poppy covered his mouth with her hand. "Don't even think about it."

She slowly lowered her hand, but Cooper gave her a wicked look. "Pipsqueak," he said, before she could stop him. Poppy shoved him back playfully.

"That's no way to seduce a woman," she warned, and he laughed.

"I'll take my chances. This woman seems pretty receptive to my . . . charms." He leaned in and kissed her bare shoulder, a trail of whisper-soft kisses that made her sigh with pleasure.

"Fine," she said. "But no seaweed down my back."

"Deal."

COOPER SETTLED BACK, Poppy snuggled in the crook of his arm. He took a gulp of wine, and felt pretty damn satisfied about how the night had turned out.

Life didn't get much better than this.

"I owe Mackenzie a drink," Poppy said, her head resting against his chest. "She's the one who told me to show up on your doorstep."

"Did she? That sounds about right." He stroked her hair, and marveled at the silky feel.

"She said you were too stubborn to make the first move." Poppy gave him a mischievous look.

He grinned. "Don't be so sure. I could have just cut your hot water again, and had you come running—naked into my arms."

Poppy laughed. "Don't even joke about it." She settled back to rest, but Cooper wondered if it were true. If she hadn't showed up that night, could he really have stayed away?

Never.

He'd been kidding himself, saying she was out of reach. Sooner or later, their chemistry would have been too much to resist. Hell, he'd sworn to steer clear from the start, but somehow, he always found a way back to her. Like a moth drawn to the flame, he couldn't stop himself from coming around. A coffee, a late night chat. A kiss that turned his world upside down.

No, it was inevitable that they'd wound up here: naked, together in his bed. The question now was, where did they go from here?

Cooper tensed. Somehow, that question had a way of

bringing back the past, but Poppy looked up questioningly, and the sight of her beautiful face made it all melt away. He didn't want to think about the future, not all the questions and disappointments it could bring, so he kissed her instead, long and slow, claiming that sweet mouth until Poppy was writhing against him.

This was all that mattered. Right here. Now. In her arms.

He pulled her closer, dragging his hands possessively over every inch of her, feeling that incredible need take over him again. Not just desire, but something more primal—to own her, make her his. Bring her such pleasure that she would never want to let go. She moaned into his mouth, and it was all the invitation he needed. He slowly eased her thighs apart and lost himself in her again.

SEVENTEEN.

WHEN POPPY WOKE again, the sun was bright in the sky outside the barn windows. She yawned, rolling over in the snug sheets. Something crumpled against her, and with sleepy eyes she reached to find a note on the pillow.

See you at June's. X

It wasn't exactly a declaration of undying love, but she'd take that scribbled X any day. Poppy stretched, feeling the satisfying ache in her limbs.

God, that man was good with his hands . . . and his mouth . . . and—

Other things.

She lay in a warm haze of memories, until her stomach rumbled, and she remembered that her clean clothes and a hot breakfast were still a drive away. The place empty, and it took a moment to adjust to the sound of trees and birdsong outside instead of the steady crashing of the waves. Poppy scrambled out of bed, her feet bare on the cold floors. She hunted around for her clothing, following the trail downstairs and back to the kitchen table. She quickly redressed, flushing as the passionate images flooded her mind.

It's a good thing that table was as sturdy as it looked.

Poppy lingered by the table. He'd cleaned up the shattered glass, but all of Cooper's paperwork and blueprints were still scattered on the floor. She carefully collected them and placed them back into neat piles, remembering how he'd swept them aside in a moment of passion.

That man sure knew how to make her heart beat faster.

She couldn't keep from smiling. It felt like her connection with Cooper had gone to a whole new level last night, and not just the physical side of things either. Seeing him here, in his natural habitat, she understood him better. Even though he'd hidden himself away out here in the woods, there was a part of him that wanted to take the leap, the same as she did. Open up to something new.

She wasn't sure what any of it meant, but it felt good to be taking that risk again. With him.

Poppy yanked on her jacket, found her keys and opened the door, only to come face to face with—

"Debra?"

Poppy blinked. One of the older women from book club was on Cooper's doorstep—hand outreached towards the doorbell. She had a crate full of apples in her arms, and Poppy stifled a groan. Just her luck that someone was making a neighborly delivery at ten in the morning!

"Poppy." Debra's eyes widened, and then a mischievous smile danced onto her face. "Good morning. I didn't know I'd find you here."

"I'm not! Here!" Poppy blurted, desperately thinking for a reason she would be emerging from Cooper's house.

A reason that didn't involve a night of torrid sex. And three orgasms.

"I . . . umm, was just dropping something off. For Cooper," she kept babbling. "He said to just leave it inside. So that's what I was doing." Poppy grabbed her purse and lunged out of the door. "Great seeing you!"

"Dearie?" Debra stopped her. "Aren't you forgetting something?"

"No! What? How?" Poppy gulped.

Debra smirked, and nodded to Poppy's bare feet.

"Oh. Right." Poppy looked around inside for her shoes. She found one sneaker tossed behind the couch, and another resting halfway up the stairs. When she re-emerged, shod this time, Debra's smile had grown.

"See you around," Poppy managed to mutter as she slinked past.

Debra laughed. "You have a great day now!"

No! Poppy glanced in the rearview mirror as she high-tailed it out of there, watching Debra recede in the distance. There was no way the other woman bought her story about an early-morning barefoot delivery. At this rate, half the town would know about her sleepover before she even made it back to the beach!

She gulped and tried not to feel like she was back in college again, doing the walk of shame back to her dorm. She was a grown adult woman, she reminded herself firmly. She was allowed to have a sex life.

An amazing, bone-melting, spine-tingling, beg-for-more sex life.

Poppy grinned. She couldn't help it. So, their secret hook-up had been busted wide open before it even had a chance to be secret. She didn't care. Because *wow*, that had been good.

And she already wanted more.

BACK AT THE COTTAGE, she found the crew working hard on the house next door. But Cooper—and his truck—were nowhere to be seen. Probably getting supplies, she guessed, and took the opportunity to have a long shower and wash her hair. She still cautiously tested the water before stepping under the spray, but thankfully, there had been no more "ice bucket" incidents since that first time with Cooper.

Her mind drifted, rinsing her hair. The shower was plenty big enough for two, so maybe Cooper could come join her one night after work, all sweaty from his labor . . .

The sound of her phone ringing interrupted her steamy thoughts, and even though Poppy was tempted to let it go to voicemail and stay happily locked in her fantasyland, she knew her hot water supply wouldn't last forever. She grabbed a towel and shut off the water, trying not to drip on the floors as she sprinted for her bedroom.

"Hello?" She picked up, and found Summer on the other end.

"Am I, or am I not, your best friend?"

"Um, yes?" Poppy trapped the phone against her ear and flipped her wet hair over, towel-drying it.

"So why am I like the last person to find out about Owen's impromptu trip to the Cape?"

"Oh. That."

"That?" Summer echoed. "Don't tell me your life is so dramatic now that your ex-fiancé showing up on your doorstep in the middle of the night to swear his undying affection and beg you back doesn't so much as warrant a text? Email? Facebook emoji?"

Poppy laughed. "OK, OK, I'm sorry! But in my defense, I've been . . . distracted."

Summer gasped. "I know that tone. Who is he? What's his name? Did he duel Owen for your affections in the middle of the Sweetbriar town square?"

"Not quite." Poppy couldn't help but laugh at Summer's dramatics. "His name is Cooper. He's . . . an old friend. And we've been getting reacquainted."

"You got laid, didn't you? I can tell it from your voice. You sound all happy and shiny and bouncing with well-banged hormones." Summer giggled. "Not that I'm not happy for you, but seriously? You go to the ends of the earth to be alone and work, and you still manage to find a hot guy. He is hot, isn't he?" she added.

"Smoldering." Poppy grinned. "He just looks at me and I feel like I'm about to spontaneously combust."

Summer sighed happily. "I remember how that feels. God, I love the butterflies."

"It's amazing," Poppy admitted. "I wasn't sure anything was going to happen. He kissed me, but then he acted like nothing happened. So I just went over there last night."

"You seduced him? Look at you." Summer sounded impressed. "I knew my bad influence would rub off one day."

Poppy laughed. "You're not so bad."

"Only because I don't have the time," Summer said, rueful. "It's hard to live wild and reckless when you have to be up at five a.m. to start baking bread for the day."

"I told you, take a vacation," Poppy said sternly. "Come visit."

"Does this Cooper have hot friends?"

Poppy paused. "Actually, yes," she said, thinking of Riley and Grayson. "Maybe it's something in the water around here, makes the men all scruffy and gorgeous."

"Scruffy and gorgeous sounds good to me, but I'll come see you just as soon as Andre gets that stick out of his snooty French ass."

"You should tell him that," Poppy said, teasing.

Summer hooted with laughter. "Can you just imagine his face? Or worse still, my mother's?"

"Maybe not." Poppy winced. Summer's mom was a famous TV chef who gave Martha Stewart and the Barefoot Contessa a run for their money. Summer had spent her life in her mother's shadow—and trying to win her approval, too. "Anyway, tell me what I'm supposed to do now, with Cooper."

"You've done it once. You shouldn't need a diagram."

"Summer! You know what I mean . . ." Poppy walked over to the window, which looked out over the construction site next door. Cooper was back: she could see his truck parked there now, and a new level of energy in the crew working on the roof. "I haven't dated a guy in years. And this doesn't even feel like dating, it's just . . . *Cooper*. You know?"

"Nope," Summer replied cheerfully. Poppy could hear pans clattering in the background, and knew she was already back to work. "But you'll figure it out. And if you run into problems, just follow my one simple trick."

"What's that?"

"Take off all your clothes. And if that doesn't work, take off all of his, too. Usually that gets you through the bumpy parts."

Poppy laughed. "Good to know."

"It'll be OK." Summer's voice turned serious for a moment. "You sound happy, that's the important thing."

"Alright." Poppy took a breath. "No awkwardness, no freak-outs, and when in doubt, get him naked again. I can do that!"

"Atta girl."

Summer rang off, and Poppy slowly lowered the phone. As she watched through the window, she saw Cooper emerge from the site. He grabbed some lumber from the back of his truck, moving confidently through the chaos back inside.

A text came. Cooper.

That towel's looking good on you.

Poppy leapt back from the window with a yelp. She didn't realize he could see her watching!

She took a breath, collecting herself, and typed a reply.

Want to come help me dry off?

I wish. Let me finish the roof today, and I'm all yours.

Poppy felt a happy shiver. *See you later.* She paused, then added an X.

Bet on it.

WAS IT JUST COOPER'S imagination, or was the clock running at half speed? His work day seemed to drag on forever, knowing that Poppy was just across the yard, curled up in that study writing all kinds of steamy scenes . . .

"You want the timber stacked inside?"

Cooper heard a voice and turned. One of his guys was waiting, looking impatient. "Sorry?"

"The timber," he said again. "You said we should bring it in now that the roof is done, in case of more rain."

"Right. Yes. Thanks." Cooper tried to get a grip. Distractions were for guys who sat around in an office all day. On site, his lack of attention could cause serious damage. "Let me help with that."

He put his head down and focused on the job, pushing all thoughts of Poppy away until the rest of the crew were packed up and clocked off. Cooper thought about heading home to shower and change, making a better impression than after a full day of sweaty work, but the temptation to see her was too strong. Besides, Poppy had already seen him covered in sawdust and three-day stubble, and it hadn't seemed to bother her yet.

He waited until the last truck drove away, then headed over and knocked on the door. No reply. He tried again, then sent a text. The reply came right away.

At the cabin. Come find me.

Cooper set off along the beach path. He was pleased the cabin was working out for her, especially now that they were hammering plywood all day long. He walked faster, and was struck with a sudden sense of déjà vu—years ago, when he was a teenager, sneaking off to meet a girl in the woods.

Back then, he'd been intoxicated with hormones, and the liquor he and his friends liberated from their parents' cabinets, sitting out by a campfire late into the night. Now, he was supposed to be older and wiser, but somehow he still felt just as reckless, his pulse kicking up at the thought of Poppy—and memories of everything they shared the night before.

He couldn't get enough of her.

Cooper emerged from the treeline and found the cabin doors thrown wide open to the shore. The light was dimming, but he could see the glow from a couple of lanterns he'd left stacked inside. Poppy was curled up in the old wingback chair with her laptop, just the way he'd imagined her. She was dressed in a sweater and jeans, focused on her screen, deep in thought. She twisted a lock of hair around her fingertips as her lips moved, reading to herself.

"Ahoy there," Cooper called, not wanting to startle her.

She looked up, and a brilliant smile spread across her face. "Hey you," she said, then looked around. "What time is it? It can't be sunset already."

"'Fraid so." Cooper reached her, and leaned in for a kiss. She tilted her head up to meet him, her lips soft and warm, even as the ocean wind whipped around them.

"I swear, I lose track of time completely when I'm writing," Poppy said. "Sometimes I'll get so deep in a chapter I'll surface later and the whole day will be gone."

"So it's going well?" Cooper asked. She nodded happily.

"I'm getting so much done—especially here. This is such a great spot, there's barely any cell reception, and no internet distracting me with cute kitten pictures and book reviews."

"You have a kitten problem?" Cooper teased. He tugged Poppy out of the chair, and then settled into it himself, pulling her back into his lap.

"A big one," she admitted. "Basically, all kinds of adorable fluffy animals. They're like crack, I could look at them all day long. Especially when I'm on deadline, and someone sends me a video of two puppies trying to climb over a wall."

He laughed, relaxing back. Sitting there, looking out at the darkening waves, with Poppy curled against his chest, he felt a sense of calm and total contentment wash over him.

He could get used to this.

"What about you?" Poppy asked, resting her head against his shoulder. "Good day?"

"Good enough." He nodded. "Aside from this little minx, tempting me in her towel . . ."

Poppy groaned. "I didn't realize you could see in from down there!"

"I guess I should just be glad you didn't put on more of a show for Billy and the guys."

"No!"

Cooper cut off her blushing protest with a kiss. It was leisurely and molten, and sent his blood raging in a heartbeat. *Damn*. This is what had been driving him to distraction all day: the thought of her, right here in his arms. Against his lips. Soft, and sweet, and yielding.

Poppy let out a sigh of satisfaction and looped her arms around his neck. "There's something I should probably tell you," she said, when they finally came up for air. "Debra caught me leaving your place this morning. She was stopping by just as I was on my way out. It didn't take much to put two and two together."

"So you're saying a new town gossip bulletin just went out," Cooper chuckled, imagining how red-faced and flustered Poppy must have been.

"I'm sorry," she said, looking embarrassed. "I don't know if you wanted to keep this . . . you know, discreet. Or even what this is. Not that you need to know," she added hurriedly.

Damn, she was adorable when she was flustered.

"I don't know what this is yet," Cooper said slowly, searching her gaze. "But I'd like to find out, if that's OK with you?"

Poppy relaxed again, and nodded. "More than OK," she smiled.

"Good." Cooper felt her shiver against him, and pulled her closer.

"It's getting cold out," she said. It was darker now, and the ocean was just a dark silhouette against the shadows.

"I'll warm you up." Cooper grinned.

She smiled, her eyes sparkling in the lantern light. "I bet you will."

Cooper chuckled, and slid one hand under her sweater. She yelped as his cool touch hit her warm skin. "You said warm!" Poppy laughed.

"Patience."

He kissed her again, deeper, the spark igniting as they grew breathless. His hands slid higher, teasing at her breasts and roving to cup the curves of her ass. Poppy moaned against his mouth and shifted to straddle his lap, rocking gently against him until he was half-crazy with wanting her.

She reached for his belt, and the last working brain cell in his head made him do the noble thing. He pulled away. "You're going to get us arrested," he warned her, even as his body screamed for more.

"It's dark," Poppy replied, with a teasing smile on her lips. "Who's here to see?"

Cooper glanced around. The beach was totally dark,

and only the lanterns could be seen flickering in the dark. To hell with noble. He leaned over and blew them out, plunging them into darkness. Poppy's laugh echoed in the tiny cabin, and then he felt her lips on his again: sweet and tantalizing. She kissed along his jaw, and leaned to nibble at his earlobe.

"I wrote a great scene today," she whispered. "But it was missing something."

"Uh huh?" Cooper tried to focus, but her hands were stroking over him and tugging his jeans open. The last thing he could do right then was think about her writing.

"I decided what I need is some research. If that's OK with you?"

"Research?" Cooper mumbled, confused. Poppy stroked him again, harder, and Cooper had to stifle a groan.

Thank god for this woman and her books.

"Happy to help," he said, as she sank to her knees. He felt her close her mouth around him, everything else in the world fell away.

This woman was heaven, and he couldn't get enough.

EIGHTEEN.

*P*OPPY WALKED WITH COOPER back to the house, her blood still singing. She couldn't believe she'd been so reckless and wanton back there, but it felt good. She felt *alive.*

"Want to grab dinner?" Cooper asked, delivering her to the front step. "I need to stop home, but I could meet you at Riley's in an hour."

"Sounds good." She smiled and leaned in to drop a quick kiss on his lips.

"Not so fast. He caught her against him, and the quick kiss turned slow and luxurious. When Cooper set her down, Poppy's head was spinning. "See you there."

He loped off to his truck, and Poppy blinked. It took her a moment to function again, and she let herself inside.

God, that man could kiss.

That man could do plenty more besides... Her thoughts turned to last night, and she couldn't help the smile that spread across her face, so wide, her cheeks ached. It turned out not settling for a life of "fine" was just about the best decision she could have made.

She hadn't known it could be so good.

Poppy managed to tear her thoughts away from

Cooper for a moment to go change for dinner. It was only the local pub, but she still wanted to look good for Cooper, so she added a bright sweater to her jeans, and carefully applied mascara and a slick of pink lip balm. There. She wasn't due to meet him for another half hour, but Poppy decided to walk up to town early. She strolled around and was pleased to see several flyers advertising the literary festival up in Provincetown next week. She always loved doing signings and events; it was a great chance to meet her readers, and other authors, too. And having this one take place so close definitely made it convenient: she could do her events and be back in bed with Cooper at the end of the day.

Or out of it . . .

She blushed, remembering her boldness down at the beach. But she couldn't help herself. Something about her connection with this man was intoxicating; it made her want to throw caution to the wind and follow her instincts.

And her instincts seemed to lead her straight to his arms.

"Poppy!"

She heard a voice, and turned to find Mackenzie waving from across the square. She was just locking up the pottery shop, so Poppy walked over. "Hey, how are you?"

"Not as good as you, I'm guessing." Mackenzie gave her a mischievous grin, and Poppy groaned.

"Debra?"

Mackenzie nodded.

"I knew it!" Poppy gulped, her cheeks burning. "How do you manage, living in a town where everyone knows your business?"

"You learn to be discreet. Aww, it's not so bad." Mackenzie gave her a sympathetic hug. "It's just that you're new, so you're a mysterious outsider, and Cooper . . . Well, Coop has a lot of friends here. We just want to see him happy."

Mackenzie began strolling in the direction of the pub, so Poppy fell into step alongside. "I know. It's just a change, coming from the city. I've lived in the same apartment for three years now, and I don't think I even know my neighbor's name!"

Mackenzie smiled. "That sounds like heaven to me."

"Sometimes." Poppy thought about it. "But when the power cut out for days and I couldn't find any matches, I wished I knew them a little better."

"Well, you won't find that here," Mackenzie said. "You're more likely to have Bert show up to fix the fuse box and Franny drop by with a casserole, just in case."

Poppy looked around. The town square was lit up in the early-evening dark: twinkling lights strung on the trees and around the gazebo. It was beautiful and peaceful, and the night was so clear, she could even see the stars. "It's a really special place, isn't it?"

"It's home," Mackenzie said simply. "I get to thinking about leaving every few years, but somehow, it never works out."

"You've lived here all your life, haven't you?"

Mackenzie nodded. "Almost. My family moved here

when I was sixteen. They're up in Truro now," she added, naming a town about fifteen minutes away. "There's more land there for the alpacas. Don't ask," she added, with a rueful face.

Poppy laughed. "OK."

They were outside the pub now. Mackenzie nodded inside. "Drink?"

"Sure. I'm meeting Cooper here for dinner, too."

"Romantic," Mackenzie teased, and Poppy laughed.

"I think it is. Maybe you're immune to it now, but this town is about as charming as it comes."

They stepped inside, into the warm. It was a cozy scene, with a fire roaring in the grate and a few people already settled in with food and drinks. They headed over to where Riley was behind the bar, still looking scruffy with too-long hair and a plaid shirt. "Look who it is," he greeted them with a charming grin. "My new favorite person."

"Uh oh." Poppy looked around. "What did I do?"

"Brought a smile to the face of the grumpiest bachelor on the Cape," Riley replied. Poppy groaned.

"Debra?"

"Actually, I heard it from Larry at the hardware store." Riley replied. "Who heard it from Franny, who heard it from—"

"I get the picture." Poppy resigned herself to living with a permanent blush.

"Remember, small towns are charming," Mackenzie reminded her. "Romantic."

"It could be worse," Riley agreed. "Mac here got

caught in a state of undress, right there in the gazebo in the middle of the square."

Poppy turned, surprised. "Really?"

"I was seventeen!" Mackenzie protested. "And how do you even know?"

"I know everything." Riley winked. He passed them two pints of beer. "I'm the friendly barkeep."

"Too friendly," Mackenzie grumbled, but she said it with a smile.

Poppy looked back and forth between them. "Have you two ever . . . ?"

Mackenzie snorted into her drink. "Um, nope."

"Mackenzie here is still waiting for Prince Charming to come swooping in," Riley teased.

"Better than having you creep out my bedroom in the middle of the night," Mackenzie shot back.

"I don't creep," Riley protested. "I make a hasty retreat."

"Same thing." Mackenzie grinned. "How is Alexa?"

"Adrienne," Riley corrected her. "And she went back to Australia."

"College starting up again?" Mackenzie teased, but Riley just winked at Poppy.

"High school, actually. Senior year."

"Pig!" Mackenzie leaned over and smacked his arm. He ducked back, laughing.

"I'm kidding! She was all grown up. Too mature for me, in the end. She said I was immature and needed to find direction in life."

"I stand corrected," Mackenzie said. "She sounds like

she has you all figured out."

"Just for that, your drinks aren't on the house to-night," Riley replied. Poppy reached for her wallet, but he waved it away. "You're fine. I still like you. You don't come into a man's place of business and judge his choices."

"Give her time and she will," Mackenzie said sweetly.

"Will what?" Cooper's voice came from behind them, and then Poppy felt his hand on her back. She turned, her heart lifting just to see him again: too handsome in a navy sweater, with his hair falling in his eyes, still damp from the shower.

"Hi," she said, smiling, and he grinned back.

"Hey, you."

She felt the pull to touch him but paused, not wanting to engage in any public displays of affection if he wasn't comfortable with it. But Cooper didn't hesitate before leaning in and kissing her softly on the lips. The rush swept through her in an instant, and she felt light-headed when he pulled back.

"These ladies were just giving me grief about my care-free bachelor lifestyle," Riley said, sliding a pint over to Cooper. "Back me up here, buddy."

"I'm staying out of this one," Cooper laughed. He took a gulp of beer. "You can't expect a leopard to change his spots."

"That's ridiculous!" Mackenzie exclaimed. "What about you? Yesterday you were saying there was no way anything was going to happen with you and Poppy, and now look at you."

Poppy arched an eyebrow at Cooper. He looked uncomfortable. "That was when I thought . . . you know, Owen . . ."

Poppy smiled. "It's OK, I get it." She'd had her own doubts too, until Mackenzie had spurred her in the right direction. Clearly her new friend was a secret matchmaker—and she wasn't stopping at Cooper.

"If he can change, so can you," Mackenzie said determinedly, looking back at Riley.

"How about you stop sticking your nose into other people's love lives, and start focusing on your own?" Riley countered. Mackenzie rolled her eyes.

"Please. I've known everyone in this town for years. I'm looking forward to my spinster lifestyle. I'm going to get five cats," she told Poppy, "and wear kaftans and have scandalous affairs with the summer lifeguards."

"Sounds like a plan." Poppy smiled.

"She lies," Cooper's voice rumbled softly in Poppy's ear. "She's always been a romantic. She'll be settled down with someone, having five kids soon enough."

"Before or after Riley gets taught a lesson in love?" Poppy whispered back.

He grinned. "I'll take that bet."

"Deal."

They shook on it. "See, they're already whispering sweet nothings," Riley said, with an exaggerated sigh. "There's no hope for him now."

"Aren't you supposed to be busy with something?" Cooper replied. "Like ordering up some food for us."

"All in good time." Riley grinned, clearly enjoying

getting under Cooper's skin.

Poppy slipped down from her stool. "As long as it has carbs and grease, I'm happy," she said. "I'll be right back."

She headed for the restroom, and took the chance to run cool water over her wrists. Her reflection in the mirror was flushed, and her eyes were sparkling with a light she almost didn't recognize.

This was what she'd been looking for.

Poppy shook off the sappy thought, and headed back out to the bar. But in the hallway, someone caught her arm and tugged her into an alcove. Cooper. He smiled, sliding his hands around her waist. "I've been waiting all night to kiss you," he murmured, drawing closer.

"You just did." She smiled, melting against him. His body already felt like it fit hers perfectly, and she slid her hands over his chest.

"Not properly," Cooper corrected her. "Not like this."

He leaned in and claimed her mouth with a searing kiss. Slow and hot and deep; his body pressing her back against the wall so she could feel every solid, taut inch of him.

He was right. That brief greeting had been only a taste of this feast. Poppy pulled him closer and surrendered to the gorgeous heat of his body and the head-spinning things he was doing with his tongue. The kiss deepened, hungry, and soon she was gasping for breath. His hands were in her hair; roving over her body, cupping her ass and pulling her closer against him.

"We can't," she gasped, coming up for air. "Anyone could come back here . . ."

Cooper kissed her neck. "And?"

"And . . . *ohh*," she sighed as his tongue found a sensitive hollow and licked against her. She sank back, dizzy with pleasure. There was no resisting, it felt too good. She smiled, giving in to his touch. "You're a bad influence."

"That's me." Cooper grinned, lifting his head. "Want to get out of here?"

"We just arrived." Poppy wavered, torn.

"And?" He yanked her closer, and she remembered in a flash what this would feel like with fewer clothes.

Far fewer.

Cooper interrupted her with another kiss, and Poppy for the life of her couldn't think of a reason to stay—at least until the doors to the kitchen swung open, and she caught the smell of something sizzling on the grill. In an instant, she was reminded she hadn't eaten all day. "And I need to eat something before I pass out," she said, finally pulling away.

Cooper kissed her forehead. "Well, we can't have that. You need your strength," he added, in a low, sexy voice. "Because believe me, baby. I've got plans."

She shivered. Now, how was she supposed to walk back into the bar and carry on like the possibility of those plans wasn't swirling in her mind? "I deserve a medal," she sighed, and he laughed.

"I'll make sure you get a prize." Cooper winked.

POPPY SPENT THE REST of the evening with a permanent

smile on her face. It wasn't just Cooper—although every glance or touch sent her stomach flipping over—but the rest of it, too. They ate at the bar, joking with Riley, and then wound up playing pool with Mackenzie and some of her friends. The warmth of the evening wrapped around Poppy, and she couldn't help feeling how lucky she was to have stumbled into this community in her moment of crisis and insecurity.

"And that is how you do it." Mackenzie played her final shot with a flourish. "Victory is mine!"

"Sorry," Poppy apologized to Cooper.

"What happened to your hustling skills?" he asked, reluctantly paying out their wager of a whole five dollars.

"Cards only," she said. "But point me in the direction of a poker table, and I'll win us back some glory."

Mackenzie laughed. "Another time. I know when to call it quits." She finished her drink and yawned. "Time for me to hit the road."

"Us too," Cooper said, drawing Poppy closer.

"We'll have to get together soon," Poppy suggested. "Have dinner, or a girls' night or something."

"Definitely!" Mackenzie agreed. "How much longer are you staying in town?"

Poppy stopped. "I . . . I'm not sure." She shot a look at Cooper. "I'm still working on my book."

"Well, just give me a call. I'm around." Mackenzie said goodbye and drifted away to talk to some people by the fire, but Poppy lingered on her question. What were her plans? She hadn't set herself a deadline for her trip to Sweetbriar Cove. Aunt June had offered an open invitation, but she would be back from her trip soon, and Poppy was racing through her book draft. She'd always seen this retreat as a temporary escape. After all, she had a life waiting for her back home. Didn't she?

"Ready to go?"

Cooper's voice brought her back to the pub. "What? Sure. Let's go." Poppy smiled and followed him to the door, but outside, she felt a flicker of insecurity. She hadn't planned on finding romance here; she hadn't planned on Cooper at all. So what would happen when she finished her draft, and it was time to get back to the real world again?

"You've got that distracted look." Cooper slung an arm around her as they stepped out into the chilly spring night. "Admit it, you're thinking about the next chapter you're working on, aren't you?"

"Busted." Poppy smiled quickly and pushed her doubts aside. There was no point worrying about the future just yet. They'd spent one night together, and yes, it was a life-changing, world-shattering night for sure, but she didn't even know what this thing with Cooper would become; it was still too fresh to tell.

She should just enjoy it now and save the questions for later. Much later.

Like after another night with him.

COOPER WAS LUCKY their highway patrol never ventured off the main roads, because he damn well broke the speed limit getting Poppy back to the cottage. All night, he'd been going half crazy with wanting her, and now they were finally alone, without Mackenzie giving him that "I told you so" look or Riley interrupting at the worst possible moment. He loved his friends, but man, they knew how to get in the way.

"Come on." Cooper yanked open the passenger door, and lifted her down from the seat. "I'm about ten seconds from undressing you, and if we're still outside, so be it."

Poppy laughed, but he could see the desire in her eyes too, and it made him pull her across the front yard in double-quick time. "We'd catch frostbite!" she protested, rummaging in her purse for the keys. It took too long, and he had to kiss her again, right there up against the door. Her mouth was so sweet and yielding; he was already hard for her, needing the release only she could provide.

Because he knew this time. He knew just how good she felt, and there was no going back from that, not with his hands already sliding under her sweater, and Poppy making that breathy moaning sound as he kissed down her neck. He felt like a man possessed, and nothing in the world could have kept him from her.

"Keys," she murmured, struggling again to find them. "Bed. Now."

But Cooper already knew they wouldn't make it that far. The minute she got the door open, he pushed her through and slammed it shut behind them, and then she was in his arms again. Kissing him. Touching him. Her sweet mouth giving him everything as they tumbled back against the stairs. He'd lost his mind, but he didn't care.

All that mattered was the hot blur of hands and mouths as he yanked off her sweater, and Poppy reached for his belt and shoved his jeans down. She moaned aloud, and damn, he had to take her. Right this minute. Right here on the stairs. He lay her out on the landing, bracing himself above her as he nudged her thighs apart and his mouth found her breast; he sucked one perfect nipple into his mouth, and she rose up, arching against him.

When he thrust inside her, it felt like coming home.

"Cooper," she gasped, and he thrust again. God, she felt so good. So right. She moved with him like she'd been made for this, every stroke, every touch driving them on together in this madness until he could feel her body clench and writhe. He was close, so close to hurtling over the edge, but he clenched his jaw and forced himself to slow. There. Deeper. Making every thrust last as watched her come undone. He needed to remember this. The color rising in her cheeks. The glaze that slipped into her eyes. And damn, the way her lips parted in a silent cry as the pleasure took her under, rushing in a shudder that swallowed him whole.

He fell against her with a cry, burying himself inside her one last time as his climax ripped through him and he wondered if he could ever get enough.

WHEN COOPER WOKE, dawn was just breaking outside on the ocean, and Poppy was sprawled beside him in bed, half tangled up in the sheets.

He sucked in a breath. Damn, she looked beautiful. He could barely remember making it to the bedroom;

they'd been too busy feasting on each other, exploring every last inch. All night, he'd worshiped her body, but somehow, he hadn't even begun to quench his thirst. Now, she looked so peaceful, it was hard to imagine she'd been the same vixen who had urged him on last night, driving him out of his mind with lust and pure, carnal need.

He gently brushed hair out of her eyes, and she stirred, yawning. "What time is it?" she asked, blinking awake.

"Early."

"Mmm . . ." Poppy rolled closer, warm and soft under the covers. "What time do you have to start work?"

"Not for a little while yet."

"Good."

Poppy slipped her arms around him, and rested her head against his chest. Cooper lay back, feeling her body rise and fall with every breath. An unfamiliar sense of peace swept over him.

It felt good to just *be* like this. A moment of still, in the midst of all the passion. No drama, no noise. No need for words, even. Just a simple calm, making everything right with the world.

He felt a rush of gratitude and tilted Poppy's chin up to kiss her. She melted into him, and if he could have kept them there for hours, suspended like that, he would have. But suddenly an angry siren cut through the calm.

Poppy broke away. "What's that god-awful noise?"

Cooper groaned. "My alarm." He hopped out of bed and looked around for his phone. "I usually go for a run before work."

"Make it stop!" Poppy buried her head under a pillow, and he laughed.

"I'm trying. Where are my pants?"

"Umm, downstairs, maybe?" Poppy bit her lip, and shot him a wicked grin. "I seem to remember losing them on the stairs . . ."

"That's not all you lost." Cooper couldn't resist diving back in bed. He rolled her under him, and Poppy shrieked with laughter. He trapped her body close, and she smiled up at him, sleepy and perfect.

"It's all a blur. Remind me?"

He kissed her bare collarbone.

"Mmm," Poppy sighed. "It's coming back to me now . . ."

He kissed his way down her chest, loving the taste of her. But the alarm didn't stop, it kept screeching like a demon, until finally Poppy sat up. "We need to find that thing, and break it into a million pieces."

He would toss it out the window himself right now, but Cooper had to drag himself away from Poppy's soft, naked body and go search for it in the hallway. He found his pants thrown over the banister, halfway down the stairs. He grabbed his phone from the pocket and quickly shut it off.

"Thank you!" Poppy called. She appeared, wearing his shirt, and bounced down the stairs to him. "Who invented that sound, anyway? It's not natural!"

"Some fiend." Cooper wrapped his arms around her. What was the matter with him? He couldn't go more than ten seconds without touching her, needing her body curled against him where she belonged.

Poppy smiled up at him. "So are you going on that run?"

He grinned. "I think I've had my workout for the day."

"That was technically yesterday . . ." Poppy said, sliding her hands up his naked chest. "It's a whole new day. And I'd hate to interrupt your cardio routine . . ."

She kissed him, and Cooper forgot everything but the warm, hot taste of her lips and how she pressed so eagerly against him.

She wanted him again. This incredible, firecracker woman was just as hungry for him as he was for her, and damn, it made him feel good.

"You're right." Cooper picked her up suddenly and braced her against the wall. "Routine is important." Poppy's eyes sparkled, and she wrapped her legs around his waist. He slipped his hand between them, stroking her until she moaned, loving the sounds she made.

Loving everything about her.

He pushed her shirt up over her head and spread her thighs wider, so ready to sink inside her and claim her body all over again—

The door opened behind them. Cooper tensed. "Whoever you are, you better have a damn good excuse for barging in right now!" he roared, without turning.

"Well, it is my house."

Poppy gasped and froze in his arms.

"Aunt June!"

NINETEEN.

*J*UNE WAS HERE. In the house. And Poppy was pinned, half-naked up against the wall about ten seconds away from an epic orgasm.

Oh god!

She pulled away from Cooper and scrambled to dress herself, but her shirt was nowhere to be seen. "June!" she cried, covering her bare chest with her hands. "I didn't know you were coming back so soon."

"Clearly." Her aunt was grinning in the doorway, swathed in a bright purple pashmina. "I see you've been making friends with the neighbors. Cooper," she nodded, her eyes sparkling with mirth.

"June." Cooper's voice was strangled. He quickly set Poppy down and refastened his belt, retrieving Poppy's nightshirt. She grabbed it out of his hands and pulled it over her head.

"How was the cruise?" Poppy babbled. "Was it fun? I never wanted to try one, you're just trapped out there for days, hostage to food poisoning and buffet tables, but I saw your photos and it looked like a great time."

June arched an eyebrow. "Not as much fun as you've been having," she said. "Coffee's on, is it? Cooper. You'll stay for a cup."

It didn't sound like a question.

June bustled off to the kitchen—leaving Poppy feeling like the worst niece in the world.

Poppy turned and buried her face against Cooper's chest.

"I can't believe we just got busted like a couple of school kids!" she cried. "She's nice enough to have me stay, and I turn her home into a brothel!"

"You were going to charge?" Cooper grinned. He plucked her bra off the door handle and handed it to her. How the hell did it get there?

"You know what I mean!" Poppy exclaimed. "I was . . . You were . . ."

"Still pretty modest, by my standards." Cooper drew her closer, his lips brushing against her ear. "If she'd arrived another couple of seconds later, well, then we'd have something to talk about."

She felt a jolt of desire, which was the last thing she needed right now. "This isn't funny!" Poppy smacked him lightly. He was grinning like it was one big joke, but this was her aunt they were talking about. She was Poppy's family, and now she'd seen her—

Poppy whimpered again.

"Shh, breathe," Cooper said, taking hold of her shoulders. He gave her a comforting squeeze. "She doesn't mind. Hell, she was paying more attention to my bare ass than whatever you were showing."

"He's right." June popped her head around the corner and winked. "Coop, would you be a doll and take that fine ass of yours to carry my bags?"

"Yes, ma'am." Cooper laughed and headed out the door. Poppy braced herself and headed for the kitchen.

Something about getting caught like this made her feel like she was sixteen again, sneaking around with her high-school boyfriend. But luckily, June didn't seem about to ground her and take away her driving privileges. "I'm sorry," Poppy said, cringing with embarrassment.

"What for?" June snorted. "It's about time you got a little sparkle in your eye. Come give me a hug—and then tell me everything." She swept Poppy back into the kitchen. "I'm sorry I didn't call," she added, depositing a still-shell-shocked Poppy in a chair. "I thought I'd come back early and surprise you."

"You sure did that." For all the bad timing, she was happy to see her aunt again. June looked tanned and relaxed after her vacation, with her shoulder-length hair tinted auburn and her trim figure dressed in her usual bright, clashing prints.

Cooper arrived back. "I put your bags up in your room," he said.

"Thanks, honey." June beamed. "Now, you come sit down and tell me all the gossip I've been missing out on. Present company excluded, of course."

Cooper cleared his throat. "Actually, I should be getting to work." He was already edging out of the room. Poppy didn't blame him, with the way June was checking him out. He shot Poppy an apologetic look. "I'll call you later, OK?"

"Are you forgetting something?" June called, just as

he was about to turn and go. He looked at them blankly. "A goodbye kiss for your girl," she said.

Cooper quickly kissed Poppy on the lips. "Good luck," he whispered, before beating a hasty retreat.

"Hmm, I can't say I like his quick escape." June frowned as the door slammed shut behind him. "A gentleman doesn't just run after being caught in a compromising position."

"June!" Poppy protested. "It's not Victorian times."

"Just as well," June said mischievously. "He'd be down on one knee after compromising your virtue like that."

"Remind me not to send you any more of those regency romances from my publisher," Poppy grinned. The first rush of humiliation was fading now. As long as she didn't think about it. She got up and gave June a big hug. "Welcome home! I missed you. Even if I could have used a heads-up before you came back."

"In my defense, I didn't think you needed the warning." June gave her a look. "Didn't you say you were looking for peace and quiet to work on your book? 'No drama,' " she mimicked.

"I guess fate had other plans." Poppy couldn't keep the smile from her face. "My first morning, a terrible noise made me go storming over next door, and, well, there was Cooper."

"He is delicious, isn't he?" June winked. "If I were twenty years younger. And that ass . . ." she sighed in appreciation.

"Hey!" Poppy protested. "No objectifying my boyfriend."

"Is that what he is, then?"

Poppy paused. "I don't know," she admitted, those thoughts from earlier in the evening resurfacing again. "It's all still pretty new. We only got together a few days ago."

June gasped. "No! And here I am interrupting! I'm surprised you even came up for air. When I met my third husband, we ran away to a little motel outside Jacksonville and didn't get out of bed for a week."

Poppy laughed. June had an illustrious romantic history, to say the least. "It's fine," she reassured her. "We'll make up for lost time at his place, don't worry."

June grinned at her. "Oh, it's good to see you like this. I knew that Owen wasn't right for you, there was no oomph to the two of you. All head, no heart."

"Owen wasn't a bad guy," Poppy defended him. "But, you're right. It feels different with Cooper. I don't think I've ever felt this way," she admitted.

June nodded approvingly. "Well, you know I'd love to see more of you. You're welcome to stay as long as you like."

"Thank you," Poppy said. "I don't know what my plans are yet, there's still plenty of writing left for me to do."

"Is Cooper helping with the research?" June cackled.

Poppy blushed. "Maybe."

"I look forward to reading all about it."

POPPY CAUGHT UP with June's cruising adventures, then

took a shower and settled in to write. Before long, the construction noise started up and a loud sawing noise was filtering through the windows. Once, it would have driven her to distraction, but this time, she heard the noise and smiled.

Cooper was working hard.

She forced herself to stay at her computer, even as she itched to see him again. It was a good thing he was on a schedule at the site, otherwise her own writing calendar would be out the window. Still, it was hard to focus with memories of their night together playing vividly in her mind. Every kiss. Every touch.

Every slow, deep thrust.

She shivered. It was hard to believe anything could top that first night, but somehow, it just kept getting better. Or rather, Cooper did. He wasn't just good with his hands. No, that man was good *everywhere*.

Poppy dragged her attention back to work, typing quietly in the study while June bustled around, getting settled back in, and the sound of construction continued steadily outside the windows. By noon, she had ten pages under her belt, and was ready for a break.

Aunt June was on the phone, broadcasting her return to everyone in town, so she took her third cup of coffee from the pot and strolled out to the back porch. It was getting warmer now, the season shifting over to spring, and the fruit trees in the garden were budding with new blossoms. Poppy breathed in a lungful of the crisp sea air, and tried not to think about the life waiting for her back home. Her little apartment had always been a refuge to cloister herself away and write, but now it somehow seemed small compared to this expanse of blue ocean in front of her, memories of the city streets dense and noisy as she looked out at the woods and gently curving bay and wide, windswept shore.

"Tell me there's still a pot brewing, and I'll give you everything I own."

Poppy turned. Cooper was strolling over from the neighboring yard. Was it just her, or did his eyes seem extra-blue in the morning sun?

"Here, take this one." She offered him her mug. "I would have sent you off with a Thermos, but you ran out of here so fast . . ."

Cooper chuckled. "Sorry about that. I, uh, wasn't expecting your aunt."

"Nobody does. She's like the Spanish inquisition," Poppy quipped.

Cooper took the mug, and a kiss too, his stubble scratching lightly against her skin. "Angel." He took a seat on the back steps beside her, and gulped it down. "So how was your interrogation?"

"June, you mean?" Poppy said. "Not too bad. Once I got over the abject humiliation of getting caught with my pants down, I mean."

"I seem to recall your pants weren't the ones that were down," Cooper corrected her with a wry smile.

"Ah, yes," June's voice came from the porch. "I recall that too. Vividly."

Poppy groaned, turning. "You're never going to let that go, are you?"

"Well, I wouldn't if I were you," June said. "Oh, relax. Cooper's man enough to take some jokes from an old dame like me."

"You're not a day over thirty-five," Cooper said with a broad grin.

"See, he's a keeper." June chuckled. "Do you want to join us for lunch, hon? It looks like you're working up an appetite."

Poppy shook her head. There was really no stopping her.

"I'll pass today, thanks June," Cooper said. "Another time."

"Count on it." The phone rang. "Ooh, that'll be Larry," June said, and disappeared back into the house. Cooper caught Poppy's gaze.

"She's a character, isn't she?"

"She was always my favorite relative growing up," Poppy confided. "She always told me the truth, not just what she thought you wanted to hear, like all the other grown-ups."

Cooper nodded. "She would stop by a lot, back when my dad was dying." He traced her hand, turning it over in his. Poppy watched him, the wry smile on his face edged with sadness. "Everyone was bringing casseroles and healthy snacks," he explained. "But she'd show up with a bottle of whiskey and his favorite ice cream. I would hear them laughing, playing cards, or gossiping. I didn't get to hear him laugh much those days."

Poppy squeezed his hand. Cooper seemed to realize what he'd said. He gave her a shrug. "She was a good friend to him. That's why I don't mind, when she, you know . . ."

"Is wildly inappropriate?"

"Something like that." He lifted her hand to his lips and kissed it, so naturally, it made her stomach flip over. "Anyway, I just stopped by to see if you wanted to head into Provincetown. I have to pick up some supplies, but we could get lunch, and you could walk around, or write?"

"That sounds great," Poppy said, smiling. "I've been meaning to drive up there. I have this vivid memory from when I was a kid, eating lobster rolls, right on the pier."

"Then lobster rolls it is."

THEY DROVE UP the coast with the windows wide open and the sea air whipping Poppy's hair into a tangle. She didn't mind. It was a perfect spring day, bright and blue-skied, and it seemed like they had the whole Cape to themselves. In a few months, the beaches would be packed with vacationers, crowding for the Fourth of July fireworks and lining up for ice cream on the pier, but for now, the road wound through lush green plains, with the empty shore unfurling lazily alongside. She hadn't thought ahead yet to her summer plans, but now the possibilities danced, tempting on the breeze. She'd thought she'd be setting up house with Owen in the city, hosting BBQs in his postage-stamp backyard and working her way through her thank-you notes for their wedding, but that plan was ancient history now. An alternate life in some parallel universe she couldn't even picture, it felt so far away.

"Penny for them?" Cooper asked, as the road forked into Provincetown.

"Nothing." Poppy glanced over. "Just thinking . . . it's funny how things turn out."

He reached over to take her hand. "It sure is."

She knew they should talk soon about what it was they were doing and if she should stay in town for longer, but Poppy didn't want to wreck the moment. For now, she was still wrapped in that delicious haze of new beginnings and wanted it to last for as long as possible. So they ate lobster rolls from that same place Poppy remembered from twenty years ago, sitting on a wooden bench overlooking the bay, and strolled the winding, old streets hand in hand, until Cooper had to make his detour to the building supplies yard.

"I shouldn't be long," he said, pulling her in for a quick kiss. "An hour, maybe? I'll call when I'm done."

"That's perfect." Poppy looked around, spying the old library just ahead. "I brought my laptop so I can squeeze in a few more words."

Cooper headed back to his truck, and Poppy hitched her bag higher and made her way over to the library entrance. It was an old converted church with soaring ceilings, and inside, she was surprised to find a replica of a schooner boat sitting slap-bang in the middle of the main floor, the sails stretching fifteen feet high. Mackenzie was right: they loved their nautical history here on the Cape. Off to one side, there was a reading room, and Poppy finally settled in to work, enjoying the quiet hum of conversation around her, and the bursts of children's voices from the story-time across the room. The hour drifted past, sunlight spilling on the floors around her, and Poppy found herself writing easily, speeding through the action on the page. She checked her plot outline and felt a sense of satisfaction. Despite her bumpy start, she had flown through the book these past couple of weeks. At this rate, she'd be done by the end of the month.

And then . . . ?

Poppy paused. All her earlier thoughts about the future bubbled to the surface again, but this time, she didn't push them back.

She could see herself here, for more than just a brief vacation.

Poppy weighed the idea cautiously. She'd only been there a little while, but already, it felt like home. Not just the way she felt with Cooper; it was more than that—the sense of community in Sweetbriar, the real feeling of belonging that had somehow wrapped around her. She knew it was impulsive to think about uprooting her life and moving halfway across the country, but still, she couldn't help imagining the days and weeks ahead, as spring turned to summer on the Cape, and their relationship deepened, and became something real. She could stay another month . . . she could rent a place for the summer . . .

Was it crazy to think like this?

She'd spent years writing about people who went to the ends of the earth for love. Moving to Sweetbriar, just to test the waters, seemed almost sensible in comparison.

But this was real life, not the stories in her books, and Poppy didn't know if she was getting way ahead of herself in pursuit of that happy ending.

She'd never felt like this before.

Another burst of children's voices cut through her thoughts. The story-time was ending, and a group of parents and toddlers were chatting among the books. One small kid in a blue jumpsuit toddled determinedly towards Poppy, and collapsed with a thud on the carpet to examine the brightly-colored scarf spilling from her bag.

"Brady!" A blonde woman detached from the group and hurried over. "I'm sorry," she said with an apologetic smile. "Brady, that's not yours."

"It's OK." Poppy smiled. Brady was tugging the scarf out of her bag, looking amazed as the colors kept unfurling. "He can play if he wants."

"Thank you," the woman said, looking frazzled. "He's just at that stage where he wants to touch everything. I swear we've childproofed the house a dozen times, but he still finds something. We might just build an addition with no outlets, no wires, nothing."

"How old is he?" Poppy asked. Brady was happily chewing on the wool. He was plump and sturdy, wearing cute little red boots.

"Coming up on eighteen months. I'm Laura, by the way."

"Nice to meet you. Poppy."

"That's such a cute name." Laura brightened. "We wanted to be surprised by the sex, but I was so sure he'd be a girl I had a whole list of flower names picked. And then this munchkin comes along." She grinned affectionately and picked him up, cradling him easily on her hip. "Do you have kids?"

Poppy shook her head. "Not yet."

Laura bounced little Brady. "Well, when you do, two words for you: safety tape."

Poppy laughed. "I'll try to remember that."

"Anyway, sorry to interrupt."

"It's OK." Poppy checked the time. It was almost two, and she was set to meet Cooper. "I need to get going, anyway." She packed up her computer and gently retrieved her scarf from Brady's chubby little hands.

"Say goodbye, Brady." Laura waved, and Brady mimicked her with a gurgle.

"He's too cute," Poppy said.

Laura smiled. "It helps when it's two a.m. and he's teething, that's for sure."

Poppy shook Brady's outstretched hand, his fist closing tightly around her finger. "Nice to meet you," she told him, and he answered by gripping even tighter. "I'm going to need that back," she joked.

"Brady," Laura scolded him playfully. "What have I told you about stealing fingers?"

Poppy gently peeled her hand away, laughing. That's when she caught sight of Cooper watching them from across the room with the strangest expression on his face.

TWENTY.

$\mathcal{C}$OOPER FELT IT like a punch in the gut, watching two parts of his life collide right in front of him. Poppy, standing there, chatting to Laura as if it were the most natural thing in the world. They laughed together, cooing over Laura's kid, and every muscle in his body turned to lead.

The woman he was falling for and the one who'd taught him his love would never be enough. What sick joke was the universe playing, throwing them together in his face like this?

Poppy looked up and saw him, waving him over with a smile. Cooper wanted to bolt, but he forced his emotions back and walked over like nothing was wrong.

"Cooper." Laura blinked, looking surprised. "I didn't know . . . Hi."

Poppy looked back and forth between them. "You guys know each other? Of course you do," she added with a laugh. "I need to get used to this small-town thing. Let me guess, you went to elementary school together?"

"No, not quite." Laura gave him a soft smile. "It's good to see you, Cooper. How have you been?"

"Fine," Cooper answered shortly. She looked good,

but then, she always did. Even the shadows under her eyes couldn't spoil Laura's natural glow. She bounced the kid on her hip, looking like she'd been born to be a mother. This was what she'd wanted. They'd planned for two kids, maybe three. Both of them had been only children, and they'd agreed they wanted a whole brood.

It came rushing back, the feelings he'd thought were behind him now. The guilt. The betrayal. Everything they'd dreamed together, and everything that had crumbled in the end. Because he hadn't been enough for her; he hadn't done enough to make her stay. His biggest failure was staring him straight in the face, and damn, it made him feel like a fool.

He'd tried to forget, but he guessed the universe had a way of reminding him. He couldn't leave this behind if he tried.

Poppy was still smiling, oblivious to the hurricane beating in his chest. "Brady here decided he wanted to nibble on my scarf," she explained. "So we were just—"

"I need to get back," he told Poppy abruptly, interrupting her. "I'm running late."

Poppy gave him a puzzled look. "Sure. Anyway, it was nice to meet you." She smiled at Laura. "And hey, if you need help on that child-proof addition, this is your guy."

"I'll keep it in mind."

He could feel Laura's gaze on him, but he looked away to avoid the blame and bitterness he was certain must still be lingering there. "The crew will be waiting for me," he said, impatient. He didn't even wait for Poppy to say goodbye before he turned and walked fast for the exit.

Outside, the street was busy, but he cut through to where he'd parked his truck without pausing to see if she'd followed. He climbed in and started the engine, gripping the steering wheel hard.

The past bore down on him, heavy with regret.

It shouldn't be this hard.

What made him think it would be any different this time?

"What was that?" Poppy climbed in, interrupting echoes of the past. "You bolted so fast, you didn't even say goodbye."

"I told you, I'm late." He drove off with a lurch, pulling a U-turn in the street to head back towards the highway. Poppy grabbed her seatbelt and buckled up quick.

"Cooper?"

He ignored her, wishing like hell he could be somewhere else right now. Alone, away from Poppy's curious stare and the confusion in her eyes.

"Cooper!" Her voice finally broke through. "Slow down. Please."

He realized he was speeding and took his foot off the gas. "Sorry," he said gruffly, and Poppy exhaled.

"Are you OK? What happened?"

He shook his head. "It's fine."

Poppy didn't look away, but Cooper fixed his eyes on the road. What could he say, anyway? *That woman you were just talking to? There was a time I thought she was the one I would spend the rest of my life with.* Besides, he already knew the first question out of her lips would be to ask why things ended between them, and Cooper didn't want to see the look on her face when he had to admit that it had all been his fault.

He'd driven Laura away. He'd ruined everything. And given time, he would wind up doing the same thing with Poppy, too.

That bullet wound in his chest got bigger. Damn. Poppy.

He was going to hurt her in the end.

He didn't want to, he'd do anything to keep her from the pain, but how the hell was it going to turn out any different? He already knew this was how it ended: with fights and recriminations. He'd loved Laura; they'd been happy once upon a time, but sure enough, the bickering had turned to yelling, and the connection between them had crumbled away until they were just two strangers in the same house staring at each other from across an unbridgeable canyon.

He couldn't bear it if he did that to Poppy, too. If he dimmed the light in her eyes, even for a second, it would be a damn crime.

He drove, lost in thought, until they were back outside June's place. He parked and shut off the engine. Poppy looked over. "Thanks for lunch," she offered. "Maybe I can come by tonight? Leave June the house to settle in. And lock the door," she added with a laugh.

Cooper felt torn in two. He wanted nothing more than to lose himself in her again, turn the clocks back to when it was just the two of them, and the real world didn't matter. But the bitter weight was pressing in his chest, and he needed space to get his head straight.

"Not tonight," he replied, avoiding her gaze. "I need to catch up on my sleep now that we're heading into the home stretch here on the job."

"OK." Poppy sounded disappointed, and the guilt hit hard. See, there he was, screwing everything up again.

He got down and went to open her door. Poppy climbed to the ground.

"So, I'll see you tomorrow?" she asked, the uncertainty clear on her face.

He nodded, but before he could head back to work, she caught his hand and tugged him closer. "You know you can talk to me, right?" she said, her eyes searching his. "I know this is still early, and we haven't said anything about . . . where this is going, or what it is. But I'm here. I want to be here."

She looked so open and compassionate, it cut him open. Then she reached up and brushed his lips in a kiss, and Cooper nearly gave up the fight. He kissed her back, deeper, and those sparks roared to life, bright and wild.

One touch is all it took with her. From the start, she'd been undeniable. He wanted her. He wanted to be the man for her.

But just like he'd teased her what seemed like a hundred years ago, you didn't always get what you want. Cooper should have learned his lesson a long time ago, but he guessed it was just history repeating.

Regretfully, he pulled away. "Sorry," he said, meaning it with every bone in his body. "I really have to go."

Poppy stepped back. "OK, I won't keep you," she said

with a smile. "But if you change your mind about tonight . . . call. I'll sneak away, it'll be just like breaking curfew."

She winked and headed up the porch steps, and Cooper let out the breath he hadn't realized he'd been holding. He wouldn't be calling her, not tonight. Not until he figured out how to deal with this mess, and all the foolish hopes he had spinning in his chest when his head knew full well that only disappointment lay ahead.

He turned and strode back to the construction site. His guys were still working, and he should be unloading supplies from the truck, but first, he went looking for a sledgehammer.

He needed to break something, right now.

TWENTY-ONE.

*P*OPPY SPENT THE REST of the week writing hard, trying to get as much of the book under her belt as possible before the Spring Fling Literary Festival. But as busy as she was, she couldn't ignore one obvious fact: Cooper was pulling away.

Oh, he wasn't being obvious about it. He sent cute texts in response to her messages and gave her brief kisses as he stopped by en route to someplace else, and even called apologetically to cancel their plans at the last minute, promising it was just a rain-check until things calmed down with work, but Poppy knew the truth. You judged a man by his actions, not his words, and Cooper's actions couldn't have been clearer. Aunt June had been right, this was the honeymoon period, and they were supposed to be stealing every moment possible together, but instead, Poppy found herself sitting up nights watching *Miss Fisher's Mysteries* on Netflix with her aunt, trying to ignore the fact she wasn't making passionate love to Cooper in his bed instead.

"Typical men," Aunt June sighed, when she noticed Cooper wasn't coming around every morning for coffee and a kiss. "Getting skittish at the first sign of commitment."

But Poppy hadn't mentioned commitment, and Cooper didn't seem the type of man to just let her down with a bump.

"I don't know . . ." She toyed with her mug. She didn't understand it. She had just been thinking that they could have a future together, but it was like he'd flipped a switch, and everything they'd shared suddenly evaporated into thin air. "He's been acting strangely ever since we went for lunch in Provincetown last week. No." She paused, thinking back. "Lunch was great, it was after . . ."

She remembered him coming to pick her up at the library, acting so harsh and rude when she was talking to—

"Laura," Poppy exhaled. How could she have missed it? And sure enough, June looked over.

"Laura Perkins? Well, that would explain it."

"Did they date?" Poppy winced, hoping it was a long-gone platonic ex, from a relationship that ended perfectly nicely, with zero acrimony or heartbreak on either side. But somehow, judging by how quickly he'd bolted, she doubted it.

June nodded. "Nice girl. They were pretty serious for a while back there, but it wasn't exactly smooth sailing. I don't know what happened in the end, but Cooper seemed real broken up about it."

And clearly, he still was.

Poppy tried to ignore the painful flicker of insecurity coming to life in her chest. Everyone had a past, and hers had shown up on her doorstep just the other week. Maybe Cooper just needed to process some things, or perhaps she was reading too much into it, and he really was just busy.

Or maybe he was still in love with Laura, and the past month had been just a fun distraction for him, and not the start of something real.

She found herself reaching for her phone again, and dialing this time.

"Hey," she said, when he answered. "How's it going over there? The house is looking great."

"Liar," Cooper chuckled, and the sound of his laughter warmed her from the inside out. "It's still a mess, but, it's getting there. I'm sorry I've been so busy," he added, "it's been one thing after another. I haven't had a moment to slip away."

The sincere apology in his voice made her pause. Had she been over-thinking this? He was busy. It happened. It didn't have to mean anything.

"That's OK," she lied. "Will you be free this weekend? It's the literary festival, and I have a couple of events. I'd love for you to be there."

Cooper paused. "I'll do my best," he said, and her heart sank a couple of inches. "We really are slammed," he added. "I've already got my crew working through the weekend, but I'll try to get away."

"OK," Poppy said quietly. She didn't even suggest she drop by after work; she already knew he'd have a reason not to. Unless he chose to talk to her about whatever was going on, there wasn't anything she could do.

Except write. And hope. And try to ignore the rejection weighing heavier in her chest with ever day Cooper breezed by with quick smile, or cut their night short after one drink at the pub to go catch up on his sleep.

How much sleep did one man need? Especially when there was a willing woman ready to bear the burden of insomnia right alongside him. And under him. All night long.

But Poppy didn't want to push. Cooper, as everyone had been telling her, was stubborn, and maybe he just needed some space to figure things out for himself. So, she bit her tongue, and accepted enough rain-checks to float a life raft, and before she knew it, it was the weekend, and she was just a few chapters away from finishing her novel. Her agent, Quinn, was overjoyed, and insisted on driving down from New York to accompany her for the day.

"Every bestseller needs her entourage," she'd declared, and Poppy was glad to take her up on her invitation.

"Look at this place!" Quinn announced as she stepped out of the car: sunglasses on, red lipstick, and a massive thermos in one hand that Poppy knew contained pure espresso. She looked around at June's cottage and the beach like an explorer surveying a foreign land. "I love it. So small-town, Hallmark movie . . . I just want to slap a 'now a major TV series' label on the cover and call it a bestseller."

"It's good to see you too, Quinn." Poppy went to greet her, accepting Quinn's trademark air kisses on both cheeks.

"I mean it. I swear I've seen this place before. Are you

sure they didn't shoot the last Nicholas Sparks movie here?" she asked, peering over the rim of her designer shades. "The one where someone dies in the end?"

"That doesn't exactly narrow it down." Poppy grinned and Quinn snorted with laughter.

"You should try that in your next book. People love a tragic ending, they weep bucketloads, then go tell all their friends."

"I prefer happily-ever-after, thanks all the same."

Quinn shrugged, unconcerned. She helped Poppy load her bag into the car, stuffed with bookmarks, postcards, and other fun freebies she always had shipped out to sign for her readers. They got in, and Quinn gave her a grin. "So, are you ready to rock this thing? I had your publisher send someone down to take care of us, full VIP treatment."

"I don't need that!" Poppy protested. "This is just a local thing."

"Are you kidding? You're a headline act, babe." Quinn started the engine. "And with your new contract negotiations coming up, I won't let them forget it."

Poppy sighed, but she couldn't deny she was glad to have Quinn fighting in her corner. The business side of her career had always made her feel slightly uncomfortable. She loved writing and would do it for free if she had no other choice, but love didn't pay the mortgage, or buy her the freedom to drop everything and come spend a month on Cape Cod when she needed, so she knew not to argue when her agent got dollar signs flashing in her laser-corrected eyes. As much as a shark Quinn was, she was Poppy's shark, and that was a blessing. At least, it was most of the time.

"Susie Atwood just left Atria." Quinn launched into her updates of all the big publishing and romance world gossip. "She got lured away when her editor switched houses. And sales on the new Kate Munroe book are terrible, it sank like a stone."

"Poor Kate!" Poppy shuddered. It was every author's nightmare to have readers suddenly stop showing up.

"Oh, she's fine." Quinn waved away Poppy's concern. "She already banked her advance check. No, it's a great opportunity. I hear her editor is looking for a new big release for 2020, something with series potential. Have you given any more through to your next book?" she seamlessly asked. "I wouldn't need a full manuscript, just a few chapters and an outline will do."

"I told you, I'm not thinking about it until I'm finished writing this one." Poppy said firmly. "Who knows, maybe I'll take some time off after, wait a while before signing something new." She'd been through the emotional wringer these past few months, and as much as a month in Sweetbriar Cove had restored her, she knew she'd need a real vacation after this book was done.

Especially if she was going to be nursing a broken heart.

But for Quinn's ear-splitting screech of a reply, you'd think Poppy had suggested throwing in the towel and never writing again.

"What?!"

"Not long! A month or two. I'm not a machine," she

reminded Quinn, "and I do have to think up an idea before you can sell it."

The other woman sighed. "I know. I just want to make sure we take every opportunity, that's all. People love your books, they really strike a chord."

Poppy smiled. "Thank you, that's sweet of you to say."

"That's my job."

"So you flatter every client?" Poppy laughed.

"Yes, but with you I really mean it." Quinn winked, then pushed her sunglasses up her nose. "Now, let's go sell you some books!"

THE LITERARY FESTIVAL had taken over Provincetown. The pier was full of booths and snack vendors, the main cobbled street was decked out with ticker tape and flags, and the sedate town hall had been transformed, with talks and panels bursting out of every room, and brightly-colored author signing tents lined up in the cooling shadow of the old Colonial building. It was a gorgeous day, and the crowds were out in force, enjoying saltwater taffy and clutching paperbacks as they went in search of their favorite authors.

Poppy loved the sight of readers in the morning.

"Now, let's see, you have 'writing the romantic hero' at eleven, then a group signing, then another panel at two . . ." Quinn consulted the schedule of events as Poppy signed in at the main stage. "And don't forget the dinner tonight. All the big publishers will be there, and you're a guest of honor."

"I am?" Poppy beamed, taking her badge. She still got a kick out of seeing her name, printed there on the schedule alongside authors she'd loved for years.

"Of course you are. Do you need a plus-one for the green room?" Quinn asked, turning. "You need a special wristband to get in."

Poppy paused. She hadn't heard from Cooper yet. "Let me check," she said, and typed out a quick text.

Do you think you'll make it today? Would love to see you.

The little ellipses appeared on screen for a moment, showing he'd seen her message and was typing a response. Then it stopped. No reply.

Poppy bit back her disappointment.

"I'll take one, just in case," she said, turning back to Quinn. "My aunt is around here somewhere, she said she was hunting down James Patterson. I don't know if that was a promise or a threat."

Quinn smirked. "It's OK, he travels with security now. Oh, Fiona! Over here!" she waved over a bright-eyed girl who couldn't have been more than twenty, laden down under a massive bag of books. "This is Fiona, from your publisher. She's been running your social media campaigns."

"It's great to meet you!" Poppy pushed her emotions aside and shook the girl's hand. "Thanks so much for all your hard work."

"It's my pleasure." Fiona beamed from under her blunt-cut bangs. "I love your writing. We all can't wait for the last book in the series."

"It's got 'bestseller' written all over it," Quinn agreed. "At least, it will once we talk about your promotion budget."

Poppy gave her a look. "Let's not talk about that to-day. Was your flight down OK, Fiona?"

The girl grimaced. "A little bumpy."

"Oh, me too! I hate to fly." Poppy carefully steered her on before Quinn could corner her to demand a national book tour and full court press.

HER FIRST PANEL was a fun discussion about how to write compelling heroes, with a group signing after. It was always a little nerve-wracking being in front of an audience, but she got to chat back and forth with the other authors, and pass the microphone along when she didn't know quite what to say. There was always safety in numbers, but when Poppy arrived after lunch at her second event, she found a stage with just two chairs, and a sign proclaiming *Poppy Somerville in Conversation.*"

"Wait, it's just me?" Poppy's nerves rose. "I thought there was a whole group."

"Sorry, didn't they tell you." Fiona frowned and scrambled to find the paper. "A couple of the authors had to drop out at the last minute, so they shifted things around."

"This is excellent." Quinn surveyed the room, which was filling fast. "You're the star attraction. Just look at all these customers."

"Readers," Poppy corrected her automatically. She looked around, her stomach churning. It was one thing to talk about her work as part of a group, but alone on stage? She felt a flicker of nerves, but Quinn gave her arm a squeeze.

"You've had crowds like this before at signings. You'll be fine," she said with a surprisingly supportive smile.

Poppy took a deep breath. "OK." She nodded. But as she scanned the crowd full of expectant faces, she realized something that set her heart sinking in her chest with more than just nerves.

Cooper wasn't here.

She knew he had work, but she'd hoped he would have found a moment to slip away to come support her. This was her last event of the day, and even though she'd forced herself to focus on meeting the readers and giving her all to the event, she'd still been holding out a hope that he would come. Because if he didn't, if he chose not to support her when she was just a few miles up the highway, well . . . whatever was making him pull away from her wouldn't just be solved with a little space.

Could this be over before they'd even begun?

Poppy's heart ached, but she didn't have time to think about it. The interviewer, a local journalist named Eliza, welcomed her with an enthusiastic handshake.

"Don't worry, this will be fun," Eliza reassured her.

"Oh God," Poppy laughed, "do I look that nervous?"

"Maybe a little." Eliza grinned. She had auburn red hair caught back in a flyaway bun, and tortoiseshell glasses. "But I'll go easy, I promise. My first question is just about the social impact of the romance genre and the sociological implications of the fantasy of gender norms."

Poppy gulped.

"Kidding!" Eliza grinned, and Poppy let out her breath in a whoosh. "Seriously, just relax. We'll chat about your writing, and your path to publication, and then open things up to questions. But, beware," she added, guiding Poppy towards the stage. "There's usually one person lurking in every audience who wants to pitch you their unpublished manuscript, so get ready to hear about their alien abduction romance story!"

LUCKILY, ELIZA WAS right—about the easy and fun part, at least. She was a skilled interviewer, and gently guided Poppy through the panel, peppering her with enthusiastic questions about her characters and experience until Poppy could actually relax and enjoy the conversation. When the time came to open it up to questions, she was surprised to find just how many of the audience were fans of her books and had thoughtful questions about how she'd written her series.

"We have time for just a couple more questions . . ." Eliza said, and Poppy realized that the hour had flown by. "How about you, in the red?"

She pointed to a woman in the front row with her hand waving high in the air. The woman bounced out of her seat and gripped the mic. "Hi, first of all, I'm a big fan," she gushed. "I've read all your books."

"Thank you." Poppy smiled. "I like this question so far."

Everyone laughed. "I was wondering," the woman continued, "the love stories you write are so . . . amazing.

They're passionate and loving and everything you could want. Are they based on real relationships you've had? Is that where you get your inspiration? Is there someone special in your life?"

Poppy took a deep breath, ready to roll out her stock answer about love being inspiring in all forms—family, friendships, and more—but then she caught sight of a familiar face in the crowd, and her heart took flight.

Cooper.

He was standing in the back of the room, leaning against the wall. She caught his eyes, and he smiled at her: that heart-stopping, eye-crinkling grin that made her insides flip over and melt.

He came.

"I . . . made it all up," Poppy said, with a flash of honesty. "For the longest time, I didn't really know what it felt like to connect with someone the way I wrote in my books. I saw it around me, every day, and I wanted it so badly for myself. That's what I poured into my books, that hope, the longing—I think we all feel it, every day." She looked around and saw people nodding along, and it gave her the courage to continue. "I wanted to believe, but it wasn't easy. When you're alone, and you're writing about love like that every day . . . well, it felt like a cruel irony, sometimes. I wondered if I would ever find the kind of relationships I was writing about, or if they even existed at all. Whether they'd always just stay confined to the pages of my books, and never be something real to me. But . . . then I did find it."

She met Cooper's eyes again, and felt it all over again.

The bond between them, that alchemy of connection and chemistry that seemed to draw her to him, every time. She smiled, hit with a sudden wave of gladness that her winding road had brought her all the way here, to Sweetbriar Cove, and the man she'd almost given up hope of finding.

"So, yes. It's real," she said, turning back to the questioner. "That passion, the feeling like you're not alone, and somebody sees you, all the way to your heart. I'm glad I kept the faith and believed all those years, because the love I've written about before is only just the beginning. I can't wait to share more of my stories with you."

The crowd broke into applause, and Eliza wrapped up the panel. "That was great," she said to Poppy, as they headed off stage. "You're a natural."

"Really? I felt like my hand was shaking so hard my mic was trembling." Poppy looked around, wanting to catch Cooper before she went to sign books. But when she looked for him, there was no sign of his tousled dark hair to be seen. She frowned, straining on her tiptoes. Maybe he was over at the signing tent already.

"Darling, fantastic." Quinn swooped in, smothering her in a hug. "I loved that part about your new book, there have already been a dozen tweets from people in the audience. They can't wait!"

"They'll have to wait a few more months." Poppy dragged her attention back. "I'm still not done with the first draft."

Quinn waved it away. "But what you have written so far is phenomenal. Now, let's go sign some books for your adoring fans!"

She swept Poppy off, but Poppy hung back, scanning the crowd one last time. She thought she saw Cooper in the hallway and lifted her hand to wave, but then he turned around and melted into the crowd, and was gone.

TWENTY-TWO.

COOPER HUNG BACK and watched Poppy as she signed books for the line of fans waiting patiently after the event. He hadn't seen her for days, and watching her like this, in her element, her smile hit him all over again. Even though there were two dozen or more readers waiting, she didn't rush anyone: taking a moment to chat and exchange a few words as she wrote her name with a flourish. Her face lit up with every new encounter, and he could see how much it meant to her to greet them all in turn, posing for photographs and accepting gifts and praise.

Her words mattered to them. Those stories he'd dismissed were a part of their lives, and that was something pretty amazing.

Like their author.

A new fan rushed forward to talk to Poppy, her arms filled with a stack of books. Poppy welcomed her like an old friend, holding up the covers to show the people with her, and hugging the reader. "I can't believe you have all the old covers!" Cooper heard her exclaim, and the woman almost cried, tripping over her words to explain how much those books had meant to her.

He felt a stab of pride. This was Poppy's gift. She connected with them, through her books, through those words she typed on every page. She put her heart out there for everyone to see, and they loved her for it.

Like he did.

The knowledge dropped through him like a stone. But of course it was true, that was the damn shame of it. He loved her. This beautiful, talented, infuriating woman was offering up her heart to him, but as much as he wanted to grab her tight and never let go, the past still had its hold on him, shackles slowing every footstep until it seemed like he'd never be free.

He wasn't made for love. That's what he'd been telling himself these past three years, and as much as he wanted to believe something different, those words seemed carved too deep to erase.

How could it be any different this time?

"Cooper!" Poppy saw him, and waved him over. She bounced out of her seat to kiss him in greeting. "You made it! This is my agent Quinn, meet Cooper."

A woman in tight black denim and a crisp blazer arched an eyebrow. "Are you the one to thank for breaking her writer's block?" Quinn gave him a red, glossy smile. "I can see why. *Hello.*"

"Quinn," Poppy giggled and elbowed her. "Sorry." She beamed, turning back to Cooper. "Ignore her. I'm glad you're here. Did you catch the panel? I won't be long signing, you can wait here, or in the green room . . ."

She was babbling, and Cooper detected a nervous flicker in her expression. He could guess why. He'd been distancing himself all week, telling himself a little space was all he needed. She'd let him be, but it was clear she knew something wasn't right.

"I don't want to interrupt. I can walk around," he said, feeling eyes on him from everyone waiting in line.

"Nonsense," Quinn interrupted. "You can keep me company, I need to find a decent cup of coffee."

Cooper smiled. "Now I know why you two get along."

Poppy flashed him a smile, and the next person edged forward. "Is this your boyfriend?" the older woman asked, beaming. "Look at you, you make such a cute couple! It's no wonder you write such romantic stories."

Cooper cleared his throat. He could feel the eyes on him—not just this reader, but the rest of the waiting line, too. "You know what, I'll go get you both that coffee," he said, already backing away. "I'll, um, see you in a bit."

He quickly turned and headed through the crowd, and it wasn't until he was half a block away that he let himself slow.

Look at him, bolting all over again.

Dammit. This wasn't Poppy's fault, none of it was. But just like last time around, he was screwing things up without even trying.

The coffee shop was just ahead, but instead of joining the extra-long line, Cooper cut around back, down to the beach. The Provincetown bay curved gently, flat golden sand leading out to the calm waters bobbing with sailboats, and the distant honk of the ferry.

He found an empty stretch of sand, and looked out

across the ocean. The Cape had always felt like home to him, but now as he gazed at the horizon, those familiar shores felt like a cage, holding him back. Living surrounded by ghosts of his past and the constant reminders of all the ways he'd failed as a man. If he'd met Poppy in another city, another time . . . could he have found a way to believe in starting over? A blank slate. A fresh start. Or would he fall short all over again, and wind up hurting the woman he loved?

A couple of kids, maybe seven or eight years old, came running past, chasing down the Labrador that charged into the waves. "Sorry!" their father called, jogging behind.

Cooper watched them play and felt a deep ache, that grief that lived behind his ribcage, a quiet constant. His father would know what to do. He always had a way of fixing things: leaking roofs, broken bicycles. "It's simple when you know how," he would say, and show Cooper where the screw needed to be replaced, or the tile replaced, but Cooper didn't know how to go about fixing himself, and his father had been gone before Cooper even knew he was broken inside.

How was he supposed to mend this mess, when all he could see was the wreckage that still lay ahead? Poppy had been searching all her life for something real, a partnership, a family. Cooper could fool himself into thinking he was the man to give it to her, but what happened when all his good intentions faded and Poppy realized he wasn't enough? Seeing the disappointment in Laura's eyes at the end had just about broken him, but

Cooper knew, it would be a hundred times worse this time around.

Poppy deserved more than this. More than him.

So what was he waiting for?

POPPY REMEMBERED HER first big public author event, for all the wrong reasons. She'd had dinner with friends beforehand at a hole-in-the-wall diner, which clearly didn't deserve the health rating posted on the wall, because by the time she'd arrived at the bookstore for her signing, her stomach was churning with an ominous shiver. All night, she had to act like nothing was wrong, when secretly she was breaking out in a cold sweat, counting the minutes until the inevitable race to the bathroom. She knew disaster was looming, she just had to breathe and smile and keep it together long enough to do her job.

And tonight was no different.

The literary festival had taken over one of the nicest restaurants in town for a big celebration dinner for the authors and publishers. Poppy was seated at a table with Cooper, Eliza, Quinn, and a few other authors; the champagne was flowing, the food was delicious—and all Poppy could feel was a terrible tangle of dread in the pit of her stomach. Cooper was acting like nothing was wrong, but she knew him enough now to know it was just that: an act.

"I didn't realize you were local!" Eliza was exclaiming from across the table. "Maybe we could set up an interview, I write for some of the Boston newspapers, too."

"Absolutely!" Quinn answered for her. "That sounds great."

"How long are you staying?" Eliza asked, pulling out her phone to check her schedule. "It's so much better to chat in person. You know, 'Author Poppy Somerville breezes into the room and orders a slice of pie that belies her slim figure,' " she quipped, and Poppy managed a faint smile.

"I . . . don't know yet. I was thinking about renting a place through the summer." Cooper snapped his head around. "You didn't say."

"It was just an idea." She forced herself to meet his eyes. "What do you think?"

The question trembled in the air between them, but she couldn't keep on hoping this was just a temporary stumble, not when her heart ached like this. She wanted to be holding hands with him under the table, leaning in to exchange private whispers, laughing through the night the way she had just a week ago, both of them giddy and excited and breathless for more.

Instead, Cooper's face was impassive. He reached for his drink and took a swallow. "I guess it's up to you," he said flatly. "I figured you would be getting back to New York after the book was done."

Poppy froze.

Was that all she was to him: a temporary distraction, already overstaying her welcome?

She took a shallow breath and turned back to the

table. "We'll see," she said to Eliza. "How about we set something up in the next week or two?"

"Perfect." Eliza smiled. "And maybe if I'm extra nice, you'll slip me an advance copy of the next book."

They all laughed. "Get in line," Quinn said. "She's got it under lock and key. No spoilers allowed."

Fiona, her publicist, nodded vigorously. "Last year someone leaked an advance copy of the Julia Chambers book. People posted the ending all over social media. It was a disaster!"

"You mean people found out they all lived happily ever after? Gee, what a surprise."

They all turned at the sound of Cooper's scathing comment.

Poppy tensed. "He's more of a non-fiction guy," she said quickly, trying to smile it away, but Cooper shook his head.

"I don't have any problem with fiction, but it should be based in reality, right?" He looked around the table. "People just don't act that way. The books should carry a warning: 'Will give you delusions of romance.' It's setting you up for disappointment."

"You mean I am," Poppy said clearly.

There was an awkward pause, and then Cooper looked away. "You said it." He drained his beer and got to his feet. "Bar's in the back, right?" he asked, then walked away before she could answer.

Humiliation flushed hot on her cheeks. Poppy wished the floor would open and swallow her up.

"If I had a dime for every time a guy complained

about romance novels," Quinn spoke up quickly. "I say there's nothing wrong with raising the bar. If they had it their way, romance would mean taking the trash out once a week and leaving the toilet seat down!"

The table laughed, and Quinn steered the conversation on, but Poppy's heart was aching. She'd heard Cooper's tirade against her work before, but she'd thought it was behind them. That the time they'd spent together had changed his tune, and opened his eyes to the real life love stories happening all around them.

Like theirs.

"Excuse me," Poppy said softly, pushing back her chair. "I'll be right back."

She wove through the dining room. There was no sign of Cooper at the bar, but she glimpsed him through the window, pacing in the alleyway out back. She opened the door and stepped outside, and the cool air hit her in a rush.

She wrapped her arms around herself, shivering. "What was that?"

He turned, his expression tight. "What do you mean?"

Poppy exhaled. He was standing right in front of her, but somehow, it felt like miles between them. "I don't want to do this," she said, trying to be strong. "Bicker about why you just attacked me in front of everyone. Because we know that's not the real problem here."

Cooper's shoulders seemed to slump.

"No. It's not."

And with those simple words, her worst fears were confirmed. It wasn't all in her mind. This was it, she realized. The edge of the cliff.

Pain sliced through her chest, but she couldn't walk away. "What happened?" she asked softly, her heart aching. "What did I do wrong?"

Cooper looked up. "You?" he said, and she saw the pained regret on his face. "No, Poppy, this isn't about you. I'm sorry, but . . ." He stopped himself, and Poppy was left to fill in the words he couldn't bring himself to speak.

But this was just a fling, after all.

But she never mattered to him the way she'd so desperately hoped.

But Poppy was all alone, again.

She swallowed back the tears already stinging in the back of her throat. "You said you wanted this," she argued. "You were the one who kissed *me*, made love to *me*. Was it all a game to you?"

Cooper flinched. "No. God, no. I'm sorry." He looked at her, so anguished it made her want to take his hands and hold him tight, but it was like there was a force field around him, keeping him back. "I don't know what to tell you," Cooper said with a sad smile. "Maybe we're just not meant to be."

"No." Poppy was surprised how loud her voice rang out, but she wouldn't let him do this. "You don't get to say that. We've barely even started. We haven't *tried*—"

"What's the use?" Cooper cut her off, harsh. "This can't go anywhere. Isn't it better just to call it quits now, before anyone gets hurt?"

Poppy stared at him in disbelief.

The breakups she'd written in her books were always big, dramatic scenes. Shouting and weeping, begging and rejection. But now she realized she'd gotten it all wrong. Her heart was breaking, and it didn't make a sound.

"Is that what you really want?" she whispered, holding back tears. It felt like yesterday that she'd woken, curled in his arms as the sun rose outside the windows. For a moment, she'd been suspended in that golden, sleepy haze, not sure if she was awake or still dreaming, until he'd pulled her closer and buried a kiss against her bare shoulder, and she'd realized that for once in her life, the dream of feeling so safe, so connected, hadn't melted away with the first dawn light.

It had been real. She'd felt it—felt his arms holding her, and his heart beating steadily in his chest—and believed it was the beginning. That she'd finally found the love she'd been hoping for, the possibility of forever in his eyes.

But she was wrong. The possibility crumbled away, leaving nothing but a man who couldn't bring himself to look at her.

"It doesn't matter what I want." Cooper's reply was hollow. "This was always how it was going to end. I'm sorry," he said again, finally meeting her gaze. "But you'll see, you deserve better than me. You deserve everything."

He bunched his hands in his pockets, and glanced back to the restaurant. "Send my apologies to Quinn and everyone," he said, stilted. "I think it's best if I go."

"Cooper . . ." His name caught in her throat. She wanted to say something, find a way to break through this wall he'd built between them, and somehow understand why he was just pushing her away. But words failed her, and he turned to walk away.

"Wait!" Poppy called, before she could stop herself. "Was it real?" she demanded, aching inside. "Was any of it real? Or was I just writing us a story that never existed?"

Cooper's face seemed to split apart.

"It was real." His voice was gruff. "Every minute. I promise you that."

He closed the distance between them in a few short strides and took her face in his hands. He pressed a kiss to her forehead, impossibly tender. "I'm sorry," he whispered again, as Poppy's head spun and her body reached to hold him. Then he released her, and turned and walked away.

This time, he didn't look back.

TWENTY-THREE.

"*P*OPPY?"

The knock came at her bedroom door, followed by Aunt June's worried voice. "Poppy, hon, can I make you some breakfast?"

Poppy rolled over and burrowed deeper under the covers. It had been three days since Cooper had left her there at the dinner—three days of Quinn plying her with alcohol and cursing all men, Poppy hiding away from the world, and her aunt trying to feed her, as if her blueberry pancakes could heal all ailments.

Which, usually they did. But this wasn't any old rejection or lost job or disappointing date they were facing. Poppy's heart was broken, and no amount of maple syrup would be fixing that wound.

"Sweetheart?" Poppy heard the door open and lifted her head. June took a step inside. "It's not good for you to be wallowing like this," she said gently. "I'll run you a nice bath, and then you can come downstairs and I'll fix you some food."

"I'm not hungry," Poppy answered listlessly, but the rumble from her stomach said differently. June brightened at the sound.

"Blueberry pancakes it is. And extra-crispy bacon. Come on, you'll feel better with some food in you."

Poppy wasn't convinced, but she'd been wearing these sweatpants for three days straight now. Maybe it was time to get showered and changed—into a fresh pair of sweatpants.

Slowly, she swung her legs out of bed. June pulled back the curtains and bustled around, tidying the room. Poppy froze by the window, her eyes going straight to the house next door. "Is he . . . ?"

"Not on the site today," June said quickly. "Haven't seen him since, well, since the weekend."

"Oh." Poppy let out a breath. She wasn't sure if she was relieved or disappointed. She'd spent days wondering if he was just outside, working away on the house and completely oblivious to her heartbreak, just a few feet away.

June gave her a brief hug. "And how about we get you out of these clothes?" she said, steering Poppy to the bathroom. "You take your time, maybe wash your hair too. I'll get started on the food."

She bustled off downstairs, and when Poppy caught sight of her reflection in the bathroom mirror, she understood Aunt June's determination to get her up and out of bed. Her skin was pasty, there were dark shadows under her eyes, and everything about her looked limp and defeated. Just like she was feeling inside.

Poppy turned on the shower, and stripped to get under the hot spray. She felt like she was moving in slow motion, and had been stuck there ever since the literary festival dinner. It had been hell making it through the rest of the evening after Cooper had walked away; she forced a smile on her face, and accepted everyone's kind words and praise, but inside, she'd been falling apart. It seemed a cruel irony to be talking about romance and happily-ever-after when her own heart was breaking clean apart in her chest. Quinn had been the one to cover for her, talking loudly and steering the conversation away. She'd grabbed a bottle of wine on their way out and stuck it in Poppy's hand for the drive home. "Write your way through it," she'd said, and it was more an order than a suggestion, but still, the heartache remained.

Now, Poppy stepped out of the shower and swathed herself in a warm cotton robe. She could already smell the bacon sizzling, and her mouth began to water. She still felt like a zombie, but at least she was a clean zombie. Trust June to find a way to pull her out of bed.

When in doubt, bacon was usually the answer.

Downstairs, she found her aunt in the kitchen with the radio playing an oldies station, and a cup of coffee waiting for her at the table. "What time is it?" Poppy yawned. She'd been sleeping in fits and starts, writing too late, and crying in painful jags.

"After ten," June replied. "Now, do you want blueberries or peaches on your pancakes? No, don't answer that. You get both."

Poppy inhaled the scent of sweet vanilla batter and the salty bacon, and began to feel more human again. "Thank you," she said, giving her aunt a hug from behind. "I know I've been a mess. I'm sorry."

"Nothing to be sorry about." June patted her. "I just wish I knew what turned the two of you around. You seemed so perfect together, what happened?"

Poppy swallowed. "I honestly don't know."

That was the part that killed her. An argument could be compromised. A problem could have a solution. But how do you compromise on someone walking away from you?

June patted her arm again. "Well, there's fresh syrup in the jug, and these are ready." She expertly flipped the pancakes onto a plate, and pushed Poppy to the table. "Eat," she ordered. "You've been wasting away. If you turned sideways, I could look straight past you!"

Poppy took a forkful of light, fluffy pancake and chewed. The warm berries burst on her tongue, and it was like a wake-up call to her senses. She took another forkful, and then another, and before she knew it, June was whisking her empty plate away for a second helping. "That's better," her aunt beamed, joining Poppy at the table. "Maybe we can go into town later, get a cup of coffee or stop by the store."

"I don't know . . ." Poppy wavered. There was a chance she'd run into Cooper in town, and the last thing she wanted to do right now was walk right past him, pretending that everything was OK.

But the thought of seeing him again was like a magnetic pull, no matter what. "OK," she said quickly. "Let go, after breakfast."

June helped herself to more fruit, and gave Poppy a smile. "Maybe it will all still work out," she offered, looking hopeful. "You never know."

Poppy sighed. "I don't think so. You didn't see him," she added. "The way he looked at me . . . He'd made his mind up. It was like we were already over and he'd just forgotten to tell me."

Poppy felt the grief well up in her chest again. It wasn't just a grief for everything she'd lost—the moments they'd shared—but for the possibilities that had suddenly been cut short.

The future she'd wanted with him, and dared to even dream.

All this time, she'd been clinging to hope, that shot in the dark at finding someone to connect with, who would see her heart and love her for it, and now that she'd had a glimpse of what that belonging felt like, it hurt even more to lose it all.

And she didn't even know why.

POPPY DEMOLISHED ANOTHER PLATE of pancakes to build her strength, then got dressed and headed into town. They shopped for groceries for dinner that night, before June got waylaid by a friend in the store. "I'll meet you at the coffee shop," Poppy told her, not wanting to interrupt, and left them to gossip alone. Outside, it was a warm, spring day, but Poppy felt a tremor of nerves, making her way across the square. She expected to look up any moment to see Cooper striding around the corner, or emerging from the hardware store. What was she supposed to say to him? How was she supposed to act now?

Maybe it was a good thing she hadn't made plans to

stay for the summer. That vision of lazy beach days and long nights in his arms seemed a million miles away. Now, she just wanted to finish up her book and get back to the city, but looking around the square, with the small green park and wedding cake gazebo, she felt a pang. Sweetbriar somehow felt like home, after just a couple of months.

A home that had her ex just up the street, she reminded herself. Cooper had lived here all his life; it was no contest who was taking Sweetbriar in the breakup.

She remembered her earlier promise to Mackenzie, and detoured via the pottery workshop to pick up some mugs. The bell above the door rang out as she entered, and Mackenzie's voice called, flustered, from the back. "Be right there!"

Poppy browsed the cute ceramics, bracing herself for the onslaught of sympathy and questions, but when Mackenzie emerged—her curly hair flying out in every direction, and a smudge of paint on one cheek—she was all smiles.

"Hey! How's my favorite romance author?" She came to hug Poppy. "I heard you were a hit at the festival. I couldn't make it to your panel, I was stuck on my booth all day, but we sold out of my nautical collection and I made out like a bandit with my *books, coffee, air* mugs. See?" She held up a chunky blue cup with swirling white letters.

"I love it!" Poppy examined the glaze. "I'll take ten."

"Ooh, big spender." Mackenzie grinned. "Either that, or your coffee habit has spiraled way out of control."

Poppy smiled. "No, I figure I should stock up on gifts before I leave."

Mackenzie's head snapped around. "Leave?" she echoed, eyes wide. "You're going back to New York? But what about Cooper?"

Poppy blinked. She'd figured the legendary Sweetbriar gossip mill would have been working overtime, and Mackenzie was just being sweet to ignore the subject, but looking at the confusion on her face, she wasn't so sure.

"I'm going home," she said slowly. "Cooper and I broke up."

"He did WHAT?" Mackenzie's voice echoed. She caught her breath. "Sorry," she said. "But I am going to murder that man." She stripped off her apron, as if she was about to march out the door right that second.

"No!" Poppy yelped. "Don't, please."

"But what about you?" Mackenzie looked back at her. "Are you OK? When was this? What happened?"

Poppy slowly filled her in on the (brief) details, Mackenzie shaking her head the whole time. "I knew it," she muttered. "I knew he'd go and do something to screw this up. It's like he's incapable of letting himself be happy. He's going to wind up bitter and alone, just like I said."

Poppy swallowed hard. The thought of Cooper alone and miserable hit her squarely in the gut. She didn't want that for him. She wanted him to be happy.

With her.

"You're taking this way too calmly," Mackenzie added, looking at her with concern. "If I were you, I'd be breaking things right now. *His* things."

Poppy managed a weak smile. "I guess I'm still in a daze." She shrugged. "I've been mostly wallowing. There was some drinking," she added, remembering Quinn. "But overall, wallowing. June finally dragged me out of the house today. I think she was getting worried."

"She was right." Mackenzie nodded. "There are seven stages to grief. First, sweatpants."

"I've definitely checked that off the list."

"Good." Mackenzie gave her a smile. "That means you're all set for stage two. Follow me."

She headed for the back before Poppy could argue. Curious, she set down her mugs and followed. The studio area was a chaotic mess of pottery, paperwork, and tools, but Mackenzie led her past the room and out of the back door, to where there was a small grassy yard with a table and chairs, and a shed-like structure in the back. "I keep my kiln in there, in case it overheats and something explodes," Mackenzie explained. "And this is where I do my anger management." She presented a corner of the yard filled with shards of broken pottery, layered inches deep.

"You don't seem angry to me." Poppy looked around. There were flowers and hearts painted on the wall, and a box full of daffodils blooming cheerfully by the window.

"That's because I work it all out here." Mackenzie smiled. "Try it." She handed Poppy a vase that chipped and misshapen. "They're my offcuts," she explained. "I smash them up and make mosaics."

"I don't know . . ." Poppy didn't feel like smashing things. Truth be told, she still felt like curling under the covers back at the cottage and never coming up for air. But Mackenzie was insistent.

"It makes you feel better, I promise. Just imagine you're throwing it at Cooper's big, stubborn head."

Poppy gulped. "Don't ask me to picture him. It hurts too much."

Mackenzie gave her a sympathetic look. "We're going to need a bigger bowl."

She took the vase from Poppy's hands and hurled it suddenly at the shed wall. It broke with a loud SMASH, the pieces flying out in every direction. Poppy jumped. "See?" Mackenzie beamed. "It's very therapeutic."

Poppy blinked. Mackenzie found her a bowl from the collection of defective pottery and passed it over. "Just toss it right down," Mackenzie insisted. "It feels good, I swear."

Poppy didn't know what else to do, so she half-heartedly lobbed the bowl at the heap of debris. It hit the wall with a gentle thud and cracked in two before sliding to the ground.

"Yeah, nope." Mackenzie frowned. "We're going to need the chardonnay."

"Did I hear my cue?"

Poppy turned. It was Aunt June, with an armful of groceries. "Ooh," she said, lighting up. "Are we throwing pots again?"

Mackenzie grinned. "June happened to be in the store when a date cancelled at the last minute," she explained to Poppy. "So we had ourselves some fun back here."

"Let me do one." June set down the bag and limbered

up, stretching. Mackenzie passed her a mug with a massive chip in it, and June hurled it at the ground. It smashed into a dozen pieces, and she clapped her hands together in glee. "It reminds me of the time my second husband was cheating," she said with a nostalgic smile. "I took everything he owned and hurled it out the second-floor window."

"You didn't!" Poppy exclaimed.

"Oh, yes I did," June replied. "When he came back from that hussy's place, it was all right there on the sidewalk in ruins."

"Atta girl," Mackenzie said. "Come on, Poppy. You can't tell me you're not a little angry right now?"

Poppy gulped. The sad haze was wearing off a little, and she had to admit, there was a burning seam of anger running through that broken heart of hers.

How could he just change his mind?

Poppy grabbed a plate from the table and narrowed her eyes. This time, when she threw it, it hit the wall with a satisfying SMASH and ricocheted into tiny pieces.

"You're right," she said, surprised. "It does feel good."

"You grab the pots, I'll go get the wine." Mackenzie grinned. "And we'll have ourselves a party."

FOUR BOWLS, TWO MUGS, and a misshapen lump of something Mackenzie couldn't even identify later, and Poppy was in touch with her anger, alright. "He just LEFT," she cried, throwing another mug at the ground in a shatter of satisfying pieces. "He didn't try to talk, or explain, or anything. He just decided it was over, and that was it. Who *does* that?"

"Men," June snorted, and took a sip of her wine. "That's who. Always acting like their word is law."

"But you don't understand, Cooper isn't like that. At least, he wasn't." Poppy's shoulders sagged, remembering. "He was so sweet to me, nothing like how he seemed in the beginning. He helped me with my book, and fixed up that cabin . . ."

Just as swiftly as it came, her anger left her. Poppy sat down at the table in a slump, the pain flooding through her all over again.

Mackenzie refilled her wine glass, and nudged it towards Poppy. "I'm sorry I pushed you guys together," she said, looking stricken. "I never thought it would all fall apart like this."

"It's not your fault," Poppy reassured her. "I wanted this. And he said he did too. But just not enough, I guess."

There was silence. Poppy swallowed. "Anyway, thanks for the distraction," she offered, giving Mackenzie a smile. "What will you do with the wreckage now?"

Mackenzie surveyed the shattered pottery. "A mosaic, maybe. Or I could glue some of the pieces together into something new. Either way, I'll make it something beautiful."

Poppy felt a pang. "Got any glue for pieces of a broken heart?" she asked ruefully.

Mackenzie gave her a quiet smile. "I'm still working on that one."

"At least you'll be able to put it in a book one day," June spoke up. "Use all of this for something creative. It's not life," she added with an encouraging smile. "It's material!"

Poppy knew she was trying to help, but she flinched at the thought of it. Channeling her hopes and dreams into her work was one thing, but the idea of sharing all the intimate details of her relationship with Cooper would be a betrayal, no matter how it had ended. "Being blissfully in love is material, too," she said instead. "Never mind starving in a garret somewhere, I do my best work when I'm happy and well fed."

Mackenzie laughed. "My kind of artist," she grinned. "Here's to comfortable, happy creation." She toasted her glass to Poppy's, but she was still a long way from happy. The afternoon with her aunt and Mackenzie may have been a welcome distraction from the empty ache inside, but it was still there: sounding like an echo only she could hear.

"I tried calling him," she admitted quietly. "He didn't pick up, and I couldn't leave a message. I didn't know what to say. I just wanted to talk to him, maybe try to understand . . ." Tears welled up in her eyes, and she wiped at them, feeling foolish. "I don't even know why I'm taking it so hard. I mean, I've barely known the man for a month. It's not like we made any promises. He never even said he loved me—"

Her voice cracked, and June reached out to squeeze her hand. Poppy flushed, embarrassed. "I'm making a big drama out of it, I shouldn't even care."

"But you do." Her aunt gave her a weary smile. "Time doesn't make a difference, not when it matters. When you find your someone. Why, I've had affairs that lasted a week that mattered more than men I knew for years. It's not about how long you spent together. Sharing something real, revealing your heart . . . that always matters, whether it's for a week or a year."

Now Poppy really had to work to keep back the tears. Her aunt was right, she knew it in her gut. But what use was that rare connection when the other person turned around and walked away?

"You should go there," Mackenzie declared. "It worked last time, didn't it? Go to him, and set him straight. Find out what he's so scared of, and don't leave until you figure out a way through it, together."

Poppy shook her head. "I can't," she said sadly. "Not this time. He's made his choice, and I can't just go chasing after somebody who doesn't want me."

"But he does!" Mackenzie protested. "I saw the way he looked at you, how happy he was. I've never seen him like that before."

"No." Poppy took a deep breath. "He's right. Maybe we just weren't meant to be."

"You don't believe that," Mackenzie said stubbornly, and Poppy's heart ached.

"No, I don't. But what choice do I have?" she asked simply. "This isn't one of my books. I can't write a love story out of thin air. Real life doesn't work that way. Sometimes things don't make sense, but they happen anyway," she said, feeling the resignation in her bones.

"Not everyone gets a happy ending."

Mackenzie's lips set in a determined line. "You're wrong. I can't believe that."

Poppy thought about how long she'd believed in true love. The hours, and chapters, and thousands of words she'd poured into that one, precious hope. She didn't regret them, not for a minute—and she couldn't regret the time she'd spent with Cooper, the glimpse of that magic she'd seen in his eyes. If she had a chance to do it all over again, she would, no matter how much it hurt now, in the end.

"Look at us, getting maudlin," she said, forcing a smile. "That's what you get for drinking a bottle of wine on an empty stomach. What do you say we go back to the cottage and make dinner? If anything can heal a broken heart, it's your soup, Aunt June."

June chuckled. "I'm one step ahead of you, hon. What do you think I was buying at the grocery store?"

"It's a plan." Poppy got to her feet. "Want to come by?" she asked Mackenzie. "It's the least I can offer, after your hospitality."

"Another time." Mackenzie gave her a swift hug. "But there's something I need to do."

"Then let's get those mugs wrapped up."

They headed for the front of the store, where Poppy picked out enough ceramics to supply all her friends and family for birthdays and holidays for years to come. Mackenzie carefully wrapped them in tissue paper and packed them into boxes. "I can ship them direct to wherever you want," she said.

"That's perfect."

"You won't suddenly bolt out of town, will you?" Mackenzie stopped to check. "Disappear in the dark of night never to return?"

"I still have a few chapters of my book left to write," Poppy reassured her. "And I promise I'll come say goodbye."

"Now you're making me emotional." Mackenzie sniffled.

"I'm going to New York, not Antarctica!" Poppy laughed. "I'll still see June, and you're welcome to come stay any time you want to visit."

"I know, but it's not the same." Mackenzie gave her a wry smile. "I was about to launch my campaign to get you moving here full-time. Although I figured Cooper would take care of that."

"Me too," Poppy said sadly. "But here we are."

Preparing to leave the place she'd just imagined setting down roots. At the end of a chapter, instead of a beginning. She couldn't turn the clock back or rewrite the past, not when Cooper refused to even try. All she could do was keep believing that her happy ending was still out there, and not bound up in six-foot-two of blue-eyed, teasing-smiled heartbreak who wouldn't even take her calls now, let alone look at her like she was the only thing that mattered in the world.

The only question she still had was, why?

TWENTY-FOUR.

COOPER DIDN'T HEAR the knocking at first; he was half a bottle of whiskey deep and it was only five p.m. It wasn't until the loud banging broke through his numb haze that he realized someone was hammering on his front door.

"I'm not home!" he yelled, but the noise didn't stop. Whoever was out there was either deaf, or stupid, or both.

Unless it was Poppy.

He was on his feet before he knew it, striding for the hallway. But he'd been horizontal on the living room floor all afternoon and his balance was screwed. He banged straight into the table and was cursing the pain shooting through his knee when he flung the door open.

"Oh." His heart sank. "It's you."

Mackenzie glared at him with murder in his eyes. "What the hell are you playing at?"

Cooper closed the door in her face.

"Cooper Tiberius Nicholson!" her voice carried. "You open this door right now. I've just spent the afternoon with Poppy crying all over the damn place because of you. The least you can do is be a man and explain yourself."

Shame crashed through him. Goddamn. He wasn't drunk enough for this. Hell, he wasn't even drunk anymore.

He cracked the door. "She was crying?" he asked, his head already pounding with guilt. Mackenzie sighed.

"She was trying to be brave about it, but yeah. You did a number on her, Coop, and I never figured you for a guy who just cuts and runs."

He swallowed. "I'm doing her a favor," he mumbled, but somehow, all his justifications didn't sound so convincing out loud.

Mackenzie clearly agreed, because she pushed past him and marched inside. She took a look around at the debris—the takeout wrappers and empty beer cans and the old record player that was skipping so he had to take the whole damn thing apart—and sighed. "Come on, Coop. What's going on?"

"Nothing," he said stubbornly. "Except you're interrupting my hangover."

"The last time I saw you guys, everything was fine. Great, even," she said. "I've never seen you happy like the kind of happy you were around Poppy. Then you just break up out of nowhere, no reason, no explanation? Cut the crap and tell me what happened. Did Poppy do something?" she demanded. "No, scratch that, the poor girl doesn't have a clue why you suddenly walked out on her. Was it Laura?" She narrowed her eyes. "Is that what this is about? Are you still in love with her?"

Cooper flinched back from her barrage of questions. "Can't you just leave a man in peace?"

"Nope." Mackenzie sat herself down on the couch. "I'm not leaving until I get answers. I've got all night."

Cooper sighed. She was the only person he knew as stubborn as he was, which meant she wasn't going anytime soon.

So he did.

He grabbed his keys and jacket, and headed for the door. "Lock up on your way out," he called behind him, and didn't stick around to hear her complaints. He got in his truck and gunned the engine.

Couldn't a man get a little peace in this town?

Not that he deserved it. She was right, Poppy didn't deserve this, and the longer he thought about the way she'd looked when he broke the news—how her face had cracked wide open and those heartfelt eyes of hers filled with tears—the more he hated himself.

Goddammit, Cooper. What the hell have you done?

He drove carefully along the highway. The sun was sinking low in the sky, and his buzz had long since worn off, leaving nothing but self-loathing and bitter regret.

It had all seemed so simple. He wasn't made for happy endings, he'd known it all along. Better to save them both from the slow-motion car wreck of a relationship, and let Poppy move on and meet a man who wouldn't let her down. But looking her in the eye and telling her it was over . . . it still sliced him clean through the chest. He'd wanted to spare her from the pain of disappointing her, but instead, he'd put a betrayal in her expression he would never forget.

He took the turn through town, down towards the

beach. He'd stayed away from the construction project all week. He'd told himself his guys could handle it, but the truth was, he didn't trust himself to be a few dozen feet away from Poppy without throwing all his good reasons aside and marching over there to try and win her back.

Especially when he wondered if his reasons weren't so good, after all.

But June's cottage was dark when he pulled up, and nobody was home. Which was a good thing, he reminded himself, as he went to check the progress on the house next door. It was coming together now: the roof on, the walls up and sturdy, and those problems with the foundation all sorted. Walking around inside, he could finally picture the home it would become—more than just renderings on a page. A little drywall, a few salvaged beams, the new flooring . . .

Some lucky family was going to be happy there.

He felt an ache just imagining it. Damn. He was getting sentimental in his old age. It was just bricks and mortar, he told himself, as he locked up behind him. The next place he built better be a bachelor pad, save him from all this "what if?" whirling in his brain. Chrome and glass, made for one—and the occasional overnight guest.

But the thought of replacing Poppy with his usual parade of summer flings took the wind out of his lungs all over again.

There was no replacing a woman like her.

The sun was almost setting by the time he was done at the house, and Cooper half-expected Mackenzie to still be sitting right there on his couch if he went home, so he drove on into Sweetbriar instead. It was a quiet night at the pub, and Grayson was the only other person at the bar. He gave Cooper a nod. "Riley's out back somewhere with that waitress. I suggest you pour yourself if you want a drink this side of midnight."

Cooper rounded the bar and selected a pale ale. It came out half foam, but what the hell. Another beer—or five—and that pickaxe in his chest might stop hurting so damn much. He took a gulp. "View's different, this side," he remarked, looking out.

Grayson studied him, his expression inscrutable. He wasn't a man of many words, but clearly had something he wanted to say. Cooper ignored him. He wasn't about to break the habit of a lifetime and spill his feelings all over the place like some sloppy drunk at last call.

"She's leaving, you know."

Cooper's head snapped up.

"Franny heard it from June, today at the store," Grayson continued. He took another sip like he hadn't just set a bombshell right down on the bar. "She has a couple of chapters left to write, but once she's done with that book of hers, she's heading straight back to New York. For good."

The axe twisted. Cooper tried not to care.

"Good for her," he muttered. "She'll be happy to get back to city life, I'd imagine. Too long in the slow lane with us."

"Uh huh."

"I mean, that was always the plan, right?" Cooper continued, clinging to his last excuse. "This was a vacation for her. Vacations end. Sweetbriar's fine for a couple of months, but what was she going to do: uproot her life move here full-time?"

"You did," Grayson countered evenly. "So did I."

"Yeah, well you have issues we're not getting into," Cooper said darkly. "Like why a man travels halfway across the world to sit in an old bookstore all day, gathering dust."

"I agree." Grayson didn't rise to the bait. "We're not getting into that."

He stayed at the bar, watching Cooper with a knowing stare, and Cooper shifted, uncomfortable. "I know what you're thinking," he snapped.

"You do?" Grayson raised an eyebrow.

"Hell, it's what you're all thinking. Mackenzie, June—the whole damn town." Cooper scowled. "You think I'm a fool to mess things up, and a coward for leaving, and a bastard for breaking her heart. Well, you can save the lectures," he added bitterly, "because believe me, I've heard them all. They've been playing non-stop in my own damn brain ever since I walked away."

There was silence. When he looked up again, Grayson was still sitting there, still watching him, still smiling that inscrutable smile that somehow was the last thing Cooper needed to see. "What?" he demanded, his voice rising. "Have you got something you want to say to me?"

"Nope," Grayson replied. "Just, I'm sorry you're hurting. I know love isn't easy to find," he added, his voice gruff.

Cooper deflated. "It wasn't love," he mumbled, taking

a gulp of beer. "It was just . . . not meant to be."

Grayson finished his drink, then got down from his stool and strolled out, leaving Cooper alone with the lie still fresh in his mouth. It didn't matter if he loved her. He'd already learned that love wasn't enough. His love, at least. You could love someone as best you could, and still fall short of forever.

You really think this is your best?

Cooper pushed aside the doubts and took another drink. It was done, either way, and soon Poppy would be three hundred miles away, and it would be like she'd never existed at all.

Except for that damn pickaxe still lodged in his heart.

TWENTY-FIVE.

*P*OPPY ALWAYS FELT like she deserved a fanfare when she finished the first draft of a book. Confetti raining from the sky, a chorus girl jumping out of a cake. Why not throw in a parade with some baton-twirling and a full brass band? She deserved it.

But this time, typing those final words was a bittersweet moment. Her series was over, her characters finally reunited. It was the end of a wonderful moment in her life—and the beginning of something new for her.

She read over the last chapter, and then backed it up—twice over, just to be safe. Then she closed her laptop screen and took a deep breath of salty sea air. It was a bright, clear morning, and she was tucked away in her writing cabin again on the beach. Except it wasn't hers, she reminded herself. It belonged to Cooper. He'd only loaned it to her temporarily.

Like him.

She tried not to feel the same swell of sadness all over again, but it rose as steady as the tide in her chest. In time, it would be better, she told herself. In time, he would be just another detour on her path to real love.

So why did she still feel like that road stopped, right

here?

Her cellphone rang, in a welcome distraction. "Hey Summer." Poppy smiled, answering the call. "Great timing. I just finished my draft."

"Congratulations!" Summer exclaimed. "We'll have to celebrate when you're back. There's a new restaurant that just opened down the block from me. The chef is an asshole, but he makes gnocchi like a dream."

Poppy laughed. "Does this mean you've already hooked up with him?"

Summer snorted. "When would I have the time? Andre's started loaning me out to bake wedding cakes for his most exclusive clientele. Between him and my mother trying to get me on her TV show, I don't have a moment to hook up with anyone—let alone another asshole chef."

"You do have a track record," Poppy agreed.

"What can I say? I fall in love mouth-first."

Poppy giggled.

"You know what I mean," Summer groaned. "Anyway, what about you, how are you holding up? Have you seen him yet?"

"No, and I'm not going to," Poppy said firmly. "I don't know how it's possible to avoid someone in a small town like this, but he's doing a pretty good job of it."

"I'm sorry, babe. Just look on the bright side: come tomorrow, you'll be gone."

"I know," Poppy sighed. Why was it the thought of leaving still made her ache? "June and Mackenzie insisted on having a leaving celebration tonight in town. I should be happy to be putting real distance between us, but I'm going to miss this place," she admitted, looking out at the bay. The waves were cresting, foam-tipped and wild from the winds, and the incredible peace she'd felt the first day arriving here was still calm around her, despite the heartache.

"I'm going to miss it too, and I haven't even been!" Summer exclaimed. "I was looking forward to all those hot bearded guys you were telling me about."

"Help yourself," Poppy said ruefully. "There's one more on the market now."

"That's decided it," Summer said, sounding determined. "As soon as you're back, we're going out. You, me, a bottle of tequila, painting the town red. What do you say?"

"I say I'm about five years too old for that."

Summer laughed. "OK, then you, me, a bottle of red wine, and a night in front of Netflix watching British costume dramas."

Poppy smiled. "Now that sounds like my kind of plan."

SHE FINISHED UP at the cabin, feeling a pang as she packed away her few items and closed up the painted wooden doors for the final time. She took the winding path back up to the cottage, her heart beating faster when she saw the construction crew was working on the house next door. She couldn't stop herself searching the group for Cooper's tall, broad-shouldered frame.

No sign of him.

She exhaled, crossing past the yard to June's, but just

as she reached the gravel driveway, a truck came around the bend, slowing as it approached.

Cooper's truck.

Poppy froze. She could see him through the windshield glass, wearing a ballcap and a messy three-day beard, and just like that, all her pep talks about how he didn't matter melted clean away.

God, she wanted him.

Hope, and trepidation, and plain desire pounded through her, and as he pulled in to park, Cooper looked over and met her eyes. For a moment they were both caught there, staring, only a few feet apart, but just as Poppy raised her hand in a nervous wave, Cooper's expression changed. He threw the truck into reverse and backed out of the driveway, pulling a wide U-turn before speeding back up the road leaving nothing but gravel flying in his wake.

Poppy swallowed back the sting of disappointment. She'd been wondering if he regretted it, but there was her answer, loud and clear.

Whatever they shared was history. It was time to move on.

COOPER WATCHED POPPY getting smaller in the rearview mirror, until she was around the bend and out of sight.

He gripped the steering wheel hard, trying to focus on the road—and not the woman he just drove away from when every instinct in his body was screaming out to stay. He'd told himself he would be fine heading back to work.

He'd stayed away too long already, and he had a job to do—no matter who was living right next door. But just the sight of her standing there, wrapped up in that red sweater with her hair dancing wildly around in the breeze, made it all come rushing back. And the expression in her eyes, so unsure and full of pain, sliced him so deep he was surprised he wasn't bleeding yet.

He'd let her down.

Cooper swallowed back the guilt and turned out onto the highway. After stewing in self-loathing all week, he had a to-do list a mile long, so he headed into Province-town. The hardware store there had plenty he needed, and the longer he could distract himself with work, the less time he'd have to spend thinking about Poppy, and that tentative smile of hers disappearing from sight. The store aisles were busy, and he soon had a couple of carts filled with the AC units he needed, and plenty of pipe for the bathrooms, too. He was halfway down the electrics aisle, when someone studying the shelf stepped back, into his path.

"Excuse me," he muttered, and the woman turned.

"Cooper!" she exclaimed, and his heart sank another inch. It was Laura, juggling three different boxes in her arms with her stroller right beside her. He braced himself for an awkward pause, but Laura just smiled. "Perfect timing," she said. "I'm trying to fix the fuse box, and I can't tell which size I need."

"You, fixing?" Cooper couldn't help but remark.

She gave a rueful laugh. "I know, but Steve's out of town at a conference in Chicago, so I'm fighting this battle alone."

"What's the problem?" Cooper asked. Her kid was straining to reach a bin of screws, but before he could say anything, Laura neatly wheeled him back, out of reach.

"No idea," she said brightly. "All I know is that when I plugged my hairdryer in, all the lights went out, and no amount of flipping them up and down does a thing."

"Sounds like you blew it out." He paused, thinking of all the times Laura had tried to fix things when they were dating—and just how badly that worked out. Left to her own devices, she'd probably wind up electrocuting herself. Or worse. "If you want, I can come replace it," he offered reluctantly.

"Oh, no it's OK." Laura looked startled. "I was going to call Hank and see if he could come out—"

"That'll take until next week," Cooper interrupted. "You know. Come on, it won't be five minutes. It's the least I can do," he added gruffly.

"Well . . . thank you," Laura said, still looking awkward. "If it's not too much trouble."

"None at all. Are you still at Seashore Drive?" he asked, and she nodded. "I can head over now, when all this is loaded. You better get both sizes, until I know what we need."

"OK," Laura said. "I'll see you there."

Cooper headed to the check-out line and got his purchases stowed away in the back. He knew where Laura lived, backing onto the nature preserve, and when he pulled up in the driveway, she was already home.

She greeted him at the door with Brady on her hip.

"Thanks again," she said, looking frazzled. "I didn't even realize, but the freezer turned off, too. If I don't get power back, we're going to be eating thawed salmon for a week. Come on in," she stood back, and beckoned him inside.

"It's no problem." Cooper wiped his boots on the mat. He couldn't stop himself from looking around, curious about the life she'd built. The small house was nothing like the one they'd shared together. It was cluttered and homey, with toys on the floor and family photos on every wall.

"The fuse box is in the basement. Sorry about the mess, you'll need this." She handed him a flashlight and the fuses, and led him to the stairs.

"I'll put this one down for his nap. Watch out for the bottom step, it gives way. That's what you get for an old house, not that I need to tell you that," she added with a flustered grin.

"They call it charm, I call it dry rot." Cooper nodded. She was nervous, he could tell, but he didn't blame her. He hadn't exactly been on friendly terms since the breakup. Sure, they were polite enough, seeing each other around, but this was the first time he could remember them being alone together in years.

Brady let out a disgruntled sound, tugging at her braid.

Well, almost alone.

"I'll get to it," Cooper gestured awkwardly, and then headed down into the basement—taking care on the bottom step. With the torch, the fuse box was easy enough to find, and luckily Laura had bought the right kind. He had the faulty ones switched out in no time, and when he flipped the switch, he saw the lights upstairs turn on.

"Angel," Laura greeted him when he emerged back up to the kitchen. She'd changed into a fresh T-shirt—not stained with baby drool—and had her hair caught up in a ponytail. "Can I get you a coffee? Tea? Half-thawed filet of salmon?"

"It's fine, I should be going." Cooper still felt out of place, but she insisted.

"Please, sit down. I've been wanting to catch up. It's been so long since . . . well." Laura steered him to the kitchen table and moved to make coffee. "How are you doing?"

Cooper slowly exhaled. "I've been better," he said, and immediately regretted it. Laura was the last person in the world he should be talking to like this, after everything he'd put her through.

"I heard," she said slowly. "About you and Poppy. I'm sorry, she seemed nice."

"She was. Is," he corrected himself, then shrugged, trying to be casual. "It didn't work out. It happens."

"You know, I was thinking, and you haven't been with anyone serious since us, have you?" Laura was watching him carefully, and Cooper felt trapped under her gaze. This wasn't like with Riley, or even Mackenzie, where he could shut down their questions and move on. Laura knew him, or at least, she used to do.

He shrugged again, and looked away. "I don't know, I've dated plenty these past years."

"But nothing that's lasted."

"You should be glad about that," Cooper tried to joke. "You always said I couldn't make you happy. The least I can do is save some other poor woman from making the same mistake."

"Is that what you really think?"

When he looked back, Laura seemed surprised.

"It's true, isn't it?" Cooper felt a wave of bitter regret. "I couldn't give you what you wanted, no matter how hard I tried. I'm just not cut out to love anyone, I guess."

He ached to say it, but there was no avoiding the truth. He'd thought he'd accepted it by now, but Poppy had thrown a wrench in that for good. She'd shown him what he'd been missing out on. What he could have had, in another life maybe.

"It's OK," he said to Laura, who was looking at him with what looked like pity in her gaze. "Some of us just aren't made for all of this." He nodded around at the photos pinned to the refrigerator door, and the pile of baby clothes, fresh from the dryer. "And if I was . . . well, don't you think we would have figured it out back when we had the chance?"

Laura looked at him for a long moment, then shook her head with a rueful smile. "Did it ever occur to you that we didn't work out because we weren't supposed to?"

He looked away. "You don't have to say that. I know I screwed us up."

Laura frowned. She came to sit beside him, reaching over to take his hand. "Seriously, Cooper, have you really been blaming yourself for that all this time? God, you're even more stubborn than I thought."

Cooper pulled back. "Hey."

She rolled her eyes at him. "We were a disaster. Come on, you know that. We were at each other's throats all the time, over who knows what? Oil and water, that's what my mom always said, and she was right. There was no saving us, but you just wouldn't give up the fight. I didn't understand it, why you wanted to keep putting us both through that misery."

"I loved you," he frowned.

"And I loved you, but I couldn't live with you." Laura sighed. "It was too hard. Remember, I told you it shouldn't be that hard."

"Hard to love me," he said, with that same damn bitter ache.

"No," she corrected him gently. "Hard to be together. Admit it, I was no walk in the park either. God, when I think about those fights we had . . ." She shook her head. "You made me crazy."

"You would act like you lost your damn mind," he agreed, and she laughed.

"You see? That's not good love. That's not what you can build a future on. Imagine it," she added. "You and me, at each other's throats every day, all that resentment and frustration boiling over. You really think that's the life you should have had? We gave it our best shot," she continued, "but you weren't the one for me, and I sure as hell wasn't the one for you. You were meant for someone else. Someone who can make you happy, without wanting to wring your damn neck every other day."

Cooper looked at her, trying to wrap his head around what she was saying. All this time he'd been blaming himself, thinking that if his love wasn't enough to make it work with her then he'd never be enough for anyone else. But now she was saying there had been no saving them.

It wasn't his fault.

Could it really be that simple?

He shook his head slowly. He wanted so much to believe in what she was telling him, but he felt like a dying man in the desert, so desperate for water he was clinging to the mirage just up ahead.

"But I tried my best, and it wasn't good enough for you."

Laura looked stricken. "I'm sorry if I made you think that," she said, squeezing his hand. "I know we both said some things in the end there, but I never meant for you to hold onto them like this. God, Cooper, you deserve to be happy. You're a good man, even if we weren't good for each other."

Cooper exhaled. He felt off balance, like the world had suddenly tilted off its axis, and everything he was so damn sure he had figured out was now up in the air again, spinning in the wind.

"You really think that?" he asked, and the naked hope in his voice would have made him ashamed if it were anyone else in the room. But for better or worse, Laura knew him from the inside out. She looked at him straight on and smiled.

"I do. And I wouldn't lie to you. If you were an asshole with no hope of redemption, I'd be the one telling you that."

He managed a smile. "You and Mackenzie, at least."

Laura brightened. "How is she?"

"Giving me a hard time."

"Good." Laura got up. "You need a kick in the ass sometimes. I had high hopes for that Poppy, it seemed like she had her head screwed on straight."

"Not so much." Cooper couldn't help but smile. "She's a total romantic. Believes in soulmates and happily-ever-afters."

Laura arched an eyebrow. "That doesn't sound like your kind of thing."

"I know." He nodded. "But she had me believing. For a while, at least."

He looked away. That was the crazy thing, that for all his bitter memories and stubborn thinking, Poppy really did make a believer out of him. With her, he could see it: why some people just belong together. No judgment, no fights. He'd never felt a peace like the moments where she was curled in his arms—and never known reckless desire like when she fixed those teasing eyes on him with a smile, tempting him to lose himself forever in her touch.

"Aww, hell," he cursed, as it hit him all over again. "I've screwed this up real bad, haven't I?"

Laura patted him on the shoulder. "I'm sure it's not too late for fixing."

"I don't know about that." Cooper thought about the way he'd acted over the past week, pushing her away, time and time again. "She's leaving to go back to New

York."

"So?" Laura challenged him. "Give her a reason to stay."

Cooper was about to detail all the ways that wouldn't work, when a loud wail came from the baby monitor. Laura sighed. "Sorry, he's teething. Won't give me an hour's peace."

"No, it's OK. I've taken up enough of your time." Cooper got to his feet. "And thank you," he said awkwardly. He hadn't been expecting to talk like this—and he definitely hadn't expected that Laura would be the one to make him see that maybe, just maybe, there was still hope for him, after all.

"Anytime." Laura smiled. "Don't be a stranger now. We're going to be renovating Brady's room soon, and I love my husband, but the man can't tell a hammer from a wrench."

"Give me a call, and I'll fit you in," Cooper agreed. He paused. "I'm glad you found it," he said, giving her a wry smile. "Steve, the baby . . . It seems like a good life."

Laura smiled. "Tell me that again when I've had more than three hours sleep."

The wailing went up a decibel.

"I'll leave you to it," Cooper said quickly. "I can see myself out."

He closed the front door behind him, listening as baby Brady's wails quieted. The cool air hit him in a rush, and for the first time since that day at the library, he felt a clarity, some damn direction after all the dark, messy self-doubt.

He wanted Poppy—not just for a night, but for every-thing. A future, a family, all those things he'd believed were out of reach until she'd come along to show him that some things really were meant to be, after all.

He needed her. He loved her. They belonged together. Now he just had to figure out how to make her see it, too—sometime in the next twelve hours.

Before she closed the book on him for good.

TWENTY-SIX.

$\mathcal{J}$T TURNED OUT, when Sweetbriar Cove said *bon voyage*, they went all out. Poppy was expecting a quiet drink at the pub with June and Mackenzie, but when they stepped through the doors, she was met with a loud, "SURPRISE!"

Poppy blinked. It looked like the whole town was crammed inside the building. "You guys!" she exclaimed. "What is all of this?"

"We wanted to give you a proper send-off." Franny beamed. "It's been so much fun having you around."

"We always love an excuse for a party," Debra added, with a twinkle in her eye.

And this was definitely a party. There were balloons, and streamers, and—

"Is that a cake?" Poppy moved closer, her mouth already watering as she took in the towering chocolate layers.

"I called Summer and had her whip one up, emergency delivery." Her aunt gave her a hug. "We'll be sorry to see you go."

"I'll just be a few hours away!" Poppy protested, but Ellie from book group gave her a look.

"You know it doesn't work like that. You stop writing, you don't call . . ." She mimed wiping away tears.

Poppy laughed. "I'll put you guys in the acknowledgements of my new book, how about that?"

"Deal!"

She was ushered to the bar, and soon plied with food and drink—on the house. There was music and laughter, and as Poppy looked around, she was struck by just how quickly this town had come to feel like home.

"What's wrong?" Mackenzie asked, nudging her gently.

"Nothing. Just thinking . . . I've lived in New York for years now, and I don't think I could tell you the name of anyone living on my block. Aside from the guy at the coffee shop," she added.

Mackenzie laughed. "It does have its charm," she agreed, looking around. "We don't do this for everyone though. You're family."

Poppy had to swallow. "You're going to make me cry!" she protested. "And it's way too early for that."

The doors swung open, and her head turned. She couldn't help it, she'd been checking new arrivals all night, wondering if he would show.

"Still no word?" Mackenzie asked quietly.

Poppy shook her head. "It's just as well," she said, trying to convince herself. "I don't even know what I'd say to him if he turned up now."

"That he's been an ass, but you love him, and you'll give him one last chance to make it right?"

Mackenzie looked optimistic, and Poppy knew she

was just hoping for the best, but it still hurt her to think of even laying eyes on Cooper again. She turned to the bar and flagged down Riley. "We're going to need some shots," she declared. "Tequila."

He whistled. "You don't play around."

"It's a party, isn't it?" Poppy forced a smile. "I may as well go out with a bang."

Two shots later, and she was beginning to regret her reckless streak. Riley had brought out the karaoke machine, and any other time, Poppy would have been hiding in the back. But somehow with that pesky tequila warm in her blood, it seemed like a good idea to take center stage for a song with Mackenzie and Ellie.

"*One way, or another,*" she sang, happily out of tune. It was an easy audience, at least: clapping along and politely ignoring just how tone-deaf her warbling was. Poppy swayed in time with the beat, just about ready to launch into the final chorus, when the pub doors opened again, and this time—God, *this time, finally*—it was Cooper walking in.

The song died on her lips.

How did he do this to her, every time? Just the sight of those blue eyes sent her spinning, from clear across the room. She fumbled, barely miming along as Ellie and Mackenzie finished the song, all the while feeling his gaze on her. Inscrutable. Remote. Or was that a hint of regret she spied in their depths?

No, she was reading too much into it. He probably only stopped by to say an awkward goodbye and pretend like nothing had ever happened between them.

Poppy's heart clenched at the thought. She needed another shot of tequila.

The moment the music cut, she headed for the bar and collapsed on a stool. "Another round, please," she told Riley, pointing to her glass, but instead of pouring, he fetched her a slice of cake.

"I'm cutting you off," he said, and passed her a fork.

"I'm not drunk." Poppy frowned, but she still took a bite. Summer's cake was always too delicious to resist.

"I know," Riley smiled. "But I think you're going to want to be sober for this." He nodded behind her, and Poppy swiveled around to look.

Cooper was taking his place at the front of the room, a microphone in his hand.

Cooper. Doing karaoke.

What?

"Just so you know." Riley leaned in. "That man hates the spotlight. So if he's doing this now, there's a damn good reason for it." He winked and wandered away, leaving Poppy with her heart in her throat as the music started.

Elvis.

He wasn't . . . He couldn't be . . .

But he was. As the familiar chords struck up, Cooper cleared his throat, lifted the mic to his lips, and began to sing.

To her.

"Maybe I didn't treat you, quite as good as I should have . . ."

Poppy was struck dumb. His voice was deep and rich,

and he found her there across the bar, his gaze locked on hers as he sang. The world seemed to fade away around them. Every word, every note—all of them straight from his heart to hers.

Was this really happening?

Poppy's heart was in her throat before the end of the very first verse. She was barely aware of the crowd watching the two of them, all that mattered was right there in front of her: the emotion in Cooper's eyes as he sang to her, his voice almost catching on the words.

"Tell me that your sweet love hasn't died . . ."

And then the song he'd chosen began to sink in. The regret in those lyrics.

It was an apology.

She would have taken a few words from him, any time, anywhere, but he was doing it here, in front of everyone. Admitting he'd been wrong, and promising to make it right. He meant every line, pouring his heart into the song. So did this mean what she'd only let herself imagine: that he was sorry for pushing her away?

Did he want another chance for them?

"You were always on my mind."

The final words faded away, and then for a long moment, the room was completely silent. Poppy felt the emotion shimmering in the air between them, and then suddenly, there was applause. Whistles and hooting broke through the spell, and Cooper finally looked away, bashful.

Someone pushed her to her feet. "Go on," June hissed, nudging her forward, but Poppy held back. Her pulse was racing, heart pounding in her chest, but still, she couldn't believe it. He'd walked away, and said there was no hope for them.

So what had changed?

Cooper cut through the crowd to her. "Hey," he said softly, and Poppy had to curl her hands at her sides to keep from reaching for him. He was clean-shaven and smart in a sky-blue button-down, and god, looking way too good to resist.

"Hi," Poppy echoed. She didn't want to hope, but it was too late for that. Hope was a thousand wing-beats fluttering in her chest, as if all it would take was a word from him, and she'd take flight. "I, um, didn't know you could sing."

"Sorry," Cooper looked bashful. "I'm kind of rusty."

"No," Poppy said quickly. "That was . . ." She trailed off, not able to put it in words just yet. And not even sure she should. She gulped and forced herself to ask straight out. "What was that?"

Cooper took a breath. "That was an apology. At least, the start of one." He took her hands in his, meeting her eyes with a look that was so full of regret and determination, it took her breath away. "I'm sorry. For pushing you away, for screwing this whole damn thing up. I'm not like you," he added with a rueful smile. "I never believed in true love, or soulmates. At least, not before you."

Oh god.

It was really happening. Poppy felt the tears stinging in her eyes, but she was too overwhelmed to keep them back. She'd written her share of happy endings, but nothing compared to the way she felt right now.

The future she'd dreamed of was standing right there in front of her.

"I love you," he said, searching her face. His voice was choked with emotion, but he didn't stop. "I promise, I'm never running from it again. You can count on me, for good this time. Will you give me another chance?" he asked. "I won't let you down."

Poppy managed a nod. "I love you, too," she said. She was in tears in front of everyone, but she couldn't care less. Not when Cooper was pulling her into his arms, and finding her lips with his own, and kissing her with enough passion to wipe away the past week without him.

A kiss to make her forget the lonely nights it had taken to get them there. A kiss to heal every bitter wound.

A kiss to build a tomorrow.

She fell into the promise of forever, his lips strong and true against her mouth. And when she finally surfaced for air, the whole room was cheering.

Poppy blushed, realizing everyone was watching, but Cooper was still looking at her like she was the only person in the world. "Will you stay?" he asked, pressing her hands to his chest. "For the summer, at least. And then, after that, we can do whatever you want. I'll move to the city, or you can be here—"

"I'm staying." She answered without thinking, but the moment the words left her lips, she felt just how right they were. Sweetbriar Cove already felt like home, and the thought of building a future here—with him—filled her with happiness.

Cooper's face spread in an enormous grin. "You're sure?"

"I'm sure." Poppy beamed back. It turned out that taking that leap was easy in the end.

Some things were just meant to be.

"You guys!" They were suddenly smothered in a hug from Mackenzie. "I knew it! I knew you couldn't be so pig-headed in the end."

"Hey!" Cooper objected, laughing.

"You know what I mean."

"Congratulations." June joined in the celebration. She squeezed Poppy's hand. "Not to take the credit, but I told you a trip away was exactly what you needed."

Poppy laughed. "You didn't know this was going to happen. Did you?" She paused, wondering. June winked, as they were surrounded by well-wishers.

"I'll have to make you blueberry pie for the next book group."

"Does this mean you'll be needing a new construction project?"

"Maybe you could set your next novel here!"

Poppy happily soaked it up. She shot a glance at Cooper, and found him smiling right back. Like it or not, the town had played a part in their relationship from the very beginning, and it was sweet to have them all rooting for success.

"What do you think?" He drew her closer and murmured in her ear. "Regretting your decision yet?"

She laughed. "As long as they learn to knock, we'll be just fine."

"Knock?" Cooper quirked his eyebrow and gave her a wolfish grin. "Baby, they'll be lucky if we answer the door for a week."

He slid his arms around her, and Poppy didn't think she'd ever been happier.

Their story was just getting started.

TWO WEEKS LATER . . .

*P*OPPY WOKE TO SUNLIGHT streaming in through the windows and the sound of a gull circling over the water. She let out a sleepy yawn. She'd been up late again with Cooper, making up for lost time. Her aunt was on another trip, which meant they'd had the run of the house—and boy, had they made good use of it. She blushed, remembering just what Cooper had done to her on the living room couch, and how his body had felt, that delicious weight pressing her into the cushions.

She rolled over. The bed was empty beside her, but there was a note on the pillow.

Morning, beautiful. Early start next door, come by when you're up.

She got out of bed and went to the window. The house next door was almost complete now, with navy shutters hanging by every window, and a stately front door. Cooper had been working late all week to install all the final touches, but he hadn't let her visit; he said he'd wanted to save it until everything was done. And if his note was anything to go by, that day was finally here.

Her cellphone rang, and Poppy fished it out off the

nightstand, smiling when she saw the caller ID.

"Hey Summer! All set for your visit?" she asked. Summer's boss at the restaurant had volunteered her to bake for a lavish wedding on the Cape, so she would be driving down tomorrow with all six layers carefully packed in a van.

"If by that, you mean have I spent the past twenty-four hours creating an epic wedding cake from scratch, then the answer is yes." Summer sounded tired. "I swear, I wound up dreaming of little sugar roses. Bags of flour grew legs and started waltzing through my mind."

"I'm sorry. But I promise, you'll have a chance to relax here," Poppy said. "I've planned all kinds of fun stuff for us. It'll be great."

"It's the only plus side to the gig. I can't wait to see you!" Summer exclaimed. "And to meet this Cooper of yours. He hasn't passed my test yet."

"There's a test?"

"You know, does he adore you? Can he provide constant entertainment and copious orgasms? Will he introduce me to other hot, single guys? The usual."

"Yes, yes, and I'm sure. You're going to love him." Poppy smiled, glancing out of the window. "I do."

"Aww, listen to you, all loved up. I'd hate you if you weren't my best friend," Summer said cheerfully. "Anyway, I have to get back to work. Chef Andre is on the warpath, again. Something about the soufflés last night, apparently they weren't airy enough for his highness."

"*Quelle horreur!*" Poppy laughed. "See you tomorrow. Drive safe!"

She hung up, pleased they would be spending time together soon. It had been surprisingly easy to pack her life in New York away and ship it all out here—she'd found a subletter no problem, and they'd even hired a moving truck for all the books she couldn't bear to leave behind—but putting hours between her and Summer was the one sour note. Still, it was only a short trip away, and she was sure Sweetbriar could tempt her friend out more often—especially now that summer was filling the beaches and bringing a salty tang to the warm breeze.

POPPY DRESSED IN JEANS and a light sweatshirt, then poured a Thermos of coffee and headed next door. The front door was open, and when she stepped inside, she found a calm expanse of polished hardwood floors, gleaming honey-gold in the sun. "Hello?" she called.

"In here!"

She followed Cooper's voice into the back, where a large, open-plan kitchen opened up on a breakfast room with a wall of windows. "Cooper!" she exclaimed, looking around. "This is amazing!"

"You like it?" Cooper came to greet her with a kiss. Poppy looked around in awe.

"Are you kidding? The light . . . and this view!" There was nothing between the house and the bay, just lush grass leading down to a white picket fence, the dunes, and the sparkling ocean. "It's incredible."

"There's a view from every room," he said, showing her to the family room, with cute built-ins and French doors out to the porch. "I managed to restore these cabinets from the originals," he added, clearly proud of his handiwork. "And all those arches and cornicing are original, too."

Poppy shook her head in amazement. "I can't believe it. It seems like only yesterday this was all just bare foundation and joists."

"And noise," Cooper said, grinning.

"That too," she laughed, remembering their first meeting.

"Come on, let me show you around." Cooper took her hand and led her through, pointing out the gorgeous marble in the kitchen, and all the historical details he'd taken such pains to preserve. He really was an artist, Poppy realized, seeing just how many tiny decisions had gone into making such a magnificent space. It was homey and spacious all at once, and she couldn't help but feel envious that some lucky person would get to call this home.

"This is my favorite room," Cooper said with a smile, as he took her upstairs and opened the door to the master suite. "It faces east, so you get sunrise every morning."

"Oh my god," Poppy breathed, taking in the amazing windows. She wandered closer, out onto the balcony overlooking the whole bay. "If I lived here, I would never get out of bed!"

"Good." Cooper wrapped his arms around her from behind. "I'll hold you to that."

Poppy twisted around. "What do you mean?"

"I thought we could live here," he said casually, like he was suggesting they go for breakfast, or watch a new show on TV tonight.

She blinked, stunned. "Are you serious?"

Cooper kissed her gently, then pulled back with a smile. "I knew from the start that this project was different. It's not just another house to me. It's a home. And . . . I'd like it to be our home. If you want."

Poppy couldn't believe it. "Yes!" she exclaimed. "Oh my god, yes. But, are you sure?" she checked, before she could run away with the idea. "I know we've been spending every night together, but moving in is a big step. I don't want to rush you."

"There's no rush." Cooper held her closer, so she could rest her head against his chest. "As far as I'm concerned, forever can take its sweet time."

She let out a breath, soaking in the feeling of his embrace, and the steady beating of his heart. He was right, she realized happily.

They had forever now, and she would savor every minute of it.

THE END

ACKNOWLEDGEMENTS

Thanks so much to the many family and friends who have been such a support. To my mom, Ann, as always; to my rock-star publicist, Melissa S. and my agent, Alyssa R. Love to The Squad, Elizabeth, and Elisabeth; Anthony C.; Cheryl A.; and Yuval.

And thank you to my readers, for inviting me into your lives. It's such a blessing to share my stories with you, and I can't wait to bring you more from Sweetbriar Cove.

www.melodygracebooks.com
email melody@melodygracebooks.com

ALSO BY MELODY

Made in the USA
Monee, IL
08 April 2020